Enemies to Lovers

Enemies to Lovers

a novel

LAURA JANE WILLIAMS

G. P. PUTNAM'S SONS
New York

PUTNAM
— EST. 1838 —

G. P. PUTNAM'S SONS
Publishers Since 1838
An imprint of Penguin Random House LLC
penguinrandomhouse.com

Library of Congress Cataloging-in-Publication Data

Names: Williams, Laura Jane, author.
Title: Enemies to lovers : a novel / Laura Jane Williams.
Description: New York : G. P. Putnam's Sons, 2024.
Identifiers: LCCN 2023053091 (print) | LCCN 2023053092 (ebook) |
ISBN 9780593719473 (trade paperback) | ISBN 9780593719480 (ebook)
Subjects: LCGFT: Romance fiction. | Novels.
Classification: LCC PS3623.I55838 E54 2024 (print) | LCC PS3623.I55838
(ebook) | DDC 813/.6—dc23/eng/20231121
LC record available at https://lccn.loc.gov/2023053091
LC ebook record available at https://lccn.loc.gov/2023053092
p.   cm.

Printed in the United States of America
1st Printing

Book design by Angie Boutin

This is a work of fiction. Names, characters, places, and incidents either are the product of the
author's imagination or are used fictitiously, and any resemblance to actual persons, living or
dead, businesses, companies, events, or locales is entirely coincidental.

For Calum McSwiggan

To say thank you for the notes on the last one

And everything before that

And aren't we having a lovely time?

And we've got no cups

And we're having a trauma

And tell me how sad you are

And it's like I knew you were already on the way to temple

And don't tell anyone, but it wasn't even hard.

I appreciate you in my life. Realsies!

Enemies to Lovers

Last Christmas

I'm so sorry, he writes on the blank piece of paper. It's more of a scrawl than legible handwriting—he's always been told he writes like a doctor, all pinched and slanted and jumbled, like he has better things to be doing than scribing longhand. But who writes by hand anymore? It's an unnecessary skill, penmanship. He's trying his best, though, to make it look thoughtful. He knows that much is important.

He pauses. Pinches the bridge of his nose. He has a headache. This doesn't feel good, to be doing this.

But he must.

It's for the best.

I have led you on, he continues. *I am not good for you. Please forgive me, and let's not speak of this again . . .*

He sighs, staring at what he has done.

"You'll regret this, you know."

He looks up. He didn't realize he was being watched.

"Maybe," he replies, and his headache gets worse as he folds the paper and writes her name on one side.

1

I am floating. I am floating on the crystal-clear water of whatever ocean laps around the sandy Greek shores of Preveza. Is it the Aegean Sea? Hmmm. I should probably know that. I'll google it when I'm back near my phone. Obviously I don't have my phone in the water. It's just me and presumably some fish, early afternoon sun bringing my skin—and if I wouldn't get laughed at by my ridiculous family for poetic hyperbole, I'd go as far as to say *my very soul*—back to life after three long years under gray Scottish skies. Actually, that's not strictly true. The university is under gray Scottish skies, and so for the most part I've been under strip lighting. Either way, this is the first time I've felt any semblance of hope, or freedom, or *possibility*, in ages. I once read that we're all solar-powered. I get that now. It's like when the sun is out and the water glistens, everything that came before melts away. So much doesn't matter here, unmoored, bobbing about, the sound of my own heart surprisingly good company. Even last Christmas and everything that happened feels far away, and after my breakdown I didn't think anything *could* be any worse than that. Only I could hit rock bottom and then discover it has a basement. Classic.

Recovery can mean different things for different people. That's what my therapist says. Having a breakdown at twenty-four is part of who I am, and two years on, it's part of what's made me the resilient, hopeful phoenix-rising-from-the-ashes that gets to float in the sea and let her mind drift, happy to be alive. I was a wreck back then. A year into my PhD and I had a depression and anxiety that got worse and worse until I was signed off sick from my course and had to spend a month in a residential care facility. Even after I left, I had to have daily visits from the crisis team—but that's when I met my therapist, and she's changed my life. Well, *I* have changed my life actually, but she gave me the tools to do it. I've done a lot of work to get better. I had to stop fighting myself. I've journaled, medicated, walked, stretched, got back into running. I've made best friends with Hope, which isn't a joke: Literally, the woman I saw waiting outside my therapist's office three times a week is called Hope. It's not a metaphor. In fact I called her Despair for a while, as we got to know each other. It made her laugh. But after Jamie slipped that note under my door at Christmas, it tested my new tools to the limit. I was so humiliated. I went home for the holidays feeling so in balance, and suddenly there he was— my brother's best friend joining us for the festivities—and the vibe between us had shifted. I was open to it.

"Am I imagining this?" he'd asked, after three days of . . . *something*.

"No," I'd said. "Knock on my door later," I eventually told him, after a family movie night where his foot ended up pressed against mine under the blanket and the nearness of him almost made me explode.

He never showed. His letter said he'd bottled it. I'd put myself out there and . . . Well, it's a good job I'd had all that therapy, because I needed every trick in the book to pull myself back together. Yeah, it was only a few days of *whatever-it-was* developing between us, but all my "positive thinking" and "soothing visualizations" had me thinking I'd actually get to have a bit of fun for once. Because, spoiler alert: Nobody wants to date the woman who had a nervous breakdown. I had thought Jamie "got it," what with his own trauma. I thought he understood me. So that's what hit hardest. I know now that I should never have trusted him, because first impressions are nearly always right: He really is a vapid womanizer, and I will never fall for his charms again because I have worked too damned hard for my self-respect.

I've not seen him since then. We've avoided each other. Which is why it pisses me off so much when, standing up, with the seabed squashing sand between my toes, the sun forcing me to squint, I notice a stranger up on the beach who looks exactly like him. There's Mum and Dad and my two brothers, Alex and Laurie, and there's Laurie's wife, Kate, too. We got in an hour ago, the owners of the villa having kindly packed us a picnic basket for an early supper, which we schlepped down here, along with some beach chairs and our towels. Just the six of us. Except . . . I'm here, so that should be *five* bodies up there on the sand.

I lower my body back into the warmth of the sea and swim as close to the shore as possible, staying submerged so I can surreptitiously dislodge a wedgie. I turn to look again, now I'm closer. It's then that I realize the sixth person up there with my family definitely isn't a passing local or a figment of my imagination.

It *is* Jamie.

And I am suddenly absolutely furious.

2

I can see, as I climb out of the water, that he's the color of baked earth after six months of sailing yachts across the seven seas for millionaires who like to leave their boats in one place but pick them up in another. He's broad—broader than he deserves to be—and the thick dent of his spine looks like somebody has taken their thumb and smudged down the center of his back: lumps and bumps and pops all around it in, places I didn't even know there could be lumps and bumps and pops. His arms are as thick as my thighs. Jesus, what a show-off. I'm all for keeping fit, but Jamie takes it too far. That time could be spent on other things, like . . . reading . . . or . . . watching *The Real Housewives of New York City*. You've got to be super-vain to work out so much. But then that's Jamie Kramer: vain as they come.

I take a breath, readying for *that look* he gives me: blank, unmoved, bored. It was always that way, until it wasn't. Years of ignoring me, then four days of . . . well, whatever Christmas was. *The Big Almost.* And then I *might* have egged Jamie's car when he pied me off. So now we're back to not speaking, as if Christmas never even happened. That's useful, really: Nobody else knows what happened, of course. Over my dead body do I want my family's pity. Kate has intuited some sort of dalliance, but even she doesn't know it all.

I will say hello, because he's my brother's best friend, my parents treat him like a son, and I know Kate will be holding her breath to see if I'm going to be polite. Quite frankly I don't want to be the source of any gossip, and let's be clear: My family loves to gossip, about one another most of all. I wring out the seawater from my hair, shake the water off my arms, and make my approach to grab a beer and acknowledge Jamie's stupid arrival.

As I walk up to the cooler that we stashed the drinks in, Jamie turns just enough that I *know* he knows I'm here, but after an almost imperceptible beat he focuses his attention fully back on Mum, without acknowledging me. I could write the book on how this will go. Mum is in sickening rapture at whatever ridiculous thing he's telling her. She's practically fawning—she finds him *delightful* and *such fun, a really lovely boy*—but I will do no such thing. This is how Jamie plays it with everyone. He lets people come to him, flexing his gravitational pull with that smile and that easy laugh. I tried to bring it up with my mother a little while ago, about how he's stealthily manipulative, and she told me not to be so sensitive, that I was reading too much into it. The implication is that *I do that because I am a bit unhinged* and so I never brought it up again. But I know I'm right. He *is* manipulative. And vain. And rude. He uses people. He used *me*.

"Oi, oi!" Laurie hollers in Jamie's direction. "Here he is, flexing his biceps as he drinks, like he's posing for hidden paparazzi."

Laurie suddenly has Jamie in a quasi-headlock, arm looped around his neck and pulling down so that he can rub his hair. Jamie pushes him off easily. I step back so I don't get caught in the crossfire.

"Don't hate the player," Jamie says with a grin and a shrug.

"I could never," Laurie says with a laugh. "Although ef me, you're showing the rest of us up a bit, don't you think?"

Jamie chuckles and throws back the rest of his beer, and I sidestep around him. The smell of salt water on my skin is gently warmed by sun so friendly it's like a happy Labrador clamoring for a cuddle. And yet that's not enough to calm the thump in my chest as I get my drink and pop the lid off, raising it defiantly in Jamie's direction as I make my way over to Kate.

"Hello, Jamie," I say, not looking at him, acting as cool and indifferent as I can manage. I've already sauntered off as he says my name in return.

"Flo."

No *hello*, no *hey*. Just intoning my name like we're lawyers in a B-list TV series and he's come to my deposition as a hostile witness. His timbre is low and gruff, like a country singer warbling about a broken heart. Would it kill him to clear his throat and enunciate properly? I'm probably not worth that to Jamie, either. Behind me I hear Laurie say, "It's so good to see you, mate. I know you're having the time of your life, but we've missed you." I don't hear what Jamie says in return. *Time of his life?* I'll bet there are women in every port, like he's had for his whole life. I've always known he's a player, right from when Laurie first brought him home and I heard them talking about their "number." Everyone knows Jamie sleeps around, but nobody judges him for it. It's as if because he looks like he does, it would be a waste if he didn't. His Lothario ways are part of his charm. Well, part of his charm for everyone but me. I'm simply mad I almost fell for it.

"Christ alive, Flo," Kate says to me as I flop down onto the stripy deck chair beside her. My bum practically touches the sand through the low fabric of the seat. I misjudged the distance and flail inelegantly about—careful not to spill my beer, obviously—trying to get comfy. I'm sure this will be further evidence to His Lordship that I'm a mess and he was right to give me the swerve.

"Oh, for god's sake," I tut as I get settled. My tone is a bit sharp. Urgh! I vowed I wouldn't let Jamie irritate me more than he has already. Kate looks at me, eyebrows raised in amusement.

"That's the holiday spirit," she coos, taking the mick out of my sudden bad mood.

"Sorry," I say, taking a long pull from my bottle. I lie about why, because Jamie's name will not pass my lips. "It's the four A.M. wake-up call to get to the airport. Blame Dad's obsession with arriving for flights obscenely early."

Kate sticks out her bottom lip and pulls a "sad" face. It's a thing we do sarcastically to stop either of us ever moaning too much. "How horrible," she teases in a silly voice.

"Shut up!" I scrunch up my face. "It was still dark when we left the house. At least we had time for a beer and a full English breakfast at the airport, I suppose. How many minutes did you and Laurie have to spare before you made it?"

"Ninety seconds," Kate shoots back. "But we did get to ride on the golf-buggy thing after security, so silver linings."

"Luck is always on your side," I say, reaching over for my beach bag. I need my sunglasses. "I have honestly never met somebody for whom all traffic lights turn green, all doors open, complimentary coffees are freely given . . ."

"Speaking of which . . ." She shrugs, noticing that I seem unable to find whatever I'm looking for. She figures out it must be my sunglasses and pulls out a second pair from her beach bag, which I take gratefully. "We did get complimentary croissants at Pret, to apologize for the wait."

"You almost missed the flight because you were at Pret?" I shriek, and she motions for me to hush. "How?"

"Shush!" she hisses, looking in my dad's direction to check he hasn't heard. She lowers her voice. "I made Laurie swear he wouldn't dob me in for it. But I needed a ham-and-cheese croissant, and you know I can't function without a coffee in the morning."

"You're preaching to the converted," I say. "Coffee is life." I gulp down my beer and take in the perfection of our surroundings: powdery-yellow sand stretching all the way around the cove, endless water, the sun lowering in the sky to envelop everything in its syrupy flame. With my back to Jamie, I can almost forget he's here—and then Mum titters at him yet again, and I'm reminded that he is. Before Kate can ask me about it, I say, "Anyway. Your 'Christ alive.' Don't let *me* distract you from taking the Lord's name in vain . . ."

"The Lord's son technically," Kate points out, and I can't help but notice that she's already glowing, looking relaxed and in the holiday mood.

I can't even imagine having relaxation so readily at hand. It will take me days, if not a full week, to get my shoulders to unclench from up by my ears. I'm just built that way. Hope says it's better to be highly strung and know it than to think you're low-key and chill when everyone around you knows the truth. I have to say, I think Hope has a point. But Kate is low-maintenance through and through, and I envy that.

Kate continues, "I was going to tell you that you look *ridiculous* in that bikini, actually. Your waist, your boobs . . . if that's what almost getting sectioned does to a girl, I might need a breakdown myself. You, my friend, have never been hotter."

I pull a face at her that's supposed to mean, *Are you seriously joking about what happened?*, but it goes unnoticed. Unnoticed or ignored, which is quintessential Kate. Of course I don't mind, not really, because these past two years she's been one of the few people to keep treating me like normal. In fact I have exactly zero friends left from "before times," because nobody knew how to handle me. I met Hope in the waiting room at the therapist's office, and we bonded over mental health and a love of *Bluey*, the kids' cartoon. Hope's theory is that when you're sad, *Bluey* is the best thing to cheer you up; and when you're happy, *Bluey* is the best thing to remind you to treasure it. She's backpacking around Europe right now. Her breakdown has led her to embrace everything that life throws at her. My breakdown has left me craving safety and sameness. We're mostly a text-based friendship for the foreseeable, although Hope's determined to get me to join her. This will never happen. I am not the YOLO, go-backpacking-for-a-summer type.

"Although," Kate muses, "I suspect that an episode of my own would involve a lot of comfort-eating, thus thwarting my desire to get as snatched as you are."

"You could arrange one of those happy breakdowns," I suggest. "Put it in the contract between you and your brain."

"Oh yes," she agrees. "Great idea. 'Dear brain, please refer to clause Three C, pertaining to getting my titties to sit as nice as Flo's in a teeny-weeny string bikini.'"

"This isn't tiny," I squeal, thrusting a hand over my admittedly very bare chest. "This is a family holiday!"

"A family holiday in Greece, where the locals look like gods. Play your cards right and you should have a *fantastic* two weeks looking like that, baby."

I arch an eyebrow. "Sex hasn't been on my mind for quite some time," I remind her.

"More's the pity," she shoots back. I don't dignify that with a response. "By the way," she adds, lowering her voice and leaning in, "how are we feeling about . . ." She nods her head in the direction of Jamie, who's now got not only Mum but also Dad and my brother Alex eating out of the palm of his hand. He's always telling some anecdote about the rich and famous that he works with, name-dropping and embellishing. I'm sure half of the stories of what allegedly happens out there on the boats aren't even true. I roll my eyes, pausing mid-derision, just in time to see Jamie crick his neck, flexing it to one side and rubbing the taut, bronzed skin of his left side. He's *so* performative.

"What?" I say, playing dumb. Kate has *sworn* she'll never tell Laurie what she knows about last Christmas, or confront Jamie about it, either, and I trust her to honor her word. I simply want to forget about it all. Jamie is around a lot, because a couple of years ago he lost both his parents in a car accident, and so Mum and Dad have unofficially made him their fourth child. I do actually have a heart, so he gets leeway for such painful trauma because, god, I can't even imagine something that devastating happening. I feel for him over that. I do . . . But he was still awful to me, and is awful to most women, as far as I can tell, so I know I'm better off keeping my distance.

"Okay," Kate says slowly. "I see what game we're playing . . ."

"There's no game," I tell her, too quickly, and even I know I sound defensive.

"Sure," she retorts.

"There's not!" I say, right as Laurie reappears from wherever he's been, asking, "There's not what?"

He plops down on the sand between Kate's legs, and she kisses the top of his head. They've been married just over a year and are disgustingly in love. Kate tells him to mind his own business, and I close my eyes to luxuriate in the heat and shut everybody else out. It's not often that I'm thankful for Laurie's interruption, but right now I am. As I inhale and exhale, letting the tiniest of sea breezes tickle my skin, I can hear the waves gently lapping against the shore. It's like a real-life Spotify playlist of "relaxation noises." Hope has issued a stern text warning me to fully enjoy everything this vacation has to offer, because she's a bit like a smoker who has given up, and thus becomes evangelical about everybody else giving up: She's embraced the YOLO lifestyle and has made it her mission to get me to do so, too.

Ahhh. Sun. Sea. Sand between my toes. A moment to reflect and recommit to relaxing. And then Laurie says, "Shall we eat?"

Of course ten minutes of silence from him is asking too much.

"I'm bloody starving. And did anyone think to bring down a speaker? We need to up the holiday vibe, now the whole crew is here!"

"I hadn't known we were waiting for anybody else to join the crew," I say without opening my eyes, trying to sound as nonchalant as possible. I practically *hear* Laurie shrug and, peeking through one eye, see him already on his feet again, heading toward the hamper to start setting out the food.

"Flo, don't be ridiculous. It was all on the family e-mail chain," he yells over his shoulder.

I open my other eye, surprised. "There's a family e-mail chain?" I say to Kate.

She pulls a face. "Babe," she replies, looking over her sunglasses dramatically, "if you're not getting those e-mails, trust me: You're better off out of it. I love your mother as much as my own, but since she retired . . ."

"She's sending you the equivalent of *War and Peace* every day?" I supply.

"Like you wouldn't believe," she replies with a sigh. "I don't know what she's going to do, now she's not working. A woman as brilliant as her . . ."

I scramble out of my seat to go and help Laurie with the food—if you don't move fast in this family, you only get crumbs.

"Hmmm," I say, waving a hand. "Fine. I'll choose my ignorant bliss."

But I have to push down a voice that quietly squeaks, *If I'm not on that e-mail chain, what else doesn't my family include me in?*

THE SUN BEGINS to lower in the late-afternoon sky, light shifting from bright white to mellow yellow. Our resident caveman, Jamie, makes a fire in preparation for when it gets dark, like we can't all just put on more clothes and use candles for ambience. He creates a little circle with pebbles and stones, somehow manages to acquire driftwood . . . and genuinely gets it going by rubbing two sticks together, like a regular Robinson Crusoe. We've still not spoken properly. Imagine crashing somebody's family holiday and not speaking to them. The audacity! Not that I *want* to speak to him. I wish Jamie was deserted on an island—an island far away from us. He's all massive hands and concentrated effort, and it's infuriating that he's already tanned and stubbled after his work on the boats, his hair all grown out, but the rest of us are so pale we practically reflect the sun. It's like the Cullen family from *Twilight* and their one mortal (and very bronzed) friend. Jamie thinks he's so cool, making fires and opening beers with his bare hands, but his beach shorts are so small they're laughable. Nobody needs to see all that. He looks absurd.

"Dare I ask how you've been passing your evenings, then?" Laurie is asking him. "Sounds like you've not been short of company this year . . ."

"Laurie," Mum warns. "Don't slut-shame the boy. It's only right he should sow his wild oats." She adds, "As long as you're careful, of course. It's not enough simply to wear a condom—you need to get checked twice a year. Condoms don't protect from everything, you know."

"Mum! Jesus."

"Oh come on, Laurie," Mum says. "I was always very sure to say exactly the same to you all, when you left for university. If you're old enough to do it, you're old enough to be smart about it."

"I'm *married*, Mum," Laurie says.

"Jamie isn't," Mum points out.

"Well, don't you worry about me," Jamie tells her. "I promise I'm a very good boy."

"My arse," says Laurie.

We busy ourselves dishing out Greek salad and an array of crusty breads, olives, and cheeses, eating off plates on our laps, the tinny notes of a summer beach playlist coming from the Bluetooth speaker Alex has thought to bring. All in, it's not a bad little setup—Jamie aside. I *definitely* do not look in his direction. I can't control when he's around, but I sure as hell can control how much of my energy I give him. And, after careful consideration, I have concluded he gets: absolutely zero. None. *Nada*. JAMIE WHO?

"Cor," says Dad, helping himself to some more of the Greek wine we've been gifted. "It's all right, this, isn't it?"

"I'll say," says Alex. "I keep wanting to check my phone for urgent alerts that mean I've got to run down to the hospital and put out another fire. But I don't. I can't believe I'm actually on holiday."

"Same," says Laurie. "I don't remember the last time I've done less than a fifty-hour week."

I sigh contentedly in agreement, which Laurie deliberately mis-reads.

"All this a bit too much like hard work for you, Flo?" he teases. "Bit more activity than you're used to, I'd imagine."

I roll my eyes. Laurie thinks it's hilarious that not only did I get a degree in English and then a master's, but as part of my PhD I've been teaching some undergraduate classes, too, and I'm now going to stay on as an associate lecturer. He thinks his being a law student was "real" studying; and me paying thousands to read books and "wank off" about them is not only a joke, but that helping others to do the same—now I'm going to be official staff—is downright hilarious.

"Laurie . . ." Mum warns, like I'm six and might cry. What is it about family holidays that makes you revert to your childhood roles: Laurie teasing his silly little sister?

"It's okay, Mum," I say. "I know Laurie continues to be intimi-dated by anyone capable of the empathy it takes to put themselves in somebody else's shoes long enough to enjoy eighty thousand words. Speaking of which, how is it going with that book on the history of soccer that you got in your stocking? You were, what, twelve pages in on the plane? That must be a whole two words a day since Christmas . . ."

"I've been saving it, for your information," Laurie bats back. "I just needed a break from work. Work is a thing that grown-ups do, where—"

Suddenly Jamie leaps up.

"Anyone want to play volleyball?" he interjects, stuffing the last of the food from his plate into his mouth and patting his bare eight-pack of a stomach, a satisfied barbarian. Because of his easy cha-risma, we all look at him, our attention his, and his alone—the brewing fight between Laurie and me vanishing like vapor. "I've got some energy to burn."

Alex lets out an enormous beer-y belch.

"So that's a yes from Alex," Dad says and chuckles, because for some reason Alex is allowed to be an absolute heathen and call it a laugh, whereas the rest of us get bound to a normal standard of manners.

"You in, old man?" Jamie asks, arching an eyebrow in Dad's direction.

"Who are you calling an old man?" Dad counters, a glimmer in his eye. "I could run circles around you and your . . . your . . ." He wafts a hand up and down at Jamie's stomach. "*Abs*. With age comes experience, remember." He drains his glass and gets up, all lithe limbs and potbelly. He's not in bad nick, Dad, for a sixty-something. He's got salt-and-pepper hair and is genuinely friendly and kind, which I think keeps men very youthful-seeming. God, there was a lecturer at university who looked like Brad Pitt—as in Brad as he is now, which is still *very* buff—but he was so standoffish and abrupt that as soon as you found that out about him, he became almost ugly. I can see how people like Dad, because he's kind. It makes me value that as a quality, above all else. "And there's a six-pack hidden under here somewhere," Dad adds, grinning and patting his own tum. "Hidden deep, like, but definitely there."

Jamie smiles. He's never given me smiles freely, on account of being an arse, but with everyone else he's charming. His teeth are pearly white and in the three seconds I forget to be obtuse and look right at him, his tongue darts out over his lips and back again. I quickly look away. He's so *aware* of himself. Urgh.

"Michael," Jamie says. "You and me as the dream team, opposite Laurie and Alex, then?"

Of course he isn't asking me to join in. *Of course* he isn't! I think it's the indifference that makes me so mad. I have to work so hard to stay out of Jamie's way, but for Jamie I don't even cross his mind. How self-centered and mean do you have to be? It truly beggars belief.

"There's life in this old dog, too, I'll have you know," Mum asserts, leaping up and going to stand with Alex and Laurie, her allegiance clear.

In unison, everyone turns to me and Kate, the expectation unspoken but written on their faces: We need to make up the numbers, because right now it's three versus two.

"I'll umpire," Kate says with a smile, like butter wouldn't melt, reaching over for more pita bread and tzatziki.

"Flo?" asks Dad.

I get up. Right. Well then. I might not have been anybody's first choice, but that doesn't mean I can't dominate the court. Jamie assumes he's the sporting champion among us, but he's miscalculated how competitive we Greenbergs can be, when it is against one another. He should know that by now. You don't need to be the size of Goliath to reign supreme—he's underestimating the smarts of David— i.e., *me.*

"I'm playing to win," I tease my new teammates, wagging a finger, letting it be known they're not to let me down. Dad winks at me, a subtle *That's my girl!* Jamie is already rigging up a makeshift court, drawing lines in the sand and hoisting up a very sorry-for-itself net that he must have found on his scavenger hunt for firewood.

"You're toast," Jamie says to Laurie and Alex. "Sorry to break it to you, but I could beat you lads single-handedly."

"Do I have to remind you of the university sports day where you broke your leg doing a simple egg-and-spoon race?" Laurie says. "Hardly the bastion of sporting ability."

"I'd been drinking," Jamie retorts. "You got a groin injury at that charity soccer match, stone-cold sober!"

"That was the mud," Laurie says. "And if you remember, we called time not long after, so it didn't happen to anybody else. That pitch was *flooded*. I did everyone a favor, really."

"Nothing to do with being on the losing side, as per?"

"Not being funny, mate," Laurie says, laughing. "But you've got Dad and Flo as teammates for this. You might be able to beat us single-handedly, but consider their help a hindering force. I'd save the big talk, if I were you."

Before I can defend myself, Kate yells from the sidelines, "I wish I had a whistle."

"Just shout loudly!" Laurie yells back.

"Okay," she bellows.

Jamie grabs the ball that Mum brought down from the villa and commands Dad to keep left and he'll keep right. I stand behind them both, awaiting my orders from our self-appointed team captain, but they don't come. That would involve Jamie acknowledging my presence, after all.

Kate yells, "Go!" and Jamie throws the ball up confidently, the muscles in his shoulders rippling like they've been told a joke, and he thwacks it over the net in the direction of Alex, who bats it back with surprising grace.

"You're moving fast, for somebody who came last in cross-country!" I rib my brother over the net.

He pretends that a dagger has gone through his heart, with a "sad" face.

"Long-distance running is for people with no brute strength," he yells back. "Your words don't hurt me, Florence."

Mum hits the ball beside him, toward Dad, who bats it back, and then to Alex, who fouls out by pushing it into the net.

"Is that the brute strength you were talking about?" I goad, and he responds by lifting the ball and hitting it so hard that Dad doesn't see it coming, and it gets him square between the eyes.

"Michael!" Mum cries out, and Dad blinks several times like he's trying to catch up with what happened.

"Mike, you okay?" Jamie asks, shooting *a look* at me, like Alex's overzealousness is somehow *my* fault. How dare he! I want to tell him to fuck off, out loud, in front of everybody. That I don't do so is a reflection of my deep inner resolve and self-discipline.

"You've got me at a disadvantage, I think," Dad mutters, rubbing his forehead. "I might have had one glass of wine too many for the A-team . . ."

"You four play," Mum pronounces, coming round to take Dad by the hand and marching him off to sit down. "Honestly, Michael," I hear her say. "You can't go getting hurt on our first bloody afternoon. Just calm down a bit, won't you?"

We loiter for a second, to make sure he's okay, before Kate bellows, "Get on with it, then!"

It's me and Jamie now, a team of two. Except Jamie obviously didn't get the memo, because although Alex and Laurie work together irritatingly well, Jamie and I don't gel at all and he keeps getting in the way of all my attempts to hit the ball. Jamie's massive, overbearing frame flashes deep tan in front of me, to the side of me, around the back of me, but Alex and Laurie score a point, and then another. I can tell it's bugging Jamie, but *still* he doesn't speak to me, still doesn't break the fourth wall of his one-man show to strategize with me. I'm going to have to break first, if there's any chance of getting the game back—and to wipe the smug look off my brothers' faces, right now I'd sit down for a tea and a chat with Voldemort.

"Stick left," I tell him, quite bossily, to be honest. But I figure it's like commanding a dog: It's all in the tone. You have to act like you're in control. "And I'll stick right."

Jamie flares his nostrils. "Always calling the shots, aren't you?" he says.

I narrow my eyes. "I beg your pardon?"

"Let's just play," he mutters.

Away we go again: I clobber the ball and get us a point. Jamie gets us another. I get us one more, and now we're back even with the boys. Ha! Take *that*, Jamie! But I can tell it has annoyed Jamie that I'm actually any good, and he starts playing the whole court again, pushing me to one side, and a couple of times we almost collide. I refuse to speak to him again—if he's not interested in team sports, why bloody suggest one?—so instead I get aggressive with the ball, flying this way and that, flinging myself toward it, so Jamie can't get it. That'll show him. I can be an ignorant asshat, too.

However. My flinging and flying are how my bikini top ends up pinging over my head, so that yes, we score, but also my tits are on full show to my entire family, because I've decided to do some sort of midair yoga in the semi-nude, purely to prove my unspoken point.

"Oh my god!" cry Laurie and Alex as I land, apparently trying to decide who is more grossed out.

"Florence, your—" my father yells, as Kate starts squealing with hysterical laughter.

I hold my arm across my boobs (they're just boobs!) and look confusedly to see where my top has gone. I don't think I could do that trick again if I tried. I'm confronted with Jamie's broad, hot frame, inches from me, sweat on his tanned, furrowed brow, eyes dark with evident disgust for what he's borne witness to.

"And Laurie calls *me* a show-off," he says, handing me his T-shirt. "Put this on." He looks over my head like he can't even bear to hold eye contact. His words are quiet but firm.

Standing this close, looking at him eye to eye in this way, something jolts through me. I can't tell if it's defiance or frustration that he's even here, but it makes my throat go dry and my mouth flop open as I think of something cutting to say, before deciding to say nothing. I wasn't going to speak to him, but my jaw drops at Jamie's attitude and I take a breath to tell him where to go—before Laurie yells, "Flo! Fucking put it on."

It snaps me to, and I do so. The T-shirt smells like cedar and musk, and I *hate* that I notice.

Before I can figure it out, Jamie commands, "Let's play!"

He claps his hands, his focus dead ahead, like a director keeping a movie set on track. Alex throws the ball into the air and Jamie lunges for it. And, just like that, I cease to exist once again.

3

I sleep in late because it took ages for me to nod off last night, even after a long day of travel and our profanely early start. I was too buzzed after the volleyball game, too wired. After we won, in a fit of glory I turned round to give Jamie a high five, but he'd already crossed the net to Laurie and Alex to give them shit, as if the victory was his alone and I was nothing.

"Told you I'd win," he'd said, laughing at them.

"Yeah, fair play," Laurie had agreed.

Kate had found my bikini top and so I took off his T-shirt not long afterward, gently folded it, and left it on top of his rucksack, without a word. I wasn't about to say thank you, only for that to be ignored, too. Does Jamie seriously not realize that I'm the reason we won?

All I could think about, after I sneaked away to my room up in the eaves, was that if Jamie is going to be on this holiday, I'm going to have to stop *trying* to ignore him and engage in some sort of level of earthly being that means I *actually* ignore him. He's going to be around for the rest of my life, I imagine, so I need to move on from my abject humiliation and arrive at cool, calm, and detached.

I have led you on. I am not good for you. Please forgive me, and let's not speak of this again . . .

Those words haunt me, but by god I have heeded them. I *won't* ever speak of them again.

I'm pulled from a painful walk down a horrid Christmas memory lane by my phone vibrating. I turn over in bed to reach for it. It's Hope.

HOPE
Morning, gorgeous! Please find attached, for your consideration, THIS gem of a German find from last night

A photo of a blond-haired muscleman, asleep, comes through.

ME
I see the souvenirs continue to stack up in scores

HOPE
You'd better not to be slut-shaming

ME
I think I was, but that was wrong of me. Although—surely snapping sleeping dudes is . . . questionable?

HOPE
Hold on, let me wake him for consent.
Okay, here's an awake one!

The blond-haired muscleman has piercing blue eyes and a boy-ish grin. His cheek is pink on the side he's apparently slept on, and he's reaching out one hand to beyond the camera, presumably to touch the photographer's leg.

ME
He's very handsome! Does he have a name?

HOPE
Hold on, let me ask him. He's already gone back to sleep
Okay, it's Gunther

ME
You didn't know that before you slept with him?

HOPE
FLORENCE GREENBERG! Enough of the judgment!!
If you were getting laid, you'd be way less uptight. You do know that, don't you?

ME
You might have mentioned it a few hundred times. I'm probably just jealous. ENJOY YOUR SOUVENIR.
Also. Jamie is here, unfortunately, crushing whatever libido I might otherwise have had . . .

HOPE
WHAT
HOW
WHY!

ME

I guess he was invited? There's a family e-mail chain I'm not on, so I missed the details . . .

HOPE

Sod it, ditch the fam and come meet me in Prague! It's not too late!

Hope has already done Paris (Jean-Pierre), Brussels (Anya), Amsterdam (Lukas and Julia, at the same time), and Copenhagen (Karl on the train there and, I believe, *two* Oscars). I would be the miserable, unadventurous friend if I traveled with Hope, which I knew from the start and that's why I said no to the trip. She's determined to sow her wild oats and make up for the time she lost to her poor mental health. All power to her! Honestly, I respect her choice, but I just don't have it in me. I wish I did.

ME

I'll bear it in mind

HOPE

No you won't

ME

You're right. I won't

I automatically pull on my running gear from the suitcase, sprawled out on the spare single bed opposite mine, because that's how I start every morning, come rain or shine. I've always loved running, but now my mental health depends on it. It was a savior after my breakdown. I don't realize that it's almost eleven A.M. until I get downstairs, though, and the heat is already fierce. If I run now, even in just shorts and a sports bra, I'll melt . . . and probably miss the start of lunch, which as we've established is a no-go. This is a family of hungry gannets and they leave no crumb behind—as will be evidenced by breakfast, where there's no doubt barely a slice of bread left. Huh. I feel oddly cross at myself. Perhaps it will be cool enough later this evening for a run. I'd hate to miss one, especially on holiday. I need to stay mentally sharp, keep my demons at bay.

I loiter at the kitchen door that leads to the veranda, deciding what to do. The villa is beautiful. This is by far the nicest family holiday we've ever been on. For as much as they annoy me, we've never been a family that grew out of all taking a trip together once a year. It wasn't really a hard choice to turn down Hope's Europe adventure and come to Greece with everyone instead. Even when we were teenagers, my brothers and I never rebelled like some of my friends did. Mum and Dad are largely good company, luckily, so we always get at least a weekend in somewhere.

Normally we all have to pay our own way, but this year Mum pulled down a tax-free lump sum of her pension to really show us a good time—her treat (!)—and also to build a "she-shed" at the bottom of the garden, so she's got somewhere special to do her pottery. It's funny, being in the terrifying stage of my life where I don't know what to do for the next thirty or forty years, while Mum has essentially lived most of her life, and gets to enjoy a retirement where her biggest decision is going to be what to have for lunch. Is there a way I can just fast-forward to retirement, too? It seems nice. Cozy. I like cozy. I've fallen into academia because it means I don't have to take a chance. I can stay where I am and keep doing what I've been doing, and that suits me fine. I worry that anything else could make me end up back how I was. The uncertain has a tendency to do that. I like to keep things as I know them to be.

The windows here have pale-blue shutters to keep the sun out in the day, and the small-but-perfectly-formed kitchen has a small two-burner stove. The entire place is a maze, with shelves filled with books other guests have left behind, and the odd board game that we'll no doubt argue over. It's all built over a million different levels, culminating in our very own private pool . . . which, of course, now that I step outside, Jamie is already in, goggles on and obnoxiously massive arms propelling him through the water at speed. Classic Jamie, showing off his physical prowess at every opportunity. Mum's there, in the shade of the vine-covered pergola, flicking through a paperback thriller she bought at the airport. I planned all my reading before we came, imbibing the "hot reads for summer" lists in all the Sunday supplements and assessing the chart positions of the latest hardback releases. As in reading, so in life: I can't risk surprises. So I've got three literary masterpieces that are "good" for me, but actually quite boring. I'll probably end up stealing Mum's thriller when she's done.

"Morning," I say as I pad over, and she looks up at me with a lazy smile, a tiny espresso cup beside her.

"Morning, darling," she tells me, taking in the sight of me. "I'm glad you slept. I think you needed it."

I try not to bristle at the uninvited suggestion that, by needing sleep, I must somehow have been in sleep deficit, which I hear as: *You must do a better job of looking after yourself, darling.* I can't help it—I'm forever searching for the real meaning behind Mum's words. She's incredible; I am not. That does not escape my attention. I pour myself the last of the orange juice and sit down to join her, changing tack to ask where everybody is.

"Oh, here, there, and everywhere," Mum says with a wave of her hand. "Kate and Laurie have gone for an explore, down past where we ate supper on the beach last night, the little lovebirds. Alex and your dad have gone into town to scope out somewhere to eat tonight and to pick up a few bits."

I chuckle. "Presumably 'a few bits' means an inflatable donut for the pool and, most likely, water pistols?"

Mum chuckles, too.

"They have previous," she notes. "So I'd imagine it does, yes. Although I hope they remember actual sustenance, too. Nibbles for the fridge and whatnot."

I give a noncommittal *hmmm*, because I don't have that much faith in my brother staying on track, and he and Dad together are a bad influence on each other. I slice open the last chocolate croissant (there's one left—a bona fide miracle) and chop up a banana, making a sort of banana-choco sandwich. Mum's focus shifts away from her book and over toward me, which I can tell means she's about to say Something Meaningful.

"Whilst we've got a moment alone, darling," she starts, turning the corner of a page and closing it.

I chomp away, the only sound between us the noises of my food and Jamie's *slap-slap-slap* through the water. I look into her blue eyes. She's very Helen Mirren: soft features that add up to be more than the sum of their parts. Her nose isn't remarkable, or her eyes or her smile, but somehow all together she's beautiful. And urgh, dare I even say it, but Mum is also kind of sexy, too? She doesn't flaunt it, doesn't try to dress like a twenty-year-old to be relevant, or whatever. But she embraces her femininity and loves a cinched-in waist or a just low-enough top. Like now, in her swimsuit and sarong: It's a one-piece, but low in the back to show off her curvy bits, and scooped to give her enough cleavage without being tacky. Her sarong is tied to one side, so it reveals a sliver of her runner's legs, and she's always got pedicured feet in a brilliant red. Oh my god. Do I mean that she's a MILF? I think I do. I mean, you've gotta hand it to her, she's definitely not become invisible in her retirement. Mum is more naturally put together in her sixties than I am in my alleged prime, that's for sure.

When I swallow, Mum adds, "I've been wanting to check in."

I know she means well. I do. But it makes shivers run down my spine, because this is the role I play now, since everything happened. I'm the delicate little doll everyone needs to look out for, which I understand, because when my breakdown was at its absolute worst I had mentally checked out. By that point what was happening was probably worse for the people who love me than it was for me. But with Mum, I feel . . . I don't know. Weak. Veronica Greenberg is superwoman: She does it all. She headed up an IT firm for thirty years, raised three kids and absorbed Jamie as her own when he needed her two years ago, too—no questions asked, even though she must have had her hands full with me and my problems. She runs every day, cooks meals from scratch, and always has a spare gift bag for presents, and extra lip balm in her handbag that she lets you keep.

And I did an *amazing* job of being like that, too, even as a little girl, even as a teenager. I wasn't surly or rebellious—I was *responsible*. I was exactly like Mum until I hit my mid-twenties and then I wasn't like her at all; and now it's all anyone wants to talk about with me, despite the fact I've been doing all right for a while now. I'm better. Mostly. I was really bad for about a year, and it's been a year of recovery. Recovery might never end; just like an alcoholic will always be an alcoholic, I might always be anxious. But I'm committed to looking after myself. I'm doing okay.

"I'm fine, Mum," I say, smiling to prove my point.

"I wasn't implying that you weren't," she protests, reaching out a hand for mine. She gives me a squeeze. "But I've been meaning to say: I don't want you to make a misstep, taking this job full time. You could take a pause, you know. There's no rush for teaching. You've been at university for so long, I worry you'll be there forever simply because it's comfortable. First Newcastle and then Edinburgh . . . If you wanted to take a year off—six months even—and come home, think about your options, you could do—"

"Okay," I tell her, nodding. I squeeze her hand back. Obviously I will never do that, never *move back home at twenty-bloody-six*. I'll bet *she* never took a career pause and never made a misstep, either. God, I'd be mortified to go back home. I wish we could talk about something other than my mental bloody health.

I finish off my banana-chocolate croissant and gulp down the rest of my juice. I look in the coffeepot, but there's none left. I'll make some more in a minute. If I walk away now, Mum will think I'm cross, and I don't want her to think that. I want us to be how we used to be, when we'd talk about TV and art, and running technique, and not my bloody *feelings*.

Jamie pulls himself out of the water in one easy swoop, grabbing the towel he left on one of the sun loungers. Now I really can't get up to make coffee: I refuse to let him chase me away. It's like I forget he's here until I don't, and that winds me all over again. *Urgh.*

"Am I interrupting?" he asks, droplets of water dripping from his sandy-blond hair onto his shoulders, rolling over the mounds of his upper arms in a way that many cultures could label seductive, but I happen to think is messy, because he's dripping perilously close to the crockery. The sun reflects in fragments off the blue of the pool, and either the birds have just started chirruping in the trees because of Jamie, or else they were chirruping all along and I wasn't paying attention. The terra-cotta floor tiles are warm underneath us, the leaves of the tall olive trees as still as soldiers on guard. The light makes him glow, like one of those salt lamps, all glimmering and hazy and . . . disgusting.

"Of course not," Mum says, and Jamie's eyes flicker toward me with *that look*: the blank, almost aggressive one. I instantly look down into my empty coffee mug. "Sit, sit, sit," Mum tells him. "You're very good to do all those lengths. Keeping fit, it really is the cornerstone for a happy life, don't you think?"

"Absolutely," Jamie replies, picking up the coffeepot like I did and finding—exactly as I did—that it's empty.

"Oh, let me," insists Mum. "I finished it, so I should brew another. Be right back."

She clasps my shoulder as she stands up and then disappears, leaving me and Jamie annoyingly alone. Jamie leans over for the jug of water, thick fingers reaching for the handle, wrapping themselves around it in a flush simple movement, like he owns the place, and I watch from under my eyelashes, horrified. I want to find a reason to leave. I don't want to be here with him, all wet from the pool, gulping down water with his Adam's apple bobbing up and down noisily. He runs a hand through his hair as I sit mute, looking at my lap, and he puts on his sunglasses. They're bright red and square-framed. They look ridiculous. So, what, he spends a couple of months a year on the seven seas and now he thinks he's some chic European?

I can't do this. The floor suddenly feels too warm, the air even stiffer. Everything is closing in. I can't sit here, as Mum gets back and starts clucking over Jamie's wellness routines and the sun grows fiercer. I just can't do it.

I'm saved by my phone lighting up, Hope's name on the screen.

HOPE
Well, that was a fun morning! What you up to? Do you want to talk about J***e being there?

ME
Lol, thanks for redacting his name. He's like the-man-who-shall-not-be-named

HOPE
We can name him if you want, but personally I don't think he deserves it

ME
He doesn't. Although! I am ignoring him in a very mature, grown-up way

HOPE
Oh, yes, the MATURE ignoring. I've heard of that!

I glance up at Jamie, who, beneath his sunnies, is musing at the far edge of the table, like he's enjoying the awkwardness, like he's seeing who will break first. It's psychopathic.

ME
What are your plans today? Send more pictures!

I don't know what I'd do without Hope. It helps, so much, to have somebody in my life who has been through what I've been through, who has seen their own personal hell and figured out how to navigate it. We went through a phase of calling people who *hadn't* had breakdowns *normies*, which we haven't done in ages . . . But seated beside Jamie, I feel he's as much of a normie as they come. The word comes to me easily. And since he's a normie, I cannot let him have a hold on me. I've come too far for that. I haven't weathered a personal hell just to let a man who didn't know a good thing when he could have had it bug me any longer.

I push back my chair to scurry away. But as I'm about to declare that I'm going upstairs to get changed, Jamie says, "It was very generous of your parents to invite me."

I freeze at being addressed directly, half standing, half seated, like I've got a tummy ache or need a poo. What am I supposed to say back? Agree with him falsely, or say I'm happy he's here . . . ? I can't lie. I've never been able to, even as a kid. Plus, it's unnerving that he doesn't sound his usual hostile self.

My phone vibrates again. It's a photo of Hope's laptop screen, a picture of *Bluey* playing on it. It's one of our favorite episodes, where Bingo has weird dreams and all the kids are up in the night and don't let their cartoon parents get much sleep. By the time I turn my attention away from my phone, Mum is coming back with the coffee. Jamie is looking at me, watching me look at my phone. I think he's spied the *Bluey* photo—more for his "Flo Is Not Worth It" evidence bag. I find myself murmuring an odd noise to excuse myself, a gurgled "Mmmmnhyansosokk," before hotfooting it back up to my room, seeking solace in my phone.

ME
Jamie being here is painful! I need some *Bluey!*

I have led you on, I remember, as I burn in shame, collapsing onto my bed. *I am not good for you. Please forgive me, and let's not speak of this again . . .*

I hate this, I hate this, I hate this.

I MANAGE TO sneak off down to the beach without having to rejoin Mum and Jamie at the breakfast table, where they've graduated to playing a game of cards. I already caught a glimpse of Dad and Alex by the rental car, unloading a plethora of floating devices shaped like wildlife and several water guns, as predicted. As I hear Mum whooping triumphantly, presumably because she's trumped Jamie, I snake my way down the winding steps from the house to the beach, a sweep of curved paradise with hardly anybody on it.

I can see some hazy dots of people at the far end, but other than that I have the place to myself. Me, the book-I-won't-actually-read, and my beach towel, printed with a Penguin Classics cover of *A Room of One's Own*, get settled in the shade of a big tree with a perfect view of the horizon. Staring at the sea, I think about my chat with Mum—about pausing instead of misstepping, and coming home instead of going straight into teaching full time. Most people would kill for a chance to pause, no matter how old they are. Look at Hope, hopping on a train to Interrail around Europe and maybe even beyond, if the mood takes her. She doesn't know what she's going to do next; she simply wants to heal and live life (her grandmother left her a substantial amount in her will, which I suppose helps). Folk take jobs they don't really want as a way to pay the rent and keep building a life. What does it say about me that I'd look a gift horse in the mouth? But the truth is that I don't know what I want to do with my life. Laurie is right—what I do is very . . . *niche*. My PhD explored representations of the ocean in early modern English literature—ironically, working on the idea that it can mirror risk and possibility. I say *ironic* because I don't do much risk-taking. The teaching was a way to earn money to pay for the PhD, and then they asked me to stay, so I said yes, just like that.

I don't know how other people do it, how they choose what to do with their lives. Is it because there are two types of people in the world—ambitious and not ambitious—and I am not? And if I'm not "ambitious," does that make me lazy? Surely there are different types of ambition: I might not want to wear power-suits and work in a sky-scraper, nor do I really think I want to be a stay-at-home mum while my partner wears a power-suit and works in a skyscraper. Can a per-son be ambitious for peace? For serenity? That's all I want. I only seem able to get it if I take a little white pill every morning and stick to the same routines, day in and day out.

When Mum said a pause can be better than a misstep, what I heard was: *I know you're scared.*

Is it that obvious?

Why isn't everybody else confused about the life they should build, like I am? I fish my phone out of my bag and text my lifeline.

ME
What do you do when you start thinking about the future? Not spinning out, but like . . . musing?

HOPE
Tell myself nobody cares

ME
Oh, cheery!

HOPE

Lol, not in a bad way. Just that like, when all is said and done,
I'm not going to be remembered in the history books. Nobody
cares what I do! People are not going to sit around me on my
deathbed and issue their final score for how well I did life

Or wait, if they do, I want the criteria to be like, how much I
followed my heart. Not like, other people's criteria—being
sensible and jobs and family and all that

ME

That's where I get stuck. I'm terrified of the end-of-life scorecard
that says I failed!

HOPE

I know, babe. All I can say is . . . I'm here, and I see you, and
you'll get there. You're doing so much better even in the time I've
known you!

"Penny for your thoughts?"

I'm so in my head trying to unpick all this that I didn't even realize Kate and Laurie have come down to the beach, too, and are
casting shadows over the pale sand with their forms.

"Just thinking about the future," I say, clicking my phone locked
and slipping it back into my bag. I try to sound breezier than I feel, as
they roll out their towels and fuss about getting sorted. They've
brought food down—bread and dips and crisps and some water—so
I can't be too mad at their arrival.

Kate laughs. "Might I advise you not to?" She throws a bottle of
water at me and then spreads out the picnic.

I chortle. "Says the woman who still looks eighteen, is a trainee lawyer, married, *and* still has a sense of humor."

She steps back from the food and holds out an arm to spray on her sun lotion. "It's true," she singsongs, rubbing the oil up and down. "I am quite the catch, aren't I, Laurie?"

"Indeed you are," he agrees, scooping up some creamy hummus with his pita. Through a full mouth he adds, "That's what makes us such a match."

I snort teasingly. "I think you got my share of self-esteem, too, you know. Surely it's not healthy to regard yourself as highly as you do."

Laurie gets up with a wink and takes the sun lotion from Kate, spraying her back without her asking. His easy gesture of love isn't lost on me. Kate's the best thing ever to have happened to him. When they fell in love five years ago, we all saw this whole other side to him: considerate and complimentary and thoughtful. He was no longer my jackass of an older brother, the one who used to burp into my water bottle for school and close the lid, so that it tasted like sick at break time. He has . . . grown up. At least for Kate. Obviously he's still a jackass to the rest of us.

Jamie appears at the bottom of the steps from the house then, too, with Laurie waving him over to what was my sacrosanct and peaceful spot and is now the official meeting point—like a family holiday is supposed to be about us all spending time together. His thighs move like honey-glazed hams stuffed into Ralph Lauren shorts, a backward baseball cap making him look like a high-school jock. He doesn't walk, but *struts*.

"Hey, man!" Laurie greets him, holding a fist so that Jamie knocks into it with his own. Jamie looks over at us and barely nods, but I have to admit it is a greeting of sorts. Duly noted that he doesn't ignore me when my brother is around, then—probably doesn't want to get into Laurie's bad books. I think that might be worse. "You feeling the holiday vibe?"

"Yeah, I am," Jamie replies. "I've just been annihilated at cards by your mum, though. She's a shark!"

"Oh yeah, Veronica Greenberg is a smiling assassin. Did you have money on it?"

"A fiver," Jamie hoots. "She saw me coming!"

"Mug," Laurie says with a laugh. "Absolute mug."

Jamie and Laurie kick a ball about, calling each other names and getting increasingly close to what even I can tell is red-card kind of behavior. Eventually Kate tells them they're getting sand in the food. They come over to the shade of the tree and sit down to nibble at the snacks, too, before Kate suddenly decides to pick up on our conversation from before.

"You know what I'd *love* for you?" she asks, licking errant olive oil from where it is running down her hand to her forearm.

"I can only imagine . . ." I say, crossing my legs and arching an eyebrow. Jamie opens a packet of dried figs, offering one to all of us. I take one, but don't eat it. I hold it, waiting for Kate's declaration.

"A gap year," she declares. "A year of doing nothing."

"I had a gap year," I remind her. "Before my degree."

"Which one?" quips Laurie, winking at Jamie to get him in on the joke, unable to resist a jab at my choice of a life in academia.

"I'm ignoring that," I tell him.

"Didn't you spend it working in the local pub, and then working on a tortoise rescue program for twelve hours a day?" Kate asks.

Jamie is looking away from us and out to sea, but I can feel him rolling his eyes at me.

"Yes," I say. "In Costa Rica. I did six months there."

"And did you actually see any of Costa Rica?" Kate presses.

More eye-rolling—I just know it.

I shrug, not liking being the topic of conversation. "I saw plenty of it. From the beach. Where I worked." When she puts it like this, Kate makes me sound so square. But I liked the turtle rescue program. I didn't need to be off every night with the others, getting drunk and coming home at four A.M. "I can't live on two hours' sleep, even when I was eighteen I couldn't!"

"Exactly." She nods, satisfied that she's proved her point, flicking her choppy blond hair over her shoulder dramatically. She's in a red one-piece swimsuit with frills on the shoulders and at the thighs, and looks like a model for Reese Witherspoon's clothing line. She's warmed up to her theme now and starts wafting a hand as she says, "You need a month in Seville learning Spanish and sleeping with sexy waiters. And then a season in a ski resort, getting drunk and sleeping with tourists. Oooooh, you could do Australia and New Zealand. Bali! If you got into yoga in Bali, I'd bet you'd meet all kinds of people. Have you ever heard of ecstatic dance? It's like sex, but with your clothes on. They're mad for it up in Ubud, I've heard."

"Kate, I don't think you want me to travel so much as get laid?" I suggest, noting that she's the second person today to tell me such a thing.

Laurie puts his fingers in his ears and starts to sing loudly. I roll my eyes. It's such a cliché—older brothers who can't imagine their younger sisters are desirable to other men. I realize Jamie is looking right at me, with that stupid look on his stupid face. It's like he agrees with Laurie: I should be an asexual being. Like he hasn't already made that crystal-clear.

"Laurie," Kate coos, once he's stopped blocking out the noise of his little sister's imaginary sex life, "Flo is very hot and deserves to enjoy being hot, both by being outwardly appreciated and inwardly pleasured. We're all adults here."

"Hmmm, are we, though?" Laurie bats back, because to him I will always be a gangly twelve-year-old.

Jamie coughs and says, "I'd rather not hear about Flo's sex life, either, thanks."

Kate ignores them both and continues to focus on me. I wish she wouldn't. I wish she wouldn't in general, but especially now that Jamie is here. I don't want him to know anything about my life. Right now I can convince myself he hates an imagined version of me, but if we keep talking about how sad and pathetic I am, I might have to admit he dislikes the *actual* me, and with everything that happened during my PhD it has taken a *lot* of work even to have this much low self-confidence. I'm a work in progress, and the hardest part about that is being okay with being "unfinished"—especially surrounded by the high achievers of my family: Laurie and Kate are lawyers; Alex is a doctor; Mum is, as discussed, Veronica Greenberg; and Dad . . . well, he's the glue that keeps us all together, god bless his heart.

Oh. Shit. Kate is looking at me like she's expecting me to speak. I think I zoned out as she continued to dissect My Life And Everything That Is Wrong With It.

"Hmmm?" I say. "Sorry. I was just having a hallucination about what it would be like to have a sister-in-law who knew how to shut up and read a book."

"Ha ha," Kate says. "I'm only trying to help. I mean, Jamie, after your parents died, you realized that life is short and so followed your bliss or whatever, didn't you?"

I can't believe she's directly referenced the death of Jamie's parents. But that's Kate. She names the elephant in the room.

Jamie takes a deep breath and shrugs in a nonchalant way that seems very practiced, if you ask me. He blows out air from between his lips, making him pout like he's saying *prune*, like I've read the Olsen twins do when they're being photographed.

"Come on," Kate presses, and I'm secretly thrilled the spotlight has turned onto somebody else. I know the bits about Jamie that he shares directly with my family when I am there, and I get occasional tidbits through the way he's spoken about when he's *not* there, but seldom do I hear about Jamie in this context, from the man himself. That's what felt so special about Christmas—that suddenly we had *so much* to learn about each other. We only scratched the surface, though. Kate smirks at him, amused by his reluctance to go on record with his life's mission statement. "Seriously," she says. "Almost six figures a year from sailing boats around the world isn't a bad way to spend your days . . ."

Almost six figures?

Jamie leans back on his forearms, sinking his overdeveloped frame into the sand because he's the only one of us not sitting on his towel.

"Not all who wander are lost," he says, and Kate hoots out a laugh. Laurie shakes his head, smirking.

"Mate, you're the luckiest bastard I know. Honest to god."

I can't tell if they're poking fun at me. Jamie earns all that money swanning about sailing for half the year? Surely not.

But once again he gives very little away, and as I take the chance to study his feet, of all things—the annoyingly clean, squared-off toenails, the light dusting of hair on his toes, which weirdly isn't repulsive so much as a stamp on his masculinity, if you're into hairy men—I feel him looking at me. *Again.* I don't know what comes over me, but I dare to match his gaze, and even though we've both got sunglasses on and I can't properly see his eyes, I am 100 percent sure we've just made eye contact. He sighs, totally over the top, then turns his head away.

"I'm going to cool off in the sea," I say, getting up and heading down to the water quickly. I'm cross that my quiet afternoon of reading has been hijacked by a group of people who don't know how to exist in sociable silence. Also, with Jamie. I'm annoyed by Jamie, and I'm annoyed that I'm annoyed by him.

As I go, Kate shouts, "Your arse looks amazing in that swimsuit, babes!"

I deliberately chose something that covers me up a bit more today, after Bikini-gate yesterday, and I spin around to give her the finger. I do it with a smile to let her know I'm only half serious, cementing the fact with an over-the-top bum wiggle.

Kate screeches, yelling out, "Yassss, queen!" I throw her a cheeky grin, pleased to have made her laugh, and that's when I see Jamie shaking his head disapprovingly. *Well, excuse me for having some fun*, I think, before diving into the cool of the gentle waves. *Like, I get it: You're mad I exist, too.*

I head out a little way and lie on my back, like yesterday, practicing the deep breathing my therapist taught me—in through the nose, out through the mouth. Bonus points if you put your hand on your heart and give a little massage of reassurance.

I'm okay, I tell myself. *I'm okay.* This is what happens: All my thoughts get noisy and loud and threaten to overwhelm me: uni, the PhD, what comes next, stupid boys being stupidly judgey with their stupid head-shakes . . .

Then there's movement in the corner of my eye. Jamie.

Okay, this dude is making it really hard to avoid him, given that he seems to be in every breath I take today. He walks with so much swagger, too, like he belongs anywhere he chooses to be. What must it be like to be that sure of yourself? I can't even begin to imagine.

"The water feels warmer here," Jamie says, when he's closer. "You've not peed in it, have you?"

"What?" I say. "*No.*"

I realize too late that he's pulling my leg, and it flusters me. I clamber out of the water in a panic. I do *not* want to have to talk to him, or try to talk to him and be disregarded, or waste energy pretending he's not there, when he's very obviously trying to get my back up by following me in. *Just leave me alone, dude.* Jesus.

I barely manage to issue a simpering "Enjoy!" but I do, because I am mature and levelheaded and determined not to be outwardly rattled. All over again I flush with frustration that the first time I have to see Jamie since everything happened is for two whole weeks on a family holiday. That is some *intense* exposure therapy, goddammit.

"Flo . . ." he says, like he's telling me off.

"No thank you," I retort, and I'm not sure what that even means. *No thank you, I do not want your words? No thank you, I do not want you?* I hear him sigh, an expulsion of air that I take to mean I have disappointed him, and I could turn round and scream at him, shout at him for being here, for daring to show his thoughtless, horrid face, but I don't. Instead I scamper up the beach, dripping everywhere, focusing on nothing but the sand in front of my feet and willing myself not to cry. It's not actually that hard when I'm this angry. I don't want tears. I want to break something.

"That was quick," notes Laurie. He and Kate are eating cherries and competing over who can spit the pits the furthest. "Did you get scared by a jellyfish?"

"No," I shoot back, settling onto my towel. I can't explain any further, so I leave it at that. I grab my sun hat and pull it over my face so that I can have a little snooze—or just have a great excuse to ignore them all.

"What's got into her?" Laurie asks Kate, in a fake stage whisper.

Kate tuts. "Leave her be, she's fine," she says.

But I'm not.

It takes everything I have in me not to cry.

4

"To family," Alex says, raising his glass so that the rest of us follow. "You all do my absolute nut in, but I love you, and I'm glad we're all here together."

The seven of us are having a quick *aperitivo* before we head out, all of us various shades of pink except Jamie, whose tan, impossibly, seems to have darkened even more, despite the fact we've only been at the villa for twenty-four hours. He's wearing cutoff denim shorts and a white tank top with huge armholes, so that half his torso is on show. Should nipples be allowed at dinner? I can't believe nobody seems to mind. There'd be an uproar if I wore something even a degree as revealing. Where is his self-respect?

"To family," we all echo, smiling. I can't speak for anyone else, but it's touched me that Alex would be so uncharacteristically sweet, even if he does let out a massive fart as he lifts his glass.

"Pardon me," he says, not meaning it at all.

"Oh my *god*, Alex!" Jamie coughs, his eyes watering at the smell.

"Mate, don't," Laurie warns him. "If we don't collectively ignore him, it only serves as encouragement. Alex doesn't register the 'negative' part of 'negative attention,' if you catch my drift."

Alex farts again.

"Told you," Laurie says. Alex grins.

As we marvel at the sunset and quaff down our beers, nibbling on crisps and some olives, I sidle up to Alex and ask, "You okay, bro?"

He furrows his brow like the question offends him and replies, "Yeah, little sister. Are you?"

"Do you know what?" I reply. I've sunk my beer already and the sunset is all pink and gorgeous and it makes my shoulders sit lower, my jaw loosen. I am *determined* to enjoy this holiday. Determined! "Yeah," I say. "I am. Like you say, everyone does my nut in, but I'm glad we're all here together."

Despite Jamie being here, I think—but I don't say it. He doesn't deserve the oxygen.

"You sound soft." He winks after he speaks, letting me know he's "soft," too.

"It's in my DNA," I retort. "Which I hear can run in the family."

Alex scrunches up his nose at me playfully, and I mirror it. He's done it to me since we were kids—always him first, as a gesture of brotherly love, and I always copy, an acknowledgment that I receive said love. Feelings without words. Alex and I have our own language that way. He's always been nicer to me than Laurie. Laurie tortured me as a kid—he still does—but Alex always found a way to distract him. He didn't outright stick up for me or tell Laurie to back off (Laurie wouldn't have responded to that), but he's always made room for me, let me be a tiny bit more of myself. Laurie has all these ideas about how I should behave and it's like I always let him down. Alex lets me be myself.

"It's a proper nice place me and Dad booked for tonight," Alex says, rubbing his hands together. "Those night-lights are strung up in the courtyard, good view, proper mom-and-pop owners, *and* we saw a sign for live music in the square, too. Oh, actually—" He looks at his watch. "Drink up, gang! It's about a fifteen-minute walk and the table's booked for half past."

"Look at you," I comment, "being all organized."

"I know," Alex says with a shrug. "I surprise myself sometimes."

"We'll make a man of you yet?" I ask.

He laughs. "Something like that, yeah. Come on. You can sit next to me if you like. Seat of honor."

We assemble, grabbing handbags and locking doors and making sure we've all got phones for the way back—it will be dark and it's not very well lit, so we'll need the lights.

"You can hold my hand if you get scared," Laurie says to Jamie with a wink.

"I'll assume the position of the thorn between roses, with Mike and Vee on either side of me, I think," Jamie bats back.

"Isn't the expression *rose between two thorns*?" Dad asks.

"You could never be the thorn, mate," Jamie tells Dad. "You're not only the flower—you're the whole damned garden."

Dad chuckles. "I can see why you do as well as you do," he says. "Smooth bastard."

Alex and Dad lead the way, since they know where we're going, with Mum chatting amiably alongside them. Laurie and Kate fall into step behind, holding hands and being in love and happy. So that leaves Jamie and me at the back of the group, the air between us thick with the sound of crickets and hostility, one foot in front of the other in unfriendly but rhythmic steps. I turn my face away from him and list what is good in my head—another trick from my therapist. There's the sweet smell of lavender in the air, a cool breeze dancing

51

through the trees. I feel pretty in my maxi-dress, in that way that's very specific to being on holiday. I didn't wash my hair because the sea salt in the ocean made it dry with waves more luscious than I could style myself, and even with a smidge of sunburn, at least my freckles are out already, splattered across my cheeks. My family is here. I am safe. I have a wonderful best friend and am lucky to be able to have therapy. And Greece is beautiful.

I'm okay, I'm okay, I'm okay.

The feeling I had at drinks earlier on intensifies: something close to happiness. My breath deepens. We'll have a great dinner tonight. My family is at its best around a table. Always has been. As long as Jamie is seated at the other end, it could even be a wonderful night. I think about what Kate said about having a Greek fling. Maybe I should keep my eyes peeled . . . it's about time my libido came out of hibernation. All of Hope's stories are making me think I deserve a little fun, too. Getting flung would feel like an achievement, in so much as letting myself actually have fun would be a first. Maybe it's my bare shoulders and wavy hair and this dress . . . I'm kinda feeling myself. It's been a while.

Crunch, crunch, crunch. The gravel underfoot makes a satisfying noise as Jamie and I walk, left-right, left-right. It's annoying that I become aware of the nearness of him, the light notes of that cedary scent I caught a whiff of yesterday on his T-shirt. I'm surprised I've not been more ribbed about that today, but then fair play if nobody wants to think about their sister's boobs. If the topic of the day has moved on, I'm in luck.

The path narrows, so everyone has to meander single file, and Jamie steps back, holding out an arm to signal I should go ahead. I *should* just keep walking, go in front and let him fall behind. But for some reason his display of gallant gentlemanly manners irritates me. I don't want his empty gestures.

Let's not speak of this again . . .

I wish the words weren't so branded on my brain.

"I'm fine," I tell the ground, my voice tight. "After you."

I sweep my arm out in front of me, and when Jamie doesn't move, I glance up to be greeted with *that look*. The muscles in my face harden, my brow lowers, and we stay like that: staring each other out. His eyes are cool, and his pecs—all too clearly visible because of that poor excuse for a "T-shirt"—rise and fall with his breath. I think he's putting it on. But also there's a tiny bead of sweat up near his hairline, and it's oddly satisfying to see it grow in my peripheral vision until it falls down his cheek. He lifts a hand to wipe it away: slowly, purposefully, his eyes alight with something I'm not so familiar with. He looks . . . sad? Well, if he is: good. Maybe he's learned a valuable lesson about how to treat people. This ice between us is his doing, after all. This is the path *he* chose.

I hold his eye. I haven't played at a staring contest since I was about ten, when Laurie would stare at me in the car on long trips, and when I'd move to look at him, he'd shift his gaze an inch so that he was actually looking past me. I'd stare at him until he moved to try and "catch me," and we'd go back and forth like that until he complained to Mum and Dad that I was bugging him, when he was the one who'd started it.

"Are you two coming or what?" Dad yells from halfway down the path.

I don't take my eyes off Jamie as I answer.

"Yeah!" I say. "Jamie's going to follow first."

He looks away. I've scored my point. In what overall game, I am unsure, but it's definitely 1–0 to me as Jamie exhales deeply and moves up in front, his head down.

"Whatever," he mutters. "I don't know why I bother."

"You don't," I shoot back, but I don't think he hears me.

AT THE RESTAURANT, our hosts are delighted by Jamie's ability to make small talk in rudimentary Greek and so we immediately become the most favored table in the house.

"Welcome, new friends," a portly chap with sweeping gray hair says as he dishes out menus and bread baskets. We order drinks and they're delivered with a few picky bits to whet our appetites, and I have to say, the smells coming from the kitchen are *outrageous*. I can't tell if I want calamari or catch of the day or moussaka . . . I feel ravenous. Not only for the food, but for feeling this contented. If I'd known Jamie was coming and had somehow turned this down, I'd have been an idiot. There's no substitute for travel, and travel with family is next-level. There are no airs and graces. That's the thing I always struggled with when I had communal living at university: to truly let somebody see you—and I mean the most unpalatable, Gruffalo-like version of you—really takes some intimacy. I've never really had that level of intimacy with people outside my bloodline. It's just not the same.

We quieten as we study the menus, and I take a moment to marvel at the exact shade of pink in the sky, and how the condensation feels on the glass of my chilled wine. I must be smiling, because I accidentally lock eyes with Jamie and the right side of his mouth curves upward, before dropping suddenly when I frown, challenging him to another staring contest. He doesn't take me up on it, but instead looks back down at his menu, although his eyes don't move, so

I'm not sure he's actually reading it. If I've unnerved him in any way, I'm pleased, because he *should* feel a fraction of what I do whenever he's around.

I know I'm supposed to be paying no mind, but it's frustratingly hard.

"Well," Mum says brightly, once we've placed our order, "what a great find, guys."

"Told you," Alex boasts. "It's mine and Dad's superpower, figuring out the best places to eat. Isn't it, Dad?"

Dad chuckles. "To be honest, son, I'm just your wingman. You find these places all by yourself."

"Batman is nothing without Robin," Laurie points out, which sounds dangerously like backing up Alex's point. He must be feeling as happy to be here as I am.

"True," says Dad. "And I have always suited red."

"Is that why you've gone for the sunburnt look?" Laurie teases, and Alex hoots out a "Whoa-ah!" We all laugh.

"Laurie," Dad says, pretending to be disinterested in the insult he's about to issue. "At least when I commit to the sunburnt look, I go all-in. Those white bits around your eyes? Not *Vogue*."

"Not *Vogue*" is Dad's way of saying "unfashionable." Why? Who can say.

"I wore sunglasses on our walk!" Laurie says, defending himself.

"Might I also suggest a hat?" Dad asks, and we all laugh again. Nobody means it. Not much, anyway.

We order, and talk about Laurie and Kate's new flat (expensive), Alex's work (exhausting), and Mum's retirement plans (undefined). It's like everybody gets equal airtime, and so I know I have to have a turn, too. I can't stand it, though. I get it: I'm the family screwup, the one not quite able to be a proper adult. Nobody needs to point it out.

In fact it would be great if we could rewrite that narrative, somehow. It's just that every time I try, I get tongue-tied and my cheeks flush. When that happens, it's like I prove Laurie's theory that, emotionally, I'm a teenager.

"How are you feeling about your PhD being finished, Flo?" Alex asks. "I'd be overwhelmed, in need of a massive break, if I got a *third* degree . . ."

"So says the doctor," I counter, trying to keep things light, and he waves a hand to bat me away.

"I don't think she likes talking about it," says Laurie, glancing at me as if daring me to disagree. Is he being protective or combative? With Laurie, it can be so hard to tell.

"Don't you?" Alex asks.

I pause in my response, because the answer is *No! I do not want to talk about myself.* But the words stick in my throat because stupidly, annoyingly, irritatingly, I've got tears pricking at my eyes. Why am I like this? I don't know what it is—why I'm on the cusp of crying. I'm having a nice time. I'm fine! Now everyone is going to think I'm *not* fine, and that's so galling. I suppose it's like pushing a bruise, talking about me, about my life. It's tender. That's why I avoid it at all costs. These tears are coming from nowhere, but they're definitely coming— and now everyone is looking at me.

There's an awkward pause and I cast a glance up to find an ally, and see that even Kate looks a bit sympathetic, a bit *poor Flo.* And that's it; an errant tear escapes and runs down my face, and I push it away but another comes, so I look down at the napkin on my lap and focus on making sure there are no more.

"Oh, darling," Mum says, as Alex whispers, "Sorry."

I shake my head, but thank *god* the waiter arrives with our main courses then, right in time. It's so much food that we have to move glasses and shift the vase of flowers in the middle of the table. We busy ourselves rearranging the tablescape, and by the time we're sorted, there's a lull in the conversation, nobody sure what to talk about next.

"I have to say," announces Jamie, as we all quietly chew our food, "I'm envious of the lot of you: accomplished, handsome tarts, you all are. Two lawyers, a medical doctor, a PhD . . . Although I must add," he says, leaning over for the salt, "obviously all control is merely an illusion." He meets my eye as he says that, and I find I can't look away. "Who has any idea of what our futures might hold?"

And he's done it. He's picked up the chat, steered it into neutral territory and, before I know it, we're back to being the version of my family I love most, talking shit about what we'd do if we *could* control the future, all the funny things we would do. He's . . . rescued me? I'd be furious at the suggestion I need rescuing, if only I wasn't, on this one occasion, so very grateful.

HOURS LATER AND the air is cool and my cheeks are warm. After Jamie expertly navigated the conversation away from me as the headline, everyone seemed to realize that I really have had enough of being picked over—even if they mean well—and made the effort to have a really good night. Mum and Dad even got up for a dance at one point, in the square where the band was playing. It must be so comforting, knowing you're with your person, that you've created this whole branch of the family tree together, that you've got a legacy, and each other. Anyway. That's my family in a nutshell: They push me to the brink and then pull me back in for warm and fuzzies. It would send a lesser woman mad. I watch my parents sway cheek to cheek; Laurie and Kate whisper sweet nothings, while Alex and Jamie are listing things they admire about each other . . .

Oh my god, they're drunk. In fact *I'm* drunk. If I'm on the verge of throwing my arms around one of them to tell them how much I love them, too, then I have definitely had one too many. *Ooooops.*

The second piece of evidence that the booze has rushed to my head? As we're tipsily traipsing back up the hill with our iPhone torches lighting the way, I'm feeling called to say thanks to Jamie. He didn't have to help me out back there. But, curiously, he did.

We automatically walk in the same configuration as on the way down, with me and Jamie bringing up the rear. As we get to where the path narrows, Jamie falls back and then catches himself, seeming to remember how aggressive I was the first time and so dropping to his foot to tie an errant shoelace, letting me go ahead. It's only when he's down there that he seems to remember he's in flip-flops.

"Hey," I say, lingering as he stands. "Cheers. For before."

I'm hoping he's catching my drift. I don't have the capacity to fully break it down.

"I didn't do anything," he says and shrugs dismissively. He issues a wave, as if I'm a gnat that is bothering him and should just buzz off. It's giving me only-speak-when-spoken-to vibes, and I am *not* into it.

"What?" I say, taken aback by his attitude.

"I said, I didn't do anything," he repeats. And because I am stunned into standing still, he takes the opportunity to overtake me after all, rising to his feet to take the hill in huge strides that mean I have to take three of my tiny steps to his one. He's practically running away from me. My anger flares like a dragon's roar.

I break into a jog to close in on Jamie right as the path widens again. Now I can overtake, so I do. And as I pass I utter one word, because why can't he simply be nice? I was giving him a compliment! Showing him my gratitude. Can't we even be civil in that way? "Farthead," I say, under my breath . . . but loud enough for him to hear clearly. God, now I *know* I'm pissed. Farthead? Who, after the age of six, says *that*?

"Excuse me?" Jamie asks, marching purposefully up behind me. I don't slow down. I am apoplectic. I know what it is: It's the dismissiveness. Well, I won't stand for it. Nobody can treat me that way, not least within my own family. I wouldn't take it from my parents, or my brothers—and if he's going to be on this trip with us, I won't take it from Jamie, either. I think that's where *farthead* came from. I should have said something much stronger, but he's annoying me like the boys did when we were young, so our go-to insult from when we were little slipped out. Anyway, if the shoe fits, etc.

"You heard me," I say, and it's like we're competitors in a "fast walkers" competition, arms at right angles, feet moving deftly. "You're a . . . farthead."

I say it plainly, as facts should be spoken clearly. I can see the house up ahead, lit up from lights strategically placed throughout the gardens. I want to get inside, head on up to my room, and take a shower to wash this . . . this *feeling* off of me.

"You're a dismissive, rude . . . farthead," I finish, as my parting shot.

I must have yelled louder than I realized—I blame the drink—because my whole family turns round then, to see what's going on. Jamie clocks this as I do, so if he's got anything to say to my pronouncement, he doesn't, saving face in front of anyone but me—his main objective in this life. I take this as another win.

"Don't mind us!" I singsong.

"No," Jamie says, sounding wounded, switching tack from the

strong-and-silent-to-me type, to ham it up now he's got an audience. "Come on, Flo, that's not fair."

Mum nudges Dad, her way of telling him to pay attention to what's happening, and he says, "Ow, Vee. That hurt!"

"Oh, for god's sake, Michael," she tuts, but I see her catch Kate's eye, and Kate pulls a face. She purses her lips, and Mum sets her mouth in a straight line in reply. What the hell is that supposed to mean?

"Who's got the key?" I ask, and Alex remembers he does and lets us all in.

Jamie is right behind me as we file through to the kitchen. He's close. Too close. Closer than he has any right to be. He hisses, "How can you go from *thanking* me to calling me names, in just two sentences? And 'farthead' at that?"

Right as I'm about to say *easily*, Dad cries out, "What the hell?"

I bang into Kate in front of me, who has banged into Laurie in front of her.

"Bollocks!" Dad cries. "The pipe has blown."

There are a couple of inches of water across half of the kitchen floor, but more than that: a burst pipe from somewhere near the sink is spraying water like we're in a Beyoncé video. I have no clue what to do.

"Mike, we need to find the stopcock," Jamie says, his voice calm and smooth, like he sees this all the time. He pulls off the scrap of fabric that allegedly passes as his top as he pushes past me, wading through the water toward the leak, ready to put the shirt over the cause of the spray. It happens in slow motion: He's the month of May in a filthy calendar of "World's Sexiest Deckhands" (World's Sexiest Dickheads?), the spray arching up to the ceiling and down over his head to wet his hair, which he flicks back off of his forehead. Very *you're worth it.* The shirt goes over the tap, but not before his torso is hosed down, so that when Jamie turns to ask Laurie to come and hold it, his body glistens with moisture.

All I can think is: *Oh, for god's sake.*

"Grab this, mate!" he says, beckoning with his free hand to Laurie.

It's like the scene from *Mad Men* where Don Draper fixes the leak at his neighbor's dinner party, all the women swooning over the sight of a strapping bloke saving the day. Kate reaches out a hand and clasps the top of my thigh in delight. Mum turns to us with a raised eyebrow of appreciation. Aren't they embarrassed to gawp so openly? The way Kate exhales makes me think obviously not.

Jamie flings back the door to the cupboard under the sink, dropping to his knees in the small lake that is growing by the second. He pauses to run a hand through his sodden hair, pushing it back from his face. I swear to god that he closes his eyes as he does so, for extra effect, like this is another big performance for him.

"Oh shit, look," I hear Alex say; he has hung back to keep dry with us girls. He's pointing to the room off the kitchen and down a couple of stone steps: Jamie's bedroom. It's even worse than the kitchen.

"Oh god," Mum says. "I'll go and search out some linens. Jamie will have to sleep on the sofa tonight . . . I'll call the landlady in the morning to get a plumber."

Whatever Jamie does under the sink works, because the fountain of water stops with a whimper. All I can see of him are his waist and legs: he's lying on his back fiddling with pipes and bolts, head hidden, with Dad handing him things from a toolbox he's found. Jamie's shorts are low, below his belly button, with a soft tuft of hair trailing down to . . . well, underneath his shorts. His legs are bent to support him, every move of his arms rippling down to his torso, shimmering as it is with water, and sweat.

I don't mean to, and it repulses me, but . . . I gasp.

"I second that," whispers Kate.

I scowl at her.

"Hey, we've both got eyes, babe. I see what you see."

Okay, fine. *Sometimes—very occasionally—*Jamie can be in the ballpark of "attractive."

Rarely.

But yes.

Every now and then. If you forget his actual personality.

Mum comes back with as many towels as she can carry and points to the cleaning cupboard under the stairs. "Get the mop, would you, love?" she says.

In the more shallow areas they sop up all the excess with the towels. I go back and forth between them, pushing water into puddles, so it's easier to get up. It's hard work, to be fair, so we're all quiet, the jovial atmosphere of earlier ebbing away. It's only when we're about done, and we all pause for breath, that I remember how furious I am at Jamie's attitude from before. Everyone is shaking his hand and slapping his back, to say good job on leaping into action—if anyone else remembers Jamie and me shouting gangbusters at one another, they've forgotten it fast. I'm going to call it a night, before I bring it back up again. I just can't be bothered to deal with all this. I am calm and serene. Thoughts of Jamie roll off me. I am untouchable. Unbotherable.

"Before you go up, Flo," Mum says, as I give her a good-night kiss on the cheek, "Jamie's going to have to bunk up with you tonight. His room is totally trashed."

"What?" says Laurie, with about as much shock as I feel.

"His room is flooded, and the sofas are all two-seater things. They're not big enough for anybody to sleep on comfortably," Mum explains. "I saw there are two beds in Flo's room when I was looking for the linen cupboard."

She looks between me, Laurie, and Jamie, and all of us have approximations of the same outrage painted across our faces.

"Oh, for goodness' sake, you're all such prudes! Laurie, first of all I'm not asking anybody to do anything I wouldn't ask of any of you. Also," she adds, her features darkening with mischief, "butt out."

Laurie gasps, practically clutching his pearls.

Mum turns to me and Jamie. "I know you like your own space, Flo, but in times of need we all have to compromise. Jamie darling, it's only a single bed you'll have, but at least that's better than the floor. Alex's room is basically a cupboard with a tiny bed in it, plus he snores like a dinosaur. Flo doesn't." She winks at me. "Well. As much."

"I'm sure Jamie doesn't want to—" I start, right as Jamie says, "That will be more than fine, Veronica. Thank you."

He shrugs at me, as if he's helpless. Surely Alex will swap, so that I can have the one-bed room and *he* can share with Jamie in the twin? I wait for him to offer. He doesn't.

I look away from all of them and stare at the ceiling. I cannot believe I have to share a bloody room with Jamie now. Why does he even have to be here?

This is *not* the holiday I signed up for. I storm off and grab my phone. I pull up my texts with Hope. You won't BELIEVE what's happened now! I type, flames practically coming out of my fingertips, I hit the phone screen so hard.

"Try looking up from that thing," Jamie says, when he spots me. "There's a whole world beyond it, you know."

Urgh.

5

5:30 a.m.

I have slept for maybe ten minutes the whole night, because Jamie's mere presence in my room has been enough to keep me awake. I cannot believe this turn of events. I cannot believe that not only has Jamie Kramer invaded my summer holiday, but now he's invaded my bedroom. And he's slept soundly, too, barely moving, his breath shallow and as if none of this is unusual or unfair at all. The moon came through the curtains to illuminate his face: the slope of his Cupid's bow, his stubbled chin, long eyelashes on carved-from-marble cheeks. He almost looks sweet when he's asleep. Of course I know better.

I tossed and turned and got madder and madder, all night, and now I need to get out of here.

I slip out from between my sheets and grab my running gear. At least it's cool enough this early to get one in, considering that I missed yesterday's. A run always sorts me out. I've been running in one way or another since I was eleven, when I started cross-country. I love that feeling of one foot in front of the other—that you don't need to know anything other than that. You simply keep going, and after the first two or three minutes it's like meditation. I never listen to music or podcasts; it's always just me and my footsteps. I've always done it because I love it, but it turns out I'm good at it, too. I've won competitions—even nationally. It's been years since I've competed, but me and a dirt track, or a nature trail, or at a push a long path beside a quiet road, and I'm happy. Much happier than when I don't run, anyway.

I pull on my running shoes by the front door and automatically follow the path down into town, the one we took last night. But I don't slip into a meditative state easily. Instead I think about the near-argument last night. I didn't mean to call Jamie a farthead per se—I was merely embarrassed that I'd acknowledged his kindness and he pied me off. That's what I get for having four glasses of wine: My judgment slipped. I'll have to get back on it today: a dignified detachment and keeping out of his way. I'll sleep on the sofa tonight, even if Mum thinks it's not possible. Jamie can take my room, unjust as that feels.

I run up past the town square to the other side of the village where life peters out again, and by lucky chance make a right up a winding path that I sense could lead back to the house in a big loop. It's longer than I'd assumed, but I don't mind. The sun is climbing in the sky by the time the villa is back in view. Honestly, running really is the best way to see a place. I clock the odd farmer in his field, the animals grazing before it gets too hot. It's nice to wake up alongside Mother Nature. Soothing. I do love to be outside, especially near the sea. Funny how I spend so much time chained to an indoor desk, then.

I slink around the back of the house, thinking I'll stretch in the shade of the veranda, and am surprised to see Kate up already, laying the table for breakfast.

"How do," she says at the sound of my approach. "Couldn't sleep?"

"Not really," I say, panting. I put my hands behind my head to force my posture upright and to get air into my lungs.

She nods. "Me neither." She notes my breathing. "Water? I'll get some ice."

"I love you," I say, regulating my inhales and exhales. "I don't tell you that enough."

She laughs lightly. "You only want me for my cold beverages."

"Doesn't take away from the depth of my feeling." I shrug, and I drop down into a runner's lunge and then flop over into pigeon pose, letting my muscles cool down and my breath get back to normal.

"So," Kate says, pouring me a drink and leaning two hands against one of the patio chairs. "Last night." I knew she was going to ask before the words left her mouth. *Of course* she wants the juicy details. "Were you and Jamie *arguing* on the way home?" She emphasizes the word *arguing* as if the notion of a cross word is somehow salacious. I mean, it *is*, but that's beside the point. I don't want to tell her too much—she already knows enough.

I don't say anything as I get up from my position on the paved ground.

Kate senses my hesitance and further offers, "You were *yelling* at each other . . ."

"Interesting," I muse. "You asked if we were arguing, when it seems that you know we were and what you actually want to know is *what about*," I say, arching an eyebrow.

She smirks. "I was warming up the witness, Your Honor."

"Badly, I might add."

She motions with a hand for me to get on with it.

I open my mouth to speak, but sigh instead. I know the best thing to do is brush it under the carpet, put it down to a few merry drinks too many, and let sleeping dogs lie. I will myself for it to be bygone. Today is a new day. Honestly, it shouldn't be this hard to get Jamie out of my system and yet. And yet.

"Was it foreplay or . . . ?"

"Foreplay?" I bat back. "Yeah. Sure. We're basically on the cusp of running off into the sunset together as lovers."

"I'm serious," she insists, giggling.

"Kate," I say, draining my glass and pouring another, to leave a dramatic pause for emphasis. "Jamie . . . well, I don't know if he hates me, but after Christmas he definitely doesn't *like* me. We're at the opposite end of the spectrum to *lovers*."

"So you're enemies?"

"I didn't say *that*," I counter, overwhelmingly aware that when you're talking to a lawyer, everything you say will be taken as evidence.

"It's a thin line between love and hate," Kate says. "Enemies to lovers and all that . . ."

"Kate," I warn.

She chews on her bottom lip and goes on. "I'm just saying, you know. I feel like there's something there. What happened at Christmas doesn't add up to me . . ."

The mention of last Christmas forces color to my cheeks and heat to my heart. Will it ever not bother me?

"Kate," I say, "Jamie is a pretentious drifter, who I tolerate because I feel sorry for him. All these women he uses and discards? It's pathetic, not to mention gross. What kind of a hole must he have in his heart to womanize the way he does?" The words pour out, surprising me, slick as oil. I can't stop them. I don't know what comes over me. It's like I'm practicing, rehearsing lines, seeing how it feels to really let rip. It's like all the anger I've had churning inside me finally gets to come out. "I tolerate him because I feel sorry for him really, but honestly, if he wasn't Laurie's friend, if he wasn't basically a surrogate son to Mum and Dad, if he was a bloke on the street who chatted me up at a bar, I'd run the other way. He's got no ambition, thinks abs are a personality trait, and has the chat of a deflated basketball with a face drawn on it. To be honest, I don't even know why you and Laurie *are* friends with him."

Kate has been stunned into silence. I don't know where all that came from, either—I've never spoken like that about anyone in my life, ever. I can tell I've gone too far because the color has drained from Kate's face and her eyes have gone saucerlike and black. I'm about to take it all back when a voice from behind me says, "Morning, all."

Oh, crap. I turn, confirming who it belongs to. Jamie. He's obviously heard every last word of what I said.

"Morning," says Kate, coming back from screensaver mode and suddenly becoming the hostess with the absolute mostest. She fetches cereals and milk, bread and some cheese, overcompensating for being the person I was saying such horrid things to by being bright and chatty and effusive. Between the clattering of cutlery and unfurling of napkins, there's no room for small talk. I know in the very corners of my mind that I should apologize, but I cannot physically bring myself to do that. Jamie would probably just pie me off again. But what haunts me, as breakfast unfurls, is that he doesn't speak, either, not even to Kate. After a while of pensive juice-drinking he peels off his T-shirt, his low-slung swim shorts letting us all know that *V* is his favorite letter of the alphabet, and slips into the pool to do his laps, leaving me to feel like absolute crap.

That was the most awkward fifteen minutes of my life. If Kate is going to point out that I should absolutely feel this way, she doesn't—but I suspect that's only because one by one everybody else files down to the breakfast table and so we don't get a private audience. Jamie continues to swim. I continue to try and mentally rationalize how maybe he didn't hear me—and fail. I know he did. I might not like him, but even I don't want to be the person responsible for making him feel crap. His ego can probably withstand it, but it isn't right. That's not who I am, saying those things.

"Here," says Alex as he arrives at the table, throwing a book down in front of me and narrowly missing my plate. "I think you'll like this. It was on the shelf by the board games."

I glance down, jam toast halfway to my mouth. As I chew, I turn it over in my hand. *Poems I Think You'll Like*, the title says. "Ha ha," I reply, swallowing.

"Legit!" Alex claims. "They're funny. Is 'irreverent' the word? Anyway. You read a shit-ton, don't you? Enjoy."

He crinkles up his nose. I crinkle mine back.

It's loosely agreed that we'll spend the day at the villa today, by the pool, with potentially a little late-afternoon walk down to the beach to stretch our legs. Alex and Dad load up the water pistols and Kate assumes a position on a giant inflatable swan, with Laurie clearing the table and Mum making a shopping list for whoever goes to the supermarket later. Jamie is still swimming. It's been forever. I think he's mad at me. I'm getting a feeling. If he is, I think it will be the first time in history I've got a reaction from him. Unfortunately, though, I'm so ashamed of myself that I can't enjoy it. I pick up my book of poems and slink off inside.

IN THE LIVING room it is cool and quiet. I curl up on one of the tiny two-seater sofas and sip my third coffee of the morning, flicking through the book. One poem in particular catches my eye. It basically says if you don't want to get riled up by a man you should either avoid him or get to know him better.

It makes me smile. My love life isn't exactly extensive, but I will say that the cure for almost every crush I've ever had has been getting to know the guy. It's like, the more you learn, the less there is to make up in your head about them. I take a photo of the page and send it to Hope.

ME
Saw this and thought of you

HOPE
Because now you know me, you're over your crush on me?

ME
My crush on you will never be over

HOPE
I feel exactly the same, gorgeous
How's it going over there? With J***e?

ME
It's . . . going. We avoid each other mostly.

I reread the poem. In the first year of my undergrad degree there was a girl in halls who was really weird with me, and then one night a few weeks in she got really drunk and I found her in the toilets crying. I gave her a tissue, helped her get home, and after that we became friends. She told me later that she'd judged me harshly, that she'd thought I was a stuck-up geek who only cared about impressing the teachers. I told her that was kind of true, but we were close enough by this point that she could see the other stuff about me, too: why I cared so much, where it came from. We've drifted since then—I've drifted from everyone since the breakdown—but if Rachel and I figured out a way to coexist by getting to know each other, then maybe this Wendy Cope is right. If I flip the Jamie script on its head, it could be a sort of exposure therapy. Huh. *Exposure therapy.* I had that thought the other night as well—that him being here is one hell of a way to confront what happened.

ME
EXPOSURE THERAPY?!
Do I need to spend MORE time with Jamie, and so release his
hold on me?

HOPE
Yes! Exactly! Exposure therapy!!!
Cure yourself of any and all emotion toward him by getting to
know him, so he can disappoint you as a man and cease to be
of any interest at all. It's foolproof! Yay, Wendy Cope.

I smile, sending back a GIF of Bluey doing a happy dance.
"Funny text?"
I look up. Kate. She's leaning against the door frame and looks uncharacteristically serious.
"Yeah, actually," I say. "My friend Hope has given me an idea for something."
She nods, not wanting to engage on anything other than what she's come in here to talk to me about. I can guess what it is, too.

"Babe," she starts, coming to rest on the arm of the sofa. "You need to fix what happened this morning. You can feel that way about Jamie all you want—and god knows, I get why—but he heard, and nobody else might be able to tell he's upset, but I can tell. And he's my friend as well as Laurie's. You overstepped. I hate to say it, but you did. Even in spite of everything."

I nod. "I know," I say. "I feel shitty about it."

"Good," she replies. "Because you should."

Bang-bang—she's not messing about. Shots have been fired. Kate's not letting me off the hook. Not that I deserve to be, but . . . I don't know. Maybe I hoped she'd tell me I'm not the monster I acted like, and that Jamie is infuriating enough to justify it? Anyway. No such luck.

"I'll take it into consideration," I say, "After a shower."

Kate nods slowly. "Okay."

"Okay."

She cocks her head at me. "I can't make you feel better about this unless you apologize, you know."

"I know!" I say, rolling my eyes dramatically. There's a feeling in the pit of my stomach, letting me know that she's right and I have let myself down. But apologize? To Jamie? That turns my stomach even more. "I will, I promise."

She leaves to go back outside and I walk upstairs, heading to *our* room. I still can't believe all his stuff is here, like we cohabit peacefully. Jamie has made his bed with hospital-precision corners, the sheet and blanket tight over his mattress. He's folded some clothes and arranged a few bits on his bedside table: a book, some lip balm, a coiled-up phone charger. It's like he's being overly tidy to prove the point that I'm not. I can't help but notice the corner of something sticking out under his pillow, too: a brown leather notebook. I'll bet it's a log of the women he's slept with, all over the world. Jamie Kramer—he who prides himself on breaking hearts.

I hop in the shower, and as I'm soaping my hair and washing my body, I turn over in my mind the idea of *getting to know Jamie better*. He did a horrid thing, but that only keeps hurting me if I let it, doesn't it? I can't quite imagine becoming best buddies, but something cordial could *possibly* be achieved. I think. Holding on to all this anger surely isn't good for me. And he's only a heartbreaker if he wins—if I act nonplussed, like properly and actually, I'll bet that will annoy him even more.

By the sink Jamie has got a neat leather toiletry bag, with toothpaste for sensitive teeth, roll-on deodorant (not spray), and interdental brushes for extra dental hygiene. All these little hints, I think, drying myself off, as to who he really is. If I did want some exposure therapy, this would be a good place to start. Like, oh, he's just a man. A man who gets body odor and needs to look after his teeth like the rest of us. There's nothing *special* about him . . .

Already I feel a bit differently. I mean, it's easier when he's not actually in front of me, of course. But in theory, yeah—I can see how learning more about Jamie could actually make him less of a threat to me, less able to annoy me. After all, I know everything there is to know about my family and I'm able to be annoyed by them without it being all-consuming—Alex has no filter when it comes to his bodily emissions, but I still think he's the kindest man I know; and Laurie is a pedant with a stick up his arse sometimes, but he's the one to call when somebody has been rude and you want another person on your side. Jamie needs to be in the same category as my brothers. I text Hope.

ME

Honestly, been thinking this over and the theory tracks. Getting to know him better? I think it will work!

I pad out of the en suite in my towel right as Jamie rounds the corner to the room. He's still wet from the pool, a beach towel slung low around his hips like he's simply too cool to dress properly. The man needs a Ken doll, complete with Ken wardrobe, so he can practice what a fully dressed man looks like. We're in the narrow corridor where the entrance to the room breaks off into the bathroom and a built-in cupboard, so unless he backs up and out, I'm hemmed in by Jamie and his show of abs.

He doesn't move.

I shift the cotton of my towel. I'm suddenly aware that underneath this simple slip of fabric I am very, *very* naked. I hold it in place tightly, just in case. Seeing my boobs during a volleyball match is one thing, but a full strip show at the bathroom door would be quite another. Plus, as if he deserves to see my boobs again.

I wait for him to leave immediately, get what he needs and then leave, or ask to use the bathroom, so *I* can leave.

He does none of those things.

Okay. This is awkward.

I feel his eyes trailing across my collarbones and up my neck, judging me, as he does. His gaze thick and unrelenting, like he's determined to intimidate me.

Exposure therapy, I tell myself. *Exposure therapy!*

I dare to make eye contact and smile. I am met with a blank stare, as per usual. I suppose he must be waiting for his apology. Fair enough.

"I'm sorry," I say. "About before. I didn't mean what I said to Kate."

Jamie narrows his eyes, and I feel about two inches tall.

"So why did you say it?" he asks. It's a simple enough question, but hell, is it loaded.

"I don't know."

My voice is small, like a school kid getting reprimanded by the head teacher. I look down at my toes, ashamed. Jamie closes the gap between us by stepping forward—just a couple of low-key enemies in towels. This is definitely an invasion of my personal space.

"Flo," he says in his low growl. My lips part. I don't know why, but I seem to be struggling to get air into my lungs.

"Yes?" I respond. My voice comes out as less than a whisper, my mouth as dry as it has ever been. I guess I'm not used to waiting for forgiveness. I glance up, waiting to see if it will come.

Jamie looks at my lips. If it was anybody else, that look would be enough to make a thousand butterflies take flight in the very lowest part of my pelvis. But this is Jamie, so that doesn't happen. I simply feel confused. This dude is *intense*.

"Like I said the other morning," he murmurs, still looking at my mouth. I think he's trying to one-up me. "I feel very lucky to have been invited here. I'm sorry you don't like me. I assumed, for me to get the invite in the first place, you must have given your blessing. If I somehow got that wrong . . . well, there's not much I can do. But I really am sorry if my being here has ruined your holiday."

I open my mouth to object and he actually has the audacity to hold up a finger to my lips.

"I'm allergic to bullshit," he tells me. "So don't. I came up here to tell you that I'll stay out of your way. I'll hang out with Laurie and catch up with him, and I'll leave you alone. I appreciate that's what you want."

I nod and he moves his finger away slowly.

"You came to find me in the shower, to tell me you're going to stay out of my way?" I ask, eyes narrowed.

His pupils dilate as he searches my face for something. We're so close I can see the smattering of freckles across his nose. All this time I thought he had blue eyes, but they're not blue, they're gray. A very, very light gray.

"Anyway," he says, shaking me out of my thoughts, "you don't like me, either. You called me a farthead. So."

"Well," I say. "That I'm *not* sorry about . . ."

"It's a very retro insult," he presses on. "I don't think I've ever been called a farthead before."

"I've called you that behind your back for years," I bat back, but before he can reply, a voice speaks.

"Oh!"

Jamie steps back and clears his throat like we've been caught. But caught doing what—talking? Tentatively finding less inflammatory ground? It's Dad, and he fills the doorway and looks between us like he's on the verge of asking if he's interrupting, before deciding against it.

"I didn't realize you weren't dressed," Dad says, but whether he means me or the half-naked Jamie opposite me, I can't tell.

"I didn't realize she was using the shower," Jamie says. "Sorry, Flo."

He motions to Dad that he needs to slip by. Dad moves, but keeps addressing us both.

"Two birds with one stone, actually," he says. "Kate has booked us all surprise massages! There are two masseurs downstairs, who are going to pummel everyone in the family into heavenly oblivion. Isn't that fun? And the plumbers have arrived, to make sure we don't get any more leaks."

Jamie has his back to me, his hands on the banister that runs in a horseshoe shape to make a balcony over the stairs. He half turns to Dad and says, "Oh, great. I'll be right there."

"Flo, you, too," says Dad. "You're up first, I think."

Jamie still lingers, even after Dad heads back downstairs, and so I say to his back, once we're out of earshot, "Was there anything else you wanted?"

"No," Jamie replies, barely looking back. He drops his chin to his chest and takes a massive breath, his girthy shoulders rising dramatically and then falling, like he's releasing anything further he might say into the ether, instead of allowing it to form words. "That was all."

6

I head down to the pool and am confronted by the most attractive man I have ever—and I truly mean *ever*—seen: tall, lithe, skin the color of a Mediterranean childhood . . . and, unfortunately, a man-bun. I recognize that no man can have it all, though, and nor should he. This fella has more than enough, even with the terrible hair. Whoa!

"Hello," he says, holding out a hand, a smile wide and true across his face. His accent betrays his roots. He must be local. "My name is Adonis. I think you are Flo?"

Adonis. The Greek god of a man is called ADONIS? Hope is going to *love* this. He is currently giving an entire new bar to the saying "If the shoe fits . . ." Maybe I'm ovulating. That's what they say, isn't it? That in the middle of your cycle you fancy people more, and are more fanciable yourself? The way Adonis (*Adonis!* I still need a minute to get over that name) is still shaking my hand and grinning at me makes me think that I am indeed a tiny bit fanciable. He's . . . appraising me. Openly. And I know I'm not supposed to enjoy being leered at, but it's so straightforward of him that I admire the gumption. My smile widens under his attention. It's like the second we shook hands he flicked a switch in me, from *off* to *definitely on*. Every fiber of my being has come alive.

"My friend Clio will be helping you today," Adonis says, gesturing to a woman I hadn't clocked before: She's older, with a gray plait and ruddy cheeks, and strong-looking hands. Exactly as I imagine a great masseuse looks, to be fair. "But I hope we can meet again later." He flashes another smile, and it feels so strange to be so freely awarded attention—and, what's more, to be reacting to it. It's nice. It makes me feel . . . well, sexy, to be honest. My cheeks flush, but I don't feel embarrassed by the desire in his gaze, not with my *on* switch. I don't think that has ever happened to me before in my life, this level of being hit upon. I don't question it. Adonis has zeroed in on me like a heat-seeking missile, and just like that, I'm open to it. This is so weird!

"Sure," I say, giving him a winning smile of my own. "Have fun . . ."

Adonis laughs. "Yes," he says, although what I said didn't even make proper sense, let alone was funny. I don't think that matters when you're flirting. It's fun to be saying words at each other. When did I last *flirt*? I mean, probably last Christmas, but let's not go there. I'm not going to overthink this. "But not too much, huh?"

Now it's my turn to laugh at something not-quite-sensical in the name of flirting. Adonis gestures to Alex to follow him, and I see Mum and Laurie looking at me with faces that might as well say: *Ew, gross!*

"What?" I ask.

"Nothing," Mum says quickly—too quickly—as Laurie says, "Where did that laugh come from? I've never heard you laugh like that in all my life." He mimics the noise that I made, and to be fair, it's not far off from the loud sound that emanated from my body as I "flirted." But so what? We can't all be smugly married. I suddenly wonder what Laurie was like to date—I'm sure he's done his fair share of OTT giggles in his time. Kate and I have never talked about how he romanced her—not really. Maybe it's time. That way I can add some ammunition to my sibling-ribbing tank. He must have done something right, to end up marrying such a baller. But I'd like to know all the things he didn't get right, please, because before Kate, my big brother was a shambles romantically. I'd like to remind him of that, but I know it sounds too defensive—and anyway Clio is beckoning me through to the back living room. I'm the first one on the massage table.

And what a massage it is. Minutes later, all thoughts of anything drift quickly away as Clio kneads and pokes and rubs me from her foldout bed. She's closed the blinds, so it is dark and shaded, and has some plinky-plonky music that sees me relax immediately. After two minutes I'm not even aware of the noise of the plumbers in the kitchen. *That* is how good she is. I was right about the strength of her hands. She finds knots in me that feel like they've been there since birth. I hover in the delicious space between waking and sleep, my body and mind peaceful and calm. I inhale and exhale, face down on the table. As Clio rubs warm oil up my left leg, starting at the calf and working her way upward in long, rhythmic strokes, I feel the tension melt away.

Hmmm . . . I wonder if Alex's massage is this good—the one with Adonis.

Adonis. I'll bet he gives *great* massages. I did notice that he has big hands. I bet they'd feel like this: firm pressure, a steady rhythm. If Adonis did this, he'd follow the line of my leg, up, and up, and up, my legs parting until he found his way between them.

Gosh.

Maybe he'd lower his weight on top of me from behind and I'd arch into him as he pushed back the fabric of my underwear. He'd find his way between my thighs and touch me, lightly at first and then with increasing intensity. He'd rub and rub, unrelenting, purposeful, all focused and determined. Never in a rush, never with any expectations. Just for me—for my pleasure. And he'd ask me, breathlessly, "Is that good?"

"Hmmm," I'd say, struggling to form the words to reply. He'd know it was good. That's part of the turn-on.

"Miss? Is that good?"

Miss?

I fling open my eyes. The clock that Clio set out as we started says almost a whole hour has gone by.

"We finished, miss. Thank you." She gives me a slight bow and gestures to my bikini top and kaftan over the back of a chair. Holy crap—I must have properly fallen asleep. *And* had a sex dream about the other masseur! Not that that is *terrible*, per se. Like I said to Kate, I've been as celibate as a nun for quite a while now, because the notion of dating as I was trying to recover and hold my life together was a step too far. I'm oddly proud of myself, truth be told, for indulging in a little fantasy. Something deep inside me is awakening after a *very* long time asleep. I feel like attention must be paid to it. It must be the holiday magic.

OUTSIDE THE SUN sits high in the sky, a king on its throne. The breeze is mild, the heat high. I am walking on a cloud, dazed after the best hour I've had in a long time.

"That was *incredible*," I tell Kate as Clio and I re-emerge, blinking, into the light outdoors. She's going to take a break and then do Mum, and after lunch it will be Kate's turn. Adonis is doing all the blokes, apparently. I find myself looking out for him, after my runaway thoughts got me all worked up.

"You look like a different person!" Kate squeals, scanning me. "That's amazing. You're . . . *radiant*. God, I can't wait for mine now. Laurie tries to rub my feet for me after a long day sometimes, but it's more of a tickle, if I'm honest. I want *pummeling*."

Pummeling. Why does everybody's language seem so filthy right now?

"How do," Alex says, wandering over and looking as jellylike as I feel. "Kate, mate. Thank you for that. I feel reborn. The hands on that man . . ." He gestures to Adonis, who gives me his apparently trademark smile as I follow Alex's finger-point.

"I can imagine," I say, and I sound like a horny housewife. I don't know what possesses me to say this to my brother, but it just slips out.

"Oh, please," Alex scoffs. "You wouldn't say boo to a goose."

I am affronted. "What do you mean? Are you so grossed out that your little sister could do sexy time that you have to pretend she's not even a woman at all?"

Alex pulls an amused face. "The fact that you call it 'sexy time' proves my point," he retorts.

"And what point is that?"

He wags a finger in my face. "That you, Florence Elizabeth Greenberg, are definitely not getting any."

"If I get Adonis's phone number, I will be," I shoot back.

"Dare you," Alex hoots. "In fact I double dare you."

Whoops. I've dug myself a bit of a hole. I've never actually hit on a man before, not really. Couldn't even believe I was flirting with Adonis. I have certainly never asked for a stranger's number . . . Should I simply walk up to him and ask? Or give him mine, on a piece of folded-up paper? Or unlock my phone and hand it to him, asking him to put in his digits?

Put in his digits. What the hell is wrong with me?

Alex busts out laughing.

"What?" I say defensively, suddenly worried that Alex can somehow hear my thoughts.

"Your face," Alex says, shaking his head. "Don't panic. You're not going to have to ask for his number, because Adonis actually gave me this to pass along."

He reaches into his pocket and pulls out a business card with a message on the back. I take it. *Text me*, it says, and his phone number is on the front.

I look up just as Adonis is heading over.

"I thought your family could perhaps come to a barbecue tomorrow night?" he says, nodding toward his phone number in my hand. He's not shy *at all*. In fact his attitude is very much of the *why* wouldn't *you want my number* variety, which I'd assumed was pushy and cocky beforehand. But he's such a happy man that it's a bit like the sun has decided to shine on me, and he's damned right: Why *wouldn't* I want his number? "Bring everybody," he adds. "It will be a big party."

I nod. Bringing everyone is way less nerve-racking than going on a one-on-one date or whatever. Don't people call it a "group hang"? Hmmm. I wonder if it's still called that if your mum and dad are there. God. Bringing my mum and dad on a date? It's like I'm thirteen. Laurie is going to *rinse me* for this.

"Sounds good," I say. "I'll text you and you can send me the details?"

Adonis's smile is wide, but somehow gets even wider.

"Yes," he says. "I think if you come, you will have a very good time. We can dance together."

I find myself chewing down on my bottom lip with a smile, nodding. He throws up his hands like a Spanish señorita doing flamenco. *There's not a self-conscious bone in his body,* I think. I laugh. I don't know what else to say. This is *very* unexpected and *very, very* cool.

"I would like to point out that I all but predicted this," Kate stage-whispers, watching me keep doing my weird grinning thing at Adonis's back as he invites Dad for his massage. He's got a fantastic arse on him. I am feeling unexpectedly amenable to the notion of a holiday fling.

"You?" I ask, but I shouldn't be surprised that Kate is trying to take the credit—that's Kate, and I love her for how she is.

"I said, on our first day, in that bikini you're bound to get attention," she says, gesturing to my swimwear. "I don't know why you have such a struggle accepting that you're fire personified, sister. Truly. If I wasn't married to your brother you'd even turn my head."

"Shut uppp," I insist, finally looking away from Adonis as he disappears with a cute wave. As I wave back, I see Jamie skulking at the side of the veranda, his brow furrowed disapprovingly in my direction. Well, let him disapprove. My love life—or my sex life, to be more accurate, since I understand those are the rules of a holiday fling—is of no concern to my actual brothers, so it certainly doesn't concern Jamie, either. I scowl at him in return, because screw him.

"Jamie! We doing this thing or what?" Laurie hollers at him as he appears from inside the house. "I'm feeling bloated as hell—I need this workout if we're going to keep eating like we've been released from prison."

"Famous last words," Jamie says to him and they head off together, Jamie looking angrily back over his shoulder.

I find my phone in my beach bag to punch in Adonis's number so that I don't lose it. I send him a text that says, Hey—this is my number! Love Flo x. Then I fire off a missive to Hope: Guess who just got a hot Greek's number! You'd be so proud!!

This is a good thing. It will be fun, a BBQ and a party, and it will take my mind off other things, like the overwhelming responsibility of being a human in this world, and also Jamie and his stupid face. I know I thought he and I could undertake some exposure therapy and become friends, but the way he just looked at me made my blood run cold. How am I supposed to get to know somebody who doesn't want to spend time with me, anyway? He *wants* to stay out of my way—that's what he said. A fool's errand, giving him any further thought. I shall focus on this plot twist, this Greek god.

My phone beeps with a message. It's Adonis. It's a kiss-face emoji. It makes me smile—again. I "like" it and throw my phone back in my bag, relaxing into a sun bed with Mum's airport thriller and a flourish.

I AM TEASED mercilessly about Adonis for the rest of the day, with Alex and Laurie and even Mum, at one point, doing impressions of me biting my lip and smiling and waving.

"Oooooh!" says Laurie in a high-pitched voice that I guess is supposed to sound like me. "A boy! My name's Flo and I fancy a boy!"

Mum especially seems pleased. She's not protective of my heart, not like a lot of mums. She's always encouraged me to *have your fun whilst you can, darling. I learned so much from my mistakes that I might even make some more!* She's one of a kind. Most mums have to rein in their kids. I wonder what it's like to feel you need to physically kick your youngest out of the nest and into the world.

Adonis comes over to say good-bye to the whole family after he does Laurie's massage, leaving early because Jamie says he doesn't want one—something about a dodgy shoulder muscle that he needs to see a doctor about. He's disappeared off inside somewhere instead.

"Bye, lover boy!" Laurie shouts after Adonis as he drives off, luckily quietly enough that he doesn't seem to hear it over the sound of the driveway gravel crunching under the wheels. "I'll miss you," he adds breathlessly, full-on taking the piss.

"Why is he your lover boy?" Dad asks, already tucking into a sundowner even though the sun is nowhere near going down.

"Didn't you hear?" Laurie asks him. "Flo got his number. She's gonna get *railed*."

"Laurie!" cries Kate, disgusted. What is it with my brothers? They either can't understand that I am a woman who actually has sexual urges, or else they do and they go way over the top commenting on it.

"What's 'railed'?" asks Dad innocently.

"Dad, don't," I say, standing up to dive into the pool. "Let's change the subject."

I cut through the water and make it all the way to the other side without coming up for air. That shouldn't impress me as much as it does, but Alex has noticed what I've done and so stands up himself, declaring bullishly, "Anyone could do that."

And that's how we both change the subject and pass the next hour: a bunch of fully grown adults having a competition to see who can hold their breath the longest. The mood is relaxed and convivial, and it's not long before everyone joins Dad in having a drink, with bags of nuts and crisps getting cracked open, too.

"Shall we stay here tonight?" Mum asks. "I don't even want to bother getting changed. I could just eat like this, to be honest. What do we think?"

"Seconded," says Dad. "I can make pasta? We've got everything in for it. Nice and easy, then, isn't it?"

"Perfect," says Mum, and Dad leans in for a kiss and the rest of us all watch, half wishing they weren't making out, and half thinking, *Oh, that's nice.* They're so in love, even after all this time. When there's space for that in my life, I'll welcome it. Must be lovely.

The Bluetooth speaker from the other night gets brought out, and although it was great getting dolled up and heading out yesterday, it's just as nice to stay by the pool, laughing and chatting and being ridiculous, everybody chipping in, getting ready for an informal dinner outside: grabbing plates and napkins, fixing drinks for one another, too.

"Can I get you anything?" I ask Jamie directly, when I head to the fridge for some more white wine. My date with Adonis has emboldened me. Talking to him directly isn't as much *exposure therapy* as it is *I actually don't care anymore.* "There's beer left," I add. "Or I'm doing the same wine as we had for *aperitivos* last night?"

The way he looks at me as he answers is so weird. It's like he can't believe I have spoken directly to him.

"No thank you," he replies.

And I should leave it at that, but I say it before I can rein myself in. I just . . . urgh! I'm trying, here! One minute he's cornering me in the bedroom, and the next he looks at me like I've asked to take a dump on his head. "Suit yourself," I tut, waving a hand.

He makes a nose—a bit like *pfffft.*

I decide not to turn back round.

———

"DIBS ON NOT DOING THE DISHES!" yells Laurie as Alex puts his last forkful of food in his mouth, which, because he's the last to finish eating, marks the end of the meal. The sun has gone down, we've drunk and eaten and laughed and ribbed each other to bits, and now we're doing what we always do: deciding who has to do the pots. Laurie puts two fists in the air triumphantly that he's got out of it first, and then pulls them back down beside him with a whoosh of victory.

"Dibs on no dishes!" follows Alex quickly, and then my mother. "Dibs on not washing up!" she trills, already laughing that she's beaten me to it. I look between them all, wide-eyed, and issue my verdict.

"Children," I sigh, shaking my head, mad that it's fallen to me.

"The rules are the rules, Flo," Alex says with a shrug, finally swallowing what is in his mouth. "Kate and Dad cooked, and the rules of calling dibs stand."

"Nobody likes a sore loser." Laurie grins. Something tells me that if I did kick up a fuss he'd like it all the more—he'd be able to prove how childish *I* am that way.

"I'm happy to take care of the dishes," Jamie says, standing up and piling the plates high on his arm like a waiter. "Mike, Kate, that was delicious. Thank you."

He heads off toward the kitchen, the muscles in his back twitching with the weight of the plates.

"Florence," Mum says. "Come on. Don't let the poor boy do it all alone. You've got better manners than that."

"Checkmate," I reply, one eyebrow raised. I don't really want to go in there with Jamie, but surely it will only take five minutes if there are two of us. "Fine."

I get up slowly, deliberately ignoring Laurie and Alex, who are *desperate* to show me their glory faces. I can feel it. I focus on getting the odds and sods from the table as their eyes beg for my attention: side plates and errant knives, and the pot that had the pasta in it.

In the kitchen a needlessly topless Jamie has filled the sink with more bubbles than any person could deem necessary, and he's elbow-deep in the dirty work of getting things clean. I put down the used dishes and cutlery to the left of him and grab a tea towel to stand to his right, where I can dry what he leaves on the rack, to make room for the next item he washes.

We stand there, side by side, in a silence that feels loaded, like there is stuff we could both be saying, but aren't. If I was Jamie, I'd be wanting to off-load a bit. Our chat earlier, upstairs—all that *I just came to say I'm going to stay away from you* stuff—derived from me having been so rude. Now he's had a bit more time to think it over, I wouldn't be surprised if Jamie asked for explicit clarification on exactly what my problem is; but then again, that would be rich, coming from him. He knows damned well what my problem is. Plus, it's not like I didn't try to be normal before, offering him a drink and whatnot. I don't think either of us can find our footing really. No wonder the air is thick with the unsaid. Pull on one delinquent thread and everything will unravel.

He washes, I dry. He washes, I dry. I can hear the clinking of glass and the hum of laughter from outside. Wash, dry. Wash, dry. It's meditative enough that I relax, a bit.

"I really didn't mean what I said this morning," I say finally, once the pots are washed and dried and stacked, ready for putting away. "I was pre-coffee and hadn't slept very well, and I was running my mouth in a grumpy moment, is all. Not that that is an excuse. What I said was inexcusable. And I'm sorry."

"Okay," Jamie says, pulling the plug on his sink full of bubbles and running the cold tap so that they deflate and disappear. We're finished, but we do not move. I throw down the towel and rest both hands on the countertop in front of me. I can see the rise and fall of Jamie's chest from the corner of my eye. His elbow knocks into mine. I am reminded of standing this close at Christmas, near the jigsaw, when I stupidly thought that maybe . . . well, I don't know. What did I think? That he liked me and we'd *be something*? Whatever it was, I was wrong. I was so wrong that I didn't come home for Mum's birthday in February, nor Dad's in March. By the time Jamie had headed off to sea, home felt safe again because I knew he wouldn't be there. But now he's here. And I'm rubbing up against the edges of a thought I would prefer to be buried and forgotten.

Let's not speak of this again.

My heart beats so insistently that it might come clean out of my chest.

"Flo," Jamie says. "Don't."

Don't? Don't what?

"I beg your pardon?" I ask.

"You're so . . ." he starts but doesn't finish.

So much for feeling relaxed.

"Look," I say, "I've said sorry for this morning, and I've resigned myself to the fact that you're here. But every time I acknowledge you, speak to you—hell, even look at you directly—it's like laser beams shoot from your eyes and if you could evaporate me into dust, then you would. What do you want me to freaking well *do*?"

He opens his mouth to reply, but then seems to think better of it.

"No," I challenge him. "Go on."

"Well," he says, spreading his palms out in front of him, demonstrating that he comes in peace. Fat chance of that, though—nothing we do is in peace. "It's just that laser beams wouldn't turn you to dust.

They'd incinerate you, perhaps force you into flames. You're mixing up your superpowers."

He says it with such a straight face that he's lost me.

"You're the weirdest fucking dude," I say. "Pick a side! Are we joking together or hating each other? Have you been diagnosed with a split-personality disorder that you'd like to catch me up on? Jesus, Jamie!"

"Sorry," he says, like I've touched a nerve. "You put me . . . on edge."

It's the most honest thing I think he's ever said to me. It takes me aback.

"Right," I say. "And what do you think you make me?"

"Angry?" he supplies.

I can't help it—I laugh in spite of myself. It comes out high-pitched and gleeful, the way all laughter that stems from astonishment does. Jamie looks at me, pleased with himself. I shake my head and roll my eyes, issuing a big sigh.

"Fuck me," I say. "You're a roller coaster. Do you know that?"

"I feel like now isn't the time to make jokes about taking me for a ride."

I roll my eyes again. "No," I reply. "But your self-awareness has been noted."

He nods slightly. Then he presses on: "Roller coasters aside . . . are you having a nice holiday?"

I inhale deeply, considering his question. "I am," I tell him. "Sun and sea—it's a balm for anyone, I think."

"Absolutely," he says.

"You?" I ask.

"Yeah." He nods.

And try as I might to search every last crevice of my brain for something to move the conversation on a bit, I come up with naught. I can see the cogs whirring behind Jamie's eyes, too. Evidently there is nothing left to say. Nothing outwardly hostile, but also nothing that means anything, either. Maybe the exposure therapy has worked, after all.

"Good job here," I announce, stepping away from the sink before things get any more uncomfortable. "We made light work of it."

"We did," Jamie agrees.

And with that, I turn on my heel and go back outside.

7

I take the sofa, like I threatened myself with. There's *no way* I can listen to Jamie lightly snore, all bathed in moonlight like an angelic five-year-old hugging a teddy bear, even if things do feel somewhat neutralized. I toss and turn, though—a bag of coat hangers would be more comfortable than this lumpy old thing.

I need to go for a run.

There's just enough light that I can make out the steps from the sitting area up to the bottom of the steps that wind up to the first floor, where everyone else's room is, and to the second floor in the eaves, where my room is. Mine and *Jamie's* room. But I only need to sneak in and grab my stuff, then sneak out without waking him. I'm light of foot. I'm not worried.

The door is open, so I pad through on my tiptoes past the bathroom and round the corner to where our two single beds are and—

"Jesus!" I utter, holding up my hands in surrender—partly to shield my face, and partly as an unconscious reaction that will let Jamie know: I had absolutely no idea he was: (a) awake and (b) stark bollock-naked. He's bent over, rummaging through a bag on the floor, and from this angle I can see *everything*. His ginormous swinging *everything*.

"What the—" Jamie gasps, scuttling to stand up. He uses a hand to cover his *ginormous swinging everything*, but to be honest, despite the size of his hands, that doesn't cover it all. His jaw drops and he swallows once, hard—a big, satisfying gulp. And I just stand. And wait. I don't know what I'm waiting for, but I daren't move, and we look at each other, shocked. I see his pupils dilate, and then he lunges for a pair of boxers and says, "Shit. Sorry. Urm . . ."

It's then that I remember to shield my eyes and look away. "Sorry," I whisper, not wanting to wake up the rest of the house. "I didn't think you'd be up."

"I couldn't sleep," he mutters, finding a pair of shorts, too. They're tiny things, the sort that only a man with thighs like his can pull off. He stands taller now he's "dressed." I am free to look now. He adds, "I was planning to go for a run."

I nod. "Same," I say.

"You're going for a run?"

"And I couldn't sleep," I reply.

And he says, "*Oh*."

I narrow my eyes at him as he moves to pull on his running shoes. "I didn't know you were a runner," I comment.

"I'm an everything," he says. "As long as it moves my body. I like to keep busy," he adds. "It helps. You know. My head, or whatever."

I roll my eyes. I almost thought we had something in common there, with the running, but he's not a runner. He's an *everything*. Well, excuse me, Your Excellency.

"Anyway," he breezes, waving a hand, "I'll leave you to it."

He's gone before I can reply.

———

I SET OFF toward the hill behind the house, because Dad mentioned that the house ring-binder with all the info about the local area says it's got great views, and although I prefer to run on the flat, occasionally pushing hard on hills feels good, just for the change. I half run, half hike, because it's steep—steeper than yesterday. But I love the feeling of my blood pumping, of all the bad thoughts and feelings leaving my body.

And then I see Jamie.

He must sense me, because there, at the top of the big hill (I mean, we could call it a mountain, to be fair, from the way I am puffing and panting), he spins round and his face falls.

"Are you following me?" he asks crossly.

"No," I say. I sound insulted. I *am* insulted. "Why would I follow you?"

He doesn't say anything.

"I'll go," I offer, already backing away. It's too early for this. I'll head back and loop into town, like yesterday. "Sorry."

I start to make my way back toward the trail. I would have liked to catch my breath more, but I can walk down, maybe find a bench on the hillside somewhere to take in the view.

"Flo, wait."

I almost ignore him, but decide against it. Ignoring Jamie isn't in the spirit of *exposure therapy*, after all. I turn round.

"You don't have to go," he says, in the same way that a person might offer to clean up after a party. He doesn't mean it.

I narrow my eyes at him.

"Nobody should be deprived of this view," he presses, gesturing around us. Finally I look up properly.

It really is gorgeous.

We're in a small clearing right at the top. There are incredible panoramic views over the sea, the bay, and then right across to the old town where we had dinner, too. I get that feeling in my chest that I had when we arrived and I took my first dip in the ocean: space. Room to breathe. Contentedness. I don't even realize I've said anything out loud until Jamie says, "I agree. Whoa, indeed."

I'm gasping, sweating, and Jamie spots it before I can think to conceal it, wordlessly handing me a water bottle that I didn't realize he'd been carrying. I take it and drink.

There's a semicircular wooden bench, designed so that no matter which bit you sit on, you can see something amazing. I meander over, sitting down with the ocean view, and let myself be for a moment. I won't be long, I just need a beat.

Jamie comes and sits beside me. We sit, not talking, simply breathing, side by side, watching the light change.

I realize that I'm glugging Jamie's water and he's not had any himself. I hand him back his bottle and he takes it with a terse smile, opening the cap to hydrate himself. We spend so long sitting there that it makes me jump when Jamie eventually speaks.

"I like it up here," he offers. "Makes my head feel quiet."

I pull a face and don't realize it's unkind until after I've done it. But like . . . Jamie needs to make his head feel quiet? *Sure.*

"What?" he asks, in that way men do when they mean, *Go on. Say what you've got to say.*

"No," I say and shrug, wishing I had sunglasses so I didn't have to look right at him. "I just . . . you make it sound like it's really hard to be you."

Jamie furrows his brow, opening his mouth to speak and then changing his mind. He takes a breath and settles on, "I don't get it. Why would you say that?"

"I don't know," I say.

"You do," he challenges. "Go on."

I shake my head and part my lips, but no noise comes out.

But Jamie won't relent. "Seriously," he probes.

"Well," I start, after some effort. "People who look like you do," I say, gesturing up and down his 8 percent body fat, "sailing across the world, apparently making all this money . . ." I realize how I sound. Intellectually, I know that everybody has some secret pain that isn't obvious to the rest of the world, but somehow that doesn't add up for him. Of course Jamie must miss his parents terribly—I don't even know how I would survive without Mum and Dad. I guess he hurt me, so maybe I'm taking my chance to hurt him a little, too. "It can't exactly be stressful for you is all I mean."

Jamie shakes his head. His face has fallen, like he expects more of me than dismissiveness—which feels rich, considering how he treats me. Of course we're not allowed to talk about that, though, are we?

"I expected you, of all people, to understand," he says, his voice saddened.

I don't get what he means. "Me, of all people?" I ask, silently marveling: *Me, the girl you so casually discarded?* Why would I have any sympathy for him?

"Yeah," he says with a nod, and he's not looking at me. He's staring at the sparkling diamonds of the ocean, his thick forearms on his distressingly massive legs. "Beautiful. Smart. Got the whole world at your feet, your whole life ahead of you, and you still had your . . ."

I nod. "Breakdown?" I supply.

"Yeah." He motions.

I almost miss the fact that Jamie has just called me beautiful and smart. He must be doing it solely to prove his point. He can't mean it.

"I wondered what you knew about that," I say, my voice as small as his was, moments ago. I mirror his body language, looking to the bay myself. Is *this* why he decided to keep his distance? Because he thinks I'm certifiably insane? I feel like this conversation is a sideways apology of sorts, if I squint and focus really hard. We're dancing around something.

Jamie shakes his head. "Only what Laurie or Kate mentioned in passing." He looks up, obviously noting the horror on my face. "Don't worry. They've been very protective of you. It's been bare-minimum details. It's none of my business."

I feel a flush of gratitude for Laurie's discretion. Who knew he had it in him?

I take a breath. "So, what?" I ask. "Are you telling me it's your turn for a breakdown now?"

He shocks me with a hoot of a laugh. "Jesus," he says, "if it was, I wouldn't be coming to you for your bedside manner, would I?"

I laugh, too. "No," I reply. "I suppose not. I don't mean to sound harsh."

"And yet," he says, eyebrow cocked.

I roll my eyes. "And yet," I say.

If this was anybody else, I'd issue a comical grin right now, to ease the tension, but I'm still not there with Jamie. We were so close to arguing, but we've pulled it back. We're almost getting on. *Almost.* That's enough. I feel like he's trying to tell me that he wants what I want, too; that he wouldn't mind finding some more solid ground between us, if we have to be around each other, anyway.

"All I mean is," he says, "that it's beautiful up here. And I'm glad you like it, too."

I nod and Jamie sits beside me, and we stay that way until the sun comes further up in the sky and my belly starts to rumble.

"Come on," he says, when he hears it. "Time for breakfast."

———

WE ARRIVE BACK at the villa, but before we go in Jamie pauses, hand on the doorknob.

"For the record," he says, his face creased in thought and reflection, "I do have problems, you know."

I go to speak, but he continues before I can say that I'm sure he does.

"I have a nice life, yeah. But I am alone. No parents. No siblings. No significant other. And I've got to be honest, Flo, it fucking sucks."

What would I have done without my family these past few years? They kept me afloat. I try to read Jamie's face, everything that is going through his mind. Is he really saying he's lonely? If he is, why push people away?

"I think that's the most vulnerable thing you've ever said to me," I say, deliberately not adding that obviously it's one of the few things he's recently said to me directly, full stop.

"You seem intent on being surprised that I have feelings," he replies. "And I can't understand why."

He's got me there. Mostly because I've never seen these feelings. And when I have come close, he's pulled away so fast I've been left with whiplash. I don't see how Jamie can accuse *me* of being the bad guy here . . .

A bunch of images crash into one another in my mind: jigsaws and cold buffets and drinks by the fire at Christmas. Lingering looks and fizzing excitement, and tears that came from nowhere. A beginning. An unspoken promise.

I take a breath, ready to ask him why, then, he *would* push me away?

The front door flings open.

We both turn to see who has interrupted us, confronted by Mum, car keys in hand.

"Oh, hello! Become jogging buddies, have you? That's exciting." She looks between us, and we must look like we've been caught doing something we shouldn't have, because she adds, "Sorry. I didn't mean to interrupt. I'm doing the bakery run. Any requests?"

"Not for me," says Jamie. "I eat what I'm given."

"Flo?" asks Mum.

"Anything with chocolate in it," I reply. "Do you need help?" I'm obviously hoping she'll say no, but Mum bursts into a massive smile. She loves it when I offer to spend time with her—and it seems she isn't capable of reading the emptiness in my offer.

"I do like the company," she says, grinning. "If you don't mind showering afterward? I don't want to hang around, you see. The good stuff goes."

I turn to Jamie. "You get first dibs on the bathroom, then, it looks like."

"Lucky me," he replies. And *goddammit*—the look he gives me. All narrowed eyes and blank stare. I think he's relieved we were interrupted. I can't, for the life of me, figure out what he wants from me. What Jamie needs. So, what: He's going to tell me his deepest, darkest secrets, but then also thank the heavens when our chat is over? I don't get it!

"See you later," I say, sounding petulant. I follow Mum to the rental car.

"Yeah," he replies. "And thanks for the chat."

I look at him. He smiles.

When we get in the car Mum asks, "What chat, darling?"

I'm too busy looking at Jamie through the window. He's not gone in yet; he's standing on the front step with his hands in his pockets and his face impassive, eyes trained on me as I do up my seat belt. I thought he couldn't wait to get inside, and now he's loitering.

"Hmmm?" I ask.

"Jamie thanked you for the chat. I just wondered what you were chatting about, is all. Unless it's private."

"We didn't really chat about anything," I tell her, as we reverse out of the drive. I lift a hand, still unsmiling. Jamie lifts his hand in return.

"Well," Mum says, pulling the car into first gear, "I'm glad to see you getting along. He's more sensitive than you think, Jamie. God bless his heart."

He falls out of view.

"I'm learning that," I say. "I think."

Mum looks at me. "Yeah?" she asks, but it's the kind of *yeah* that doesn't need an answer. We drive the rest of the way in silence, thoughts of Jamie lingering in the air between us.

8

I step out of the shower and pour baby oil onto my still-wet skin. Kate reckons that is where her glow is coming from—she glistens, subtly, and it makes her look radiant, so she's given me her bottle to try it (with explicit instructions to put a towel down; apparently baby oil and tiled floors won't mix well, if I want to stay upright). I'm feeling nervous, but good nervous, I think. I text Hope for a pep talk.

ME
Tonight is the night! Are you proud of me?

HOPE
BBQ night with the Greek god? OF COURSE I AM PROUD! This is a big step for you.

ME
Thanks, pal
Adonis keeps calling me "pretty lady," though, every time he texts
That's a lot, don't you think?

HOPE

How fit is he, on a scale of one to Captain America?

ME

Off-the-scale fit, to be fair

HOPE

Well then, he can call you whatever he likes!
Have you shaved your legs?

ME

Yes.

HOPE

Your bikini line?

ME

Hope!

HOPE

You didn't answer the question

ME

. . . yes. NOW NO MORE QUESTIONS!

FROM THE BATHROOM I hear Jamie come into our room, and I pause like a squirrel sitting upright in the face of danger, listening to him open drawers and unzip bags, the rustling of fabrics and the sound of an aerosol, maybe hair spray? I know he hasn't used the bathroom yet, because everything was bone-dry when I got up here, but I don't know where Jamie has been since our run this morning—or if he's even coming tonight.

ME
Urgh, Jamie alert. I'm hiding in the bathroom and he's just come up to our room

HOPE
How was it this afternoon? So weird, your little run together
But at least it's progress on the exposure-therapy front!

ME
Well, is it, though? By the time I got back from the shop with
Mum, he'd gone off "exploring" with Laurie and I've not seen
him since
I keep thinking about what he said, though, about having
nobody
Obviously he's got us, like the Greenbergs, as a family unit . . .

HOPE
Do you think you should maybe get Laurie, or somebody, to
reiterate that to him? Couldn't hurt (not that I'm not still mad at
him for what he did, but also: bless him)

"Do you need the bathroom?" I yell through the door to Jamie. I could open it a fraction to make sure he hears, but I think we've done enough interacting while half dressed. The movement stops.

"No," he yells back. "I showered in Alex's room. The bedroom is all yours—I'm going down for a drink."

I try to listen for any subtext in his words, any hidden depths to his tone. I come up blank.

" 'Kay," I shout back, and I hear footsteps that seem to stop, right on the other side of the door. I reach out to the wood. I swear I can see his shadow under the crack, in the space between the door and the floor. Is he going to say something?

Jamie clears his throat then, drawing me out of my thoughts, and keeps moving. I listen, frozen to the spot, as his noise echoes all the way down the hall and eventually disappears entirely. I clear the steam from the mirror with my hand and look at myself.

I put on some blusher and lipstick, and comb my hair back from my face to pile high on my head. I'm going to wear my backless maxi-dress, so having my hair up will show off my shoulders, and I find some studded earrings in my makeup bag that add sparkle to the look. I take a picture and send it to Hope.

HOPE
Approval granted!

I find a gold bracelet to wear where I'd normally put on a watch, and top up my lipstick, but I can't shake the growing feeling of unease in my chest. I feel anxious, my head full of all these scenarios and hypotheticals: What if Adonis invited me as a joke? What if he tries to take things too far? What if I go off with him, but get lost? What if Dad disowns me for being a slut?

This is what my brain does. It makes me catastrophize and spin out, no matter how positive I try to be. It manufactures worst-case scenarios and tells my body to panic in preparation. I will myself to breathe, like the therapist taught me. *I'm okay. I'm okay. I'm okay.*

"Flo!" Laurie bellows up the stairs. Footsteps. "Flo!" he shouts again.

"Coming," I scream back. "Give me a minute."

I look in the mirror one last time, remembering to breathe and listing everything I like about myself in my head. I am kind. I listen well. I am a good daughter. I am an accomplished runner.

"Florence!" Laurie yells up the stairs once more, and I bolt down to join everyone.

Jamie is there, looking tense but handsome in a shirt and chino shorts. It's the most covered up I've seen him all holiday.

"Nice of you to grace us with your presence, Your Highness," Laurie says, curtsying deeply, and I scowl at him.

"Sorry if I'm holding you back from your Adonis man-crush," I say.

"Hardly," shoots back Laurie, rolling his eyes.

Mum slaps my arm, dispersing the sibling tension. "*I'm* desperate to go and stare at him again," she says, giggling. "Now come on, or all the food will be gone."

Jamie chuckles. "This is the most food-obsessed family I have ever known," he says, and we make brief eye contact before he looks away quickly. Does he regret confiding in me this morning? I'm getting *let's not repeat that* vibes. I try to smile, but he's already looking away, his hands on Alex's shoulders, jostling him out of the door. I swear to god, it's one step forward, two steps back with him.

"We going out drinking after dinner?" I hear him asking Alex. "See what trouble we can get into?"

"I'm bloody starving," says Dad, further proving Jamie's point about us being food-obsessed.

Kate links arms with me as we follow the path to the main town, with instructions to turn off halfway to get to the part of the beach where the party is.

"And honestly," she's saying, "I could have spent a hundred euros, easy, couldn't I, Laurie?"

Laurie isn't listening. He's explaining something about his job to Dad, who is doing his level best to look like he: (a) understands and (b) is interested. That's love.

"Anyway," Kate presses on, "I just *have* to go with you. You'll love it. Most souvenirs can be tacky, and something you end up throwing in the back of a cupboard at home, but it's almost like there's a buyer or something for this market—like somebody in charge of curating it all? Honestly, I was blown away. Maybe we could go the day before we leave? You have room in your suitcase, don't you?" I can't get a word in edgeways, which suits me fine. A couple of times I feel Jamie watching me, but when I look up, his glance has changed direction.

THE BEACH IS set back from the road, and it has been transformed from what it looked like the other night, when we could see it from the mom-and-pop restaurant. There are strings of lights and a big makeshift dance floor with a live band, and a DJ station next to them. Fish is being grilled, and there are a few high tables festooned with ice buckets of beer and wine. There are kids and grown-ups of all ages, locals and tourists alike.

"Hey! Hi! Hello, friends," Adonis says when he spots us, opening his arms wide in greeting, all man-bun and arms. He kisses everyone hello and then reaches me. "Pretty lady," he says, kissing each cheek. I flush with something familiar from yesterday—happiness, I suppose, at his openness and positivity. This is going to be *fine*. I shouldn't have let myself worry. I deserve to have a little fun, especially after everything I've been through. Who knows what adventure I might have, if only I let myself. And so I resolve, right here and now, to eat with this kind man and drink with this kind man, and later, if he asks for a dance, I shall do exactly that with this kind man, too.

"Can I take her?" Adonis asks my dad, with a weird sort of respect.

And Dad gestures with a hand and says, "By all means. Have a nice time, you two!"

Laurie says something that the rest of the family giggle at, but I can't hear, so I just shoot him a look. Jamie has turned away and doesn't watch Adonis lead me off, like the others do.

"This dress," says Adonis, as he orders us drinks at the bar. "You look so beautiful, Flo."

"You keep calling me pretty lady," I tease him. "I was beginning to think you couldn't remember my actual name."

Adonis's wide, happy face crinkles in dissatisfaction. "You think I wouldn't be so respectful as to remember your name?" he says, and I feel bad for ribbing him. I only half meant it.

"I'm nervous," I explain. "I'm making stupid jokes because I'm intimidated by how hot you are." There. I've said it. That's something else my therapist taught me: If in doubt, tell the truth—plainly, and without fear.

Adonis looks at me. "Hmmm," he muses. "I think, if I may . . ." He pauses for permission. I nod gently. "Okay, so I think you maybe have what many of the tourists who come here have," he says. "You are too much here . . ." And with that he touches my temple with two fingers. "And not so much here." He lowers his hand to my heart.

I nod again, harder this time, noting how his touch is an inch lower than it needs to be—but I like it.

"Ding, ding, ding," I trill. "Correct. I don't suppose you have the cure, do you?"

I am given that smile again.

"Dancing," he tells me, offering a hand. "Come. We can drink later."

And that is that. I don't know how long we're up there for, but to begin with there is only us, and after six or seven or eight songs everybody else is up dancing, too—including, I can't help but notice, Jamie with some brunette girl.

Adonis does some silly moves to make me laugh, which I mirror and add to. And as we both get bolder he comes closer, taking a hand and putting the other on my waist so that we dance together, occasionally twirling me or dipping me, all of which serves to make me focus entirely on the here and now, which is spectacularly welcome.

"You really are pretty, lady," Adonis says to me over the music, and I believe him when he says it. I *feel* pretty, dancing this way, being in the moment like this. I put my arms round his neck and sway to the rhythm with him, and he breaks away again to spin me—out away from him and then back toward him. It's like a movie or something. I think of what Hope said, in her texts. If she was here, at the party with us, she'd be waving her arms from the side of the dance floor with a cheer, a signal to go for it, to really let go and have fun.

"God," Kate intones in my ear, from where she's dancing beside us. "He's *so* fit. I'm jealous."

Laurie pulls a face but laughs, too. "I heard that!" he warns her playfully.

I spin and spin on the dance floor, enjoying the cool air rippling off the water and onto my sweaty body, the feel of Adonis's hand on my bare lower back. Round and round I go, splaying my arms out, tipping my head back, laughing until I'm so dizzy I have to excuse myself to get some water.

"I'll be right back," I say to Adonis, my fingertips lingering on his forearm, and relishing his hand on my hip before he nods and says, "Okay, pretty lady." I'm starting to enjoy the way he says that.

I head off to the makeshift bar and lean on the counter as I wait for my turn. The guy is changing a barrel, I think, and motions that he won't be long. I smile and mouth *Okay*, curious as to how I'd say that in Greek. I'll ask Adonis. I turn so that I can see everyone on the dance floor—Mum and Dad have got up there now, dancing cheek to cheek, like they do, and both of them grinning inanely and happily. I like seeing it. I like this night.

"I could almost be jealous of your dancing partner."

Jamie.

"I don't know what I'm supposed to say to that," I tell him.

"No," Jamie concedes, and irritation prickles at my neck.

"I saw you talking with a few women before," I say. "Seems like you're having a nice night."

It isn't a question.

"I don't know what I'm supposed to say to *that*," Jamie retorts.

Thankfully, we're interrupted by the barman, and Jamie gestures to me to go first.

"Water, please," I say.

"Two," Jamie adds, holding up a peace sign.

The barman grabs two bottles and Jamie slips him cash.

"On me," he says, cracking open his lid.

"Thank you," I say grumpily, like I don't want to be around him, but I don't move. Neither does he.

"It's none of my business," Jamie says. "But your man there, I think there's a tourist in every port, so to speak."

I look over to where he has gestured, to Adonis being greeted by two blonde girls with deep tans and crop tops. They air-kiss on each cheek and one of them keeps her hand on his hip, lingering, like she's used to touching him.

"You're right," I reply.

Jamie puzzles. "And you're . . . okay with that?" he asks.

"Oh," I tell him, "I don't mean you're right about a woman in every port. You're right that it's none of your business."

"Message received and understood," he says, putting two fingers to his forehead in a captain's salute. We both look out across the dance floor, watching Adonis chat with a group of girls, including the one Jamie was dancing with earlier. She must feel our eyes on her, because she looks up, raising a hand at Jamie and blushing, coyly.

"Well," I say.

"Well," he repeats.

My eyes settle on the ground just in front of our feet, my mood sullen. So Jamie has opinions about who I spend my time with, when he's off flirting, too? That's absurd. I shoot a look at him, annoyed and confused. We lock eyes and I'm shaking my head, a gentle *What the fuck?* Jamie's eyes roam my face, deciphering what I can't find the courage to actually say. And then the most annoyingly strange thing happens.

Jamie shifts his body to block my view of the party and reaches up to my face. I can't help but look at him now. I hold my breath and his hand comes toward me, reaching for an errant piece of hair that's come loose from my updo, gently pushing it behind my ear. His face softens as he does it, but he doesn't smile.

"He's lucky to have you, if that's what you want," he says gently. For a moment he looks wistful. I get a strange thought at the very back of my brain, a hazy alert that he regrets passing on me himself.

But then the thought disappears—a helium balloon I have accidentally let go of, floating away up to the clouds.

"I agree," I say, with more conviction than I feel.

"Florence!"

Adonis appears at my shoulder and instantly takes a hand and spins me round.

"Hey," I say, feeling the disjointedness between Jamie's solemn stare and Adonis's high energy.

"You're the prettiest girl here," he says to me, pulling me close and rocking me back and forth in a dance. "Do you know that?"

I shake my head and crease up my face.

"Really," he says. "Everybody is saying so."

"Okay," I say with a chuckle. "Now I know you're laying it on thick."

"Laying it on thick?" Adonis questions, and it makes me laugh harder.

"Being charming," I clarify, and Adonis raises his eyebrows and smiles in agreement.

"I am very charming, yes," he says, and he cups my face with a hand, his thumb stroking my cheek. Okay, then: Contact has been achieved. I look up at him from beneath my eyelashes, not feeling brave enough to look at him head-on. Did he just see Jamie do the same?

"Come on," he says, voice lowered. "I want to show you something."

I turn round to where Jamie was standing, remembering that we were in a quasi-conversation, but he's no longer there. I can't see him anywhere in fact.

"Okay," I reply, and Adonis takes my hand to lead me away from the crowd.

———

AROUND THE CORNER to the beach is the entrance to a cave, where we go down a steep ramp into its belly. Adonis uses the torch on his phone, and it lights up what can only be described as an *enchanting* display of Mother Nature. Rocks emerge from the ground in thin spikes, like icicles coming from the wrong direction. Some are as big as Adonis, others about up to the knee, a sandy-orange color with ridges.

"What is this?" I marvel.

"Stalagmites," Adonis says. "It is . . . I think you say . . . a deposit? Of the minerals? It comes from the water."

"It's beautiful," I say.

"I thought you might like it."

"It's like being underwater," I go on. "Or how I imagine the bottom of the ocean to be, you know? Like we could float through in our diving gear, looking at all the fish."

I tread carefully through it all, holding on to Adonis's arm.

"This is my favorite part," he says, his torch on a mural painted onto one of the flatter parts of the cave wall. It is intricately done. Whoever painted it spent hours on it, probably coming back day after day until it was finished. It's of a man, lying on the beach with the waves crashing behind him, and a woman curled around him, holding him tightly. They both have their eyes closed, as if they're sleeping.

"It's Hero and Leander," Adonis tells me. "You know this?"

I shake my head. "It's Greek mythology?"

"You are correct," he says. I keep my eye on the art as he leans in to explain. "Hero was a priestess of Aphrodite. She was not allowed to be with men. She lived in a temple on the other side of the village to Leander. When, one day, he saw Hero, he immediately fell in love. She was the most pretty lady he had ever seen."

I find myself smiling, even though this is so cheesy.

"Leander was a good man, with a kind heart and a devotion to Hero. Soon she fell in love with him, like he was in love with her. Every night Hero would light a lamp for Leander, to guide him across the river so they could spend time together. For a while they were very happy. But one night the wind was strong, and it blew out the lamp Hero had lit. Leander persisted because it was important to him to see his love. But because of the wind, and because he could not see the lamp, he lost his way and drowned."

"He died?" I say. "That's so sad."

"With grief, Hero threw herself into the sea and drowned, as well. Somehow, though, they found each other, and we know this because their bodies were found just like this, on the beach, in a tight embrace. This is how they were buried, too."

"Whoa," I marvel.

"I think the right people come together, always," Adonis says. "In the end." He turns to me, only partially illuminated by our torch. He's smiling. He's *flirting*.

"I think you're correct." I smile back. "The right people always do come together in the end."

I stare at him, daring myself not to look away. Adonis's smile fades until he is serious, and he reaches out a hand to my waist to pull me closer. I step toward him. I look up.

"Oh, shit—sorry," comes a woman's voice, giggling in shock at walking in on two people who very obviously aren't catching up about the weather. It's one of the blondes from earlier, the one who kept her hand on Adonis's waist. "I think my secret spot is otherwise engaged," she says to someone in an American accent. I'm frozen to the spot in horror.

The person she is talking to is Jamie.

He looks at me, and I hold his gaze in the moonlight. Something about it makes my heart sink, and I hate myself for it.

"Let's go," Jamie says to her, and Adonis and I leave not long afterward.

9

Hot. I am very, very, hot. My eyelids feel glued shut by sleep, my skin sticky with slumber. The thin bedsheet is twisted in a ball at my ankles, and something is on my head. I squint open my eyes: It's the pillow. I'm on my stomach, legs and arms splayed, head pushed under the pillow, like I'm trying to free-fall out of a moving airplane and am blocked by the bother of my single bed. Crawling upright, I can tell it's mid-morning by the way the light hits and how warm it is. I tried to sleep on the tiny sofa last night because I couldn't bear to see Jamie, after that look he gave me in the cave. But it was so uncomfortable that at three A.M. I crept back into the eaves and slipped into my own bed. Jamie had been fast asleep. He's not here now. With one eye gingerly open, I take in his made-up bed.

I finally make it down for a late breakfast.

"Good morning, sleepyhead," Dad says, as I emerge into the unblinking sun. He's at the table, reading the same book of poetry that Alex gave me to read the other day.

"Morning, Dad," I say groggily, and he pours me a coffee, because he knows me and loves me and wants me to be happy.

I take it with a smile. "You're my favorite, Dad, do you know that?" I tell him, and he laughs.

"Best job in the world," he replies.

I lift the mug to my lips as I check out what everyone is up to. Jamie is doing laps. Was he doing those when I first came down? I don't remember seeing him in the pool five seconds ago. I track him back and forth until he passes everyone else at the side of the pool, their legs in the water, sun reflecting onto them in waves of light. Mum sits next to Alex, who sits next to Laurie, who sits next to Kate, who is next to . . .

Adonis?

"Flo!" he says, clocking me as I clock him. "Good morning!" He unfolds himself and everyone watches him pad over to me, and I swear my brothers are *smirking*. This is the line they cross that takes them from lovable rouges to freaking annoying. Adonis opens his arms, apparently for a hug, and as my arms go behind his back, I give Alex and Laurie the finger. I see my mother scowl. Kate says something to everyone and they all look away.

"What are you doing here?" I ask.

"I wanted to see you," he says. "To see if I can take you out? On my bike, and then later we can have lunch."

I feel the eyes of my family turn toward us again with vested interest. They were only pretending not to listen.

"Oh!" I start to say, and I'm aware that Jamie has stopped swimming and is sitting with the others now, too, watching. "I was going to grab something here . . ."

I don't know why I stumble. Last night was perfectly fine—we went back to the dance floor and hugged good night, and Adonis texted before bed to tell me to sleep well.

But then Laurie yells, "Go on the adventure, Florence!"

Laurie is encouraging this? Now *there*'s a plot twist.

Adonis grins, pleased to have familial support. All the words I could possibly say next stick in my throat. I want to hang out with him, I want to have a nice time. It's just . . . well, I don't know. A date in the middle of the day? I've never done that before! This is a *lot* of firsts happening.

"Urm . . ."

"Go on, Flo!" shouts Alex.

My mother adds, "For god's sake, Florence, it's only lunch."

I *feel* like I catch Jamie's eye, but between my sunglasses and his, I can't be sure. He gives an almost imperceptible shrug of the shoulder, which feels very much like *I'm not bothered what you do.* He had a fun night, too, no doubt, exploring the caves himself with that girl. Not that it bothers me, of course. And it's not like I need him to care.

"Okay," I say, because why not? The whole family cheers—except Jamie, who slips wordlessly back into the water.

I don't even put on shoes. I just grab my tote bag and climb onto Adonis's motorbike behind him.

"We're going to have fun!" he says, over the thrum of his engine starting.

I tell myself it's true: We are. But, oddly, I find myself looking back to the house as we pull away, half hoping Jamie has re-emerged to see this "fun."

WE TRAVEL DOWN the winding road that takes us to the main coastal path, and once we're away from the prying eyes of my family it's much easier to relax: the wind in my hair, my arms around a man who is determined to buy me lunch—I will myself to do as Laurie jeered when he yelled, *Go on the adventure.* It *is* pretty cool. I feel badass. The tension I've felt in my head since waking up melts away with reassuring effortlessness.

Adonis asks over his shoulder if I'm okay, the breeze carrying his words. I tell him I'm great and I mean it. I'm trying to be Holiday Flo. Holiday Flo meets fit men and hops on their motorbike, and doesn't get stuck in her head. By the time he pulls into a small patch of tarmac at a shack of a restaurant, I'm smiling and I can't stop. I think it might be a physical impossibility for *anybody* to ride down a path on the back of a motorbike without it being life-affirming.

Adonis takes my hand with not a scratch of self-consciousness and is welcomed in the restaurant like a son, arms open and cheek-kisses freely given. He talks in rapid-fire Greek, breaking only to tell me, "Flo, we are in the home of the best gyros on the island. I'm glad you are hungry."

"I can tell from the smell," I reply, rubbing my stomach for the benefit of the staff in case they don't speak English. A woman with ruddy cheeks and an apron chuckles, understanding my meaning.

Adonis seems pleased that my humor translates. "Come on," he says. "They'll bring it to us."

We cross over the small road that we arrived on, to the sand of the beach, where there's a handful of tables set up under beach umbrellas, all the seats facing the water. We sit, and the food comes quickly: meat seasoned to perfection, stuffed into fresh and fluffy pita bread. It's served with tomatoes, onions, fried potatoes, and the zingiest tzatziki I've ever tasted. We have tiny thimbles of chilled white wine, and I've got no idea what we talk about. We don't, really. Adonis alternates between watching the boats out on the sea-line and watching me eat, which I do with abandon. It's in my blood not to care about eating daintily or withholding my enthusiasm: I go for it, deep-throating the deliciousness with unladylike gusto. I suppose I should be trying a bit harder to be good company, but I can tell Adonis doesn't need that from me. It's funny how little we say to each other—how neither of us feels the need to fill the silence.

I lick sauce from my fingers and use a napkin to get at some runaway oil down my elbow. Side by side we sit, and if there's one thing I keep coming back to on the trip, it's how consistently amazing I feel by the water. *This* is holiday: great food, a great view, a little lunchtime wine. And yes, a handsome man (with a man-bun . . . I still can't fully get past that).

When we're done and our plates are cleared, Adonis asks if I want to go to the waterfall, and I'm so chilled, so sated, so *happy*, that there's only one response.

"Hell, yeah!" I tell him, in the style I imagine Holiday Flo most suits, and this time it's me who takes *his* hand.

THE WATERFALL IS even further down the coastal path, and it is beautiful—magical, even—hidden through a jumble of forest that suddenly gives way to a huge clearing, with a waterfall that's about ten feet high and seems to come from the sky somehow, surrounded by bundles of rock that have been smoothed by the passage of time. There's nobody else there. We are alone.

"Here," says Adonis, steering me toward a rock big enough and flat enough for two people to spread out comfortably, where he pulls out the wine left over from lunch and two plastic cups, and we cheers and settle into the show that Mother Nature is putting on.

"I can't believe you get to live here," I tell him. "This is so peaceful."

"Yeah," he says. "But of course nobody enjoys where they are from."

"They don't?" I reply, before I recognize the truth in what he says.

"I'd like to leave here," he tells me. "Work in Athens, or maybe Lisbon. I have heard many good things about Lisbon from my cousin who is there."

"Well, if that's what you want, I am sure you'll make it happen," I tell him. "May the odds be ever in your favor."

He smiles. "And what do you want, Flo?" he asks, leaning in slightly.

"I don't know," I reply. "Inner peace?"

"You don't have inner peace?"

"Absolutely zero," I say, and then, "Whoa. Actually, that's the most honest thing I've said out loud in ages. You make it easy to tell the truth."

He nods. "You don't have people to tell the truth to?" he asks.

I shake my head. "Not really," I say. "I had a . . . thing, a while back. A breakdown, really. And once you lose it like that, people are always looking for signs that you're going to lose it again. So you kind of . . . stop saying things that are too honest. Don't want to scare anyone."

"What happened?" he asks, and the way he looks at me—the way I am here, now—I suddenly *yearn* to unburden myself, to say everything that's been building up in me, so that I don't have to be weighed down by it anymore.

"Everything?" I offer, after a beat. "I was doing my PhD, and by the second year I was . . . paralyzed with dread, totally overwhelmed. And one morning I just couldn't go into the library. I couldn't physically get my feet to move; it was like a net blocking me from getting to the door and . . . I had to go home. And I got back to my flat and locked myself in my room, and I cried and cried and cried. And once that happened, I couldn't stop. I was on the verge of tears at every moment of every day. I lived and breathed inferiority. I felt ugly—I covered my mirror in my room with a scarf, so I didn't have to see myself. I was convinced people were talking about me, gossiping whenever I left the room about what a terrible person I am, so I stopped going out, to spare people the drama of having to be near me. And it all made me feel so stupid and immature. I kept thinking: Why can't I be like everyone else—all those girls who were more like grown women, sophisticated and moving through life with such certainty and ease.

"I just got so defeated by . . . life. I stopped being able to meet deadlines or appointments. Time stopped being normal: Minutes felt like hours, but whole days could go by and I wouldn't even have realized. By the time the university called my parents, I was already pretty bad. They took me to the doctor and he diagnosed burnout, but it wasn't that. I kept getting worse and eventually I had to be hospitalized, where they sedated me and let me rest, and then I was allowed back to uni under the supervision of a therapist, who helped me remember how to put one foot in front of the other, you know? Take it one day at a time?"

"And what about now?" Adonis asks. "How are you now?"

I take a deep breath. "It's so funny," I say. "In England we're always asking people how they are, but I don't think anyone ever answers honestly."

"You can be honest with me," Adonis says.

"I'm . . . better. I spend a lot of time reading, because things feel safe in books. I don't feel very brave. My family teases me for going back to university to teach, but I have no idea how to branch out and do anything different, you know? I have this sort of . . . good-girl syndrome, where I want to be liked and approved of. And I know it's a fruitless endeavor, but I still try. And if I can't be a good girl, I just do nothing. Because I don't want to fuck up. And rejection—oh my god, rejection is a big thing for me. If I get even a whiff of it, I struggle so much. I mean, I'm better than I was, but . . . it takes a lot for me not to spiral. I feel like I have to work twenty times harder than the average person to keep neutral, if that makes sense."

"I think you're brave," Adonis says. "It sounds like you won't believe me, but . . . you are not alone."

"Thank you," I tell him. I can't believe I've given him such a monologue. I'm grateful to be able to put all these feelings somewhere. I've been carrying them for so long that I'm tired. They're heavy. And boring, too. I'm sick of being so selfish, so concerned with my own self. "You're a good listener," I say. "Thank you. I'm sure you thought I might be better company than this."

"You are wonderful company," he tells me. "Please, don't worry."

I decide to believe him. At the very least, maybe I'm making him feel better about his life.

"Do you bring many girls here?" I ask him. I don't know where it comes from—but the way he's drinking his wine, laid out on the rock, he looks so very much at ease, like he's here all the time.

He grins at me. "One or two," he tells me. "If we're telling each other the truth."

"I appreciate that." I nod, noting how little I'm bothered. I don't feel jealous. It's almost a relief—confirmation that this doesn't have to mean anything except practice at having a good time.

We're interrupted by the ringing of my phone.

"Mum," I say, answering. "Hey. How are you?"

"Darling! Are you having a lovely time?"

I look at Adonis, laid out on the rock like a merman.

"Yeah," I say, and he gives me a smile. "Thanks. What's up?"

"I wondered if you were coming out to dinner with us tonight? No pressure or anything, darling—don't rush home. It's just if you'll be back late, we'll already have left, you see. I don't want you to feel abandoned."

"That's kind of you to check," I say. "I had a big lunch actually, Mum," I go on. "And we're at a waterfall. Exploring. Leave me a key under the mat at the front door?"

"Done," she says. "See you later." She pauses. "Or not," she adds, and I could die.

"I'll be back, Mum," I say, rolling my eyes. "Thanks for the encouragement, though."

I hang up, and Adonis asks if everything is okay. And it's so annoying, but as is my way, hot tears prick at my eyes, so I can't speak, only nod. And then he looks at me all full of sympathy, and one tear falls over my waterline, a solitary escapee running straight down to my chin before I wipe it away, uttering, "Sorry. It's just, she's like, the best person I know. And I suppose from everything I told you, I wish I was stronger, you know? To be more like her? It's a bit embarrassing to be a less amazing version of her. Like when you trace a picture at school and make a faint copy of the original. It's like that."

"You feel," Adonis supplies, "not good enough because you are not like her?"

I nod again. "I suppose that's about it, yeah," I say. "That feeling of inferiority is never far from the surface. Erupts without notice."

He considers this and, after a beat, says, "I think Veronica is a very good woman. But so is Flo. I think you should think about being a very good Flo, instead of a not-so-good Veronica."

I blink at him, shocked.

"I've had a therapist for two years," I say, "and she's never summed it up as well as that."

Adonis pulls me in for a hug, holding me tight. I can feel, from the placement of his arms and the way he rubs my back, like Mum does when we're sad, that it isn't sexual. It's fraternal. Reassuring, asking nothing in return.

"Better?" he asks, when I've let a few more tears pass.

"Better," I say, wiping my eyes. "Adonis, you're a very kind man." He smiles, gives a little shrug. "I'm sorry I'm a hot mess."

Adonis tells me not to worry and suggests that I get in the water, let this magical place wash away my tears. So I do. I slide into the water and push off a rock to go down deep, holding my breath to see if I can touch the floor. I can't, and I bob back up to the surface for more air. I swim to underneath the waterfall, letting the water hit my head, and tip my chin up like I'm in any other shower, except I'm not. I'm here, in a cove set back from the road, in Greece, with a man with a topknot who is called, implausibly, Adonis—and the freedom of it, the newness of it, lets me see life from a new angle. What if all I have to do is be the best Florence, instead of imitating Mum? What would that look like?

I'm not sure in this moment, but asking the question is heady.

I let the waterfall wash away everything that I have ever let hold me back, baptizing myself anew.

I'm okay, I tell my heart, and she swells in my chest in agreement, beating hard and steady and full of life. It feels good. It feels so, *so* good to be finally letting go.

10

HOPE

So, are you going to see this Greek god again?

ME

We didn't discuss that! When he dropped me off, we just said
bye
Do you think that's bad?
If he wanted to see me again, he would have told me, wouldn't
he?

HOPE

Don't be so passive!
I think you played it cool
Leave him wanting more, you know?

ME

So I did it right?

HOPE
There is no "right"
What are you guys doing today?

ME
Family snorkeling.
We literally just got here, flippers and all!
You?

HOPE
Going to bed—it was another all-nighter! I'm watching the Bluey
where Bandit gets a mullet.
It's calming me down ☺
I'll text later!

Down on the beach, we dump all our rented snorkel stuff on a
big blanket.

"Is this sanitary?" asks Alex, squinting at it. "I mean, I get rented
diving gear, but a rented snorkel? Have we hosed all this down with
disinfectant?"

Laurie reaches over to ruffle Alex's hair teasingly and says, "It's
salt water out there, isn't it? That's a disinfectant."

"Hmmm," muses Alex, pushing him off. "I don't think you understand how transmission works."

"Oh, take a day off," pooh-poohs Laurie. "We'll be fine! The guy
I got this off said it's so worth it. We just have to be careful not to go
too far out, because apparently the water gets tricky up there around
the other bay. Not that any of us are strong enough swimmers to get
out that far."

"Hey!" I say. "I am PhD-qualified when it comes to the ocean, remember?"

"Writing about it," Laurie points out. "Not swimming in it."

"Can't tempt you into a competition, then," Jamie asks, shielding his eyes from the sun with a big hand and surveying the sea. If I took a picture of him, he could go in a swimwear catalog. "I reckon I could get to that island out there. I'll bet there's all sorts around. You can see how it gets deep for a bit, but then shallows out, where the water gets clearer again."

"I don't want *any* of you going out that far," Mum chastises him. "You might be grown-ups, but you're all my babies, and that is too far for a non-Olympian. Got it?"

We all look at each other with suppressed smiles. There's something about a parent putting their foot down when you're no longer a child. It's . . . quaint.

"Yes, boss," Jamie says, snapping a salute, and the rest of us grumble, "Okay, Mum."

"Anyone for sustenance before the grand adventure?" Dad offers. "I brought down sandwiches and crisps, and some fizzy pop?"

It's largely agreed that nobody wants to eat before swimming in case it makes them sink, as per the old wives' tale, and so we put on our snorkels and masks and flippers, hooting with laughter at the ridiculousness of it.

"Oh my god, Michael! Take a picture," Mum insists before we all go in.

"God," complains Kate, "I don't know if I can walk on sand to where you are." She's down by the water's edge, and has to waddle toward us in exaggerated steps because of her flippers, bowlegged and rocking left and right.

"You look a right muppet!" Laurie teases, and Jamie hits his arm.

"Too right," Kate says with a nod, acknowledging Jamie's objection to Laurie's words. "See? Jamie knows you're sailing close to the wind, calling me a muppet."

"Yeah," defends Laurie. "But you're *my* muppet." He holds out a hand and steps toward her, pulling her in for a bear hug. "My sexy, sexy muppet." He nuzzles into her neck, and Alex pushes between them, separating them, as he complains, "Okay, that's enough foreplay here, thank you."

Jamie slips in next to Alex, leaving me to stand beside him on the end.

"Closer!" Mum says, art-directing the shot from Dad's side. "Like you've actually met before, darlings . . ."

I take a small step so I'm closer to Jamie, and then another when Mum insists. And then I feel his palm on my lower back as he snakes his arm around me, and I'm so shocked by the intimacy of it that I squeal.

"You all right over there?" asks Kate, leaning forward and talking across everyone's chests.

"Yes, yes," I singsong. "Sorry. I thought I felt a spider."

For the next photo, Jamie's palm loiters away from my bare back, and when we're done and Mum is satisfied, he mutters, "Sorry." I murmur something back about it being fine, and we wade out into the water one by one, kicking off into the deep blue sea.

IT'S BEAUTIFUL. THE water is so clear that you can see loads, and as we pad out and the water gets deeper, the fish become more colorful: flat ones with stripes, big fat ones in oranges and reds, and shoals of tiny little minnow-type things that travel together like an undulating, shimmering cloud. The water is super-calm, and for a while I open my arms and legs so that I float, letting myself be carried by it as I pretend I'm just another fish, minding her own business.

"Ouch!"

I'm under the water, so as the shriek leaves my mouth, it makes me swallow a lungful of salt water, which makes me spit and splutter, which makes me take my head out of the water so that I can actually breathe. What the hell?

A dark shadow passes my eyeline and scares the living shit out of me, so I lurch toward the nearest rocks peeking out of the sea, throwing myself on them before I can get eaten alive and bashing my elbow so hard that the skin splits and I start bleeding all down myself.

"Dammit," I say, trying to ignore the raging sting in the very same arm that I have to use to pull myself up, out of the water. I've ended up right on the very edge of the peninsula that I promised I wouldn't swim out to.

And so has Jamie.

"Jesus, Flo!" he says, bobbing out of the water. "Why the hell have you come out this far?"

I dart my eyes across the water and realize the dark shadow was him—it was Jamie.

"You scared me half to death," I yell by way of reply. "I thought you were a shark!"

Jamie reaches up to the rock and pulls himself out of the water with a lot more ease and grace than I did. He pulls off his mask and snorkel and drops them onto the flattest bit of earth, and sits there, panting.

"Are you okay?" I ask, confused.

"No, I'm not okay! Flo, do you have any idea how dangerous it is out here? We literally all talked about it twenty minutes ago."

I squint and look out into the direction we came from.

"You've come out way too far," Jamie continues. "I kept waiting for you to swim back toward us, but you didn't; you kept being carried by the current and you didn't even notice."

I've never seen Jamie like this. He is *livid*. Absolutely livid.

"Sorry," I say. "I was just . . ." I don't know how to finish that sentence. Do I really want to admit to having been pretending I was a fish? I change tack. "Anyway," I say, "you didn't need to follow me."

"Well," Jamie counters, "I did, didn't I? What if something happened?"

I bat back, "Because I can't look after myself?"

"I didn't say that," he says plainly.

"It's what you meant, though, isn't it?" I ask.

Jamie squints at me, faintly shaking his head. "I came to make sure you were okay, and that makes *me* the bad guy?" he asks.

And I throw up my hands, which could mean yes, or I don't know, or more likely why the hell are we even arguing right now?

I sigh and sit down a few feet from him, dangling my legs over the edge. It's a bit like hanging off the edge of the world.

"You're bleeding," Jamie says, looking over at me.

"Yeah," I reply, reaching my arm round to try and get a better look. It's worse than I thought actually, and it's throbbing. "I did it when you scared me," I say, "and I was trying to get to safety."

Jamie rolls his eyes and sighs, getting up to come over for a better look.

"Can you swim back?" he asks.

"Yes," I say, although I don't sound very sure. The thought of getting back into that water makes me feel nauseous. The shoreline is in the far distance. I can't admit out loud that I'm glad he's here, but . . .

I'm glad he's here. I didn't realize how far I'd come, and now I see it, I feel embarrassed. "I mean, how far do you think it is?" I say.

Jamie shrugs. "Half a mile, maybe. Laurie *did* try to warn us about the current."

I roll my eyes. "Okay, *Dad*," I say. "I fucked up. So shoot me."

"It's easier to get you back to shore alive," he quips. "Deadweight is heavier, and all that."

"I don't need *carrying*," I specify. "It's fine. I'm going to catch my breath and I'll be right there. You can go. You don't have to wait. Honestly." Obviously I don't mean this.

Jamie stands up then and suddenly rips off the net part of his shorts, underneath the fabric. "Come here," he insists, holding one end between his teeth. "Wrap it up in this."

I'm so shocked that I hold my arm out wordlessly and watch him work. He wraps the fabric around my arm three times and then knots it, his mouth perilously close to my skin as he focuses. He's careful and gentle, and when he's done, he delicately lifts my arm back down to my side.

"Thanks," I say. "Although isn't it going to get wet and effectively do . . . nothing? Not to sound ungrateful."

Jamie laughs. "I thought I was being some big, manly hero," he says. "But yes, I think you're right. I just wanted to try and help."

I look at him.

"Why?" I ask. The words fall out of my mouth.

I feel like Jamie understands the meaning behind what I've actually said because he looks down, as if he's embarrassed or ashamed. I've got so many questions about why he distanced himself from me, but it feels weak to ask. I don't want him to know how much it hurt. And yet.

"Because it's the right thing to do," he says eventually.

I nod. "Let's go back," I say, gesturing my head toward the shore. "I'm sorry if I made you worry," I add.

"I'm still worried," he says. "It's a long way back, you know. Let's go slow and steady and pace ourselves."

"After a break."

He nods. "You want to rest a bit more first?"

I don't like having to admit to needing it, but if we're going to go half a mile, I think it would be sensible to rest first. I really regret not having had some of the food Dad brought down, now.

I sit back down again and Jamie does the same.

"Can't complain about the view, can we?" I say. "It's pretty special."

"Agreed." Jamie nods. "I hear you went to a pretty nice waterfall yesterday? You're really seeing Greece from all angles."

I shrug. "Yeah," I reply. "I'm trying to embrace Holiday Flo."

"Holiday Flo?"

"Yeah, you know, like . . . letting loose a bit, having more fun. Going to waterfalls with Greek masseurs."

Jamie considers this.

"Sounds like she has fun," he decides. "Although, for the record, I do like Original Flo."

"She sounds like a bag of Doritos," I say, laughing. "Original Flo, Holiday Flo."

"Is Holiday Flo coconut-flavored?"

I laugh again.

"Coconut and regret. You know—for swimming out so far."

It's Jamie's turn to laugh. "Yeah," he says. "That'll do it."

I laugh, too, and it's not even that funny, but the laughing snowballs. He's laughing, and I'm laughing, and then we're looking at each other and laughing. I'm embarrassed that I swam out so far, and he's shaking his head like he gets it and won't push the issue, and it's ridiculous, really, that we're here and stranded on this little rock, in the middle of the sea, just him and me when . . . well, him and me when there is "us," if that makes sense. But laughing together, it makes an "us," a team. Jamie's still an arse, of course. But at least he's an arse I can laugh with.

"Look!" he shouts, pointing, and I follow his finger. "It's Laurie."

Laurie is, miraculously, in a speedboat. He's got a face like thunder and is shaking his head, like a cross father. He cuts the engine and lowers an anchor, and when he's done he turns and yells across the way, "Are you two fucking insane? Mum is about having a heart attack back there! You've been gone for nearly an hour."

Jamie looks at me with a grave face, so I have no choice but to fess up.

"It was my fault," I say. "Jamie was trying to help me."

"I'd have bloody let you drown," Laurie shouts. "Get down here and swim to the ladder."

We do as we're told in the kind of silence school kids fall into outside the headmaster's office. Jamie reaches up to the small ladder and hoists himself up, turning round to lean over and hold out a hand for me, easily taking most of my weight so that I don't have to climb much myself.

"Are you injured?" asks Laurie, looking at my arm.

I hold it out. "Jamie bandaged it," I say.

Laurie shakes his head. "You're a liability, Florence, I swear down," he says.

"Hey," Jamie replies, hitting Laurie's arm. "It could have happened to any one of us, mate."

Laurie narrows his eyes, unhappy at being contradicted, but

choosing not to say anything about it. He turns on the engine, and as the speedboat powers up, I yell, "Where did this even come from?"

Laurie takes a breath. "Veronica Greenberg gave a guy further down the beach two beers and the rest of the egg salad in exchange for fifteen minutes' use," he says.

Before I can ask if that's really true, we speed off back to shore.

I DON'T GO out that night. I'm tired after all that swimming and my arm hurts, and I need some alone time. I've spent days with my family, wishing they'd let me get some peace and quiet—if Alex isn't bombing into the pool, then Laurie is pontificating about something annoying, or Mum is chatting loudly with Kate, or Dad is whistling as he sorts out the towel on his sun lounger. It is constant noise. They assume I'm going out to meet Adonis, but I've just stayed home, alone. He hasn't texted me, but I'm kind of relieved about that. If he'd asked me to go out, I'd have gone, but for a few hours I need to be by myself. Although now, wandering through the house alone, I miss everyone already. It's not a holiday home without them; it's simply a place where we stay. I should have pulled myself together. This is the second dinner in a row I've missed.

I flick on some lamps downstairs to make it cozier, quickly shower and put on my PJs with a cotton dressing gown that I found in the linen cupboard, to preserve my modesty this time. I don't know where the Bluetooth speaker is, so I can't put on music, but I hum to fill the silence, rummaging through the fridge and picking at leftover pasta, drinking two glasses of water, picking up and putting down Laurie's book about soccer, which he's obviously made no further headway on. I sneak a peek into Jamie's room to see if it has dried out at all. It smells musty, like wet dog. I don't think he'll be moving back in any time soon.

Flopping down at the kitchen table, I text Hope to pass the time.

ME
Snorkeling was good!
Jamie isn't bugging me today, either
I think we might be heading for some sort of truce . . .

Nothing. Hope doesn't text back. She's probably too busy having a fantastic time, and I can't fault her for that.

By nine P.M. I feel pretty shattered. I'm kind of bummed they're all still out. Part of me assumed they wouldn't take too long, because they wouldn't want to be out without me. Apparently that isn't so. I suppose I'll go to bed, then, try to fall asleep in the bedroom before Jamie gets home . . .

I MUST HAVE drifted off, because it startles me when I hear voices downstairs. They're back.

"Flo?" It's Kate, in the stairwell. "Are you there?"

"Hello?" I say, right as there's an almighty crash. I head down and round the corner to see Dad swaying by the kitchen table, an assortment of fruit at his feet, from the broken fruit bowl that is also there.

"Ooooops!" he giggles—yes, *giggles*—as he catches sight of me.

"Whoa," I say. "You guys seem . . . happy."

Alex and Laurie are laughing hysterically at Dad's clumsiness, drunk as he is. My eyes flicker to Jamie: he's blinking a lot and his eyes are unfocused. He's pissed as well.

"They had a competition," Kate explains, ducking down to pick up Dad's mess. "They've been on every possible after-dinner drink this place has. Tsikoudia, mastika, ouzo, tentura . . ."

Laurie waves a finger as Kate puts the broken fruit bowl in pieces on the table, and the fruit that's rolling everywhere in a pile at the side of the sink.

"And tsipouro," Laurie adds cheerfully.

They all look green, and very unsteady on their feet. I don't know what else to do except make some black coffee and sort out glasses of water. It's kind of funny, that they've out-drunk one another in this way—although, drunk people aren't my favorite. In my undergrad years I learned quickly that the people who got most blotto weren't the fun ones; it was the people with sadness underneath their smiles. Happy people generally don't get arseholed, is my working theory.

"Drink this," I say, handing out various liquids. "None of you can go to bed as you are. You need to sober up a bit—you'll choke on your own sick otherwise."

Kate snort-laughs, shaking her head like she can't believe the state of them.

"You didn't want to join them?" I ask.

She tuts. "I can't," she replies, and her eyes flicker down to her stomach, where she's resting a hand. The penny drops for me and Mum at exactly the same moment.

"You're pregnant?" we scream in unison, and she nods.

"Only eight weeks. We just found out . . ."

"I'm going to be an auntie!" I cry, and Mum and I dance around Kate, laughing and smiling and thrilled.

I genuinely couldn't be happier for her—and for Laurie, who now has his head resting on his hands on the table, like he might fall asleep. No wonder he's been acting like a child this holiday; soon he'll be a dad and he'll have to start being the grown-up. The thought makes me smile. He has no idea what's coming. I cannot *wait* to see it.

Mum—equally sober as Kate—sits beside her and starts gabbling about when she was pregnant with Laurie and what it was like: the cravings, how her body changed, how the last month of it all sent her crazy with the waiting, but she missed being pregnant almost right away.

"Excuse me," Jamie mutters, getting up and spinning round to the kitchen sink, where he promptly throws up with a loud groan—loud enough to jerk Laurie upright.

We watch in horror as he throws up again, and then once more for good measure. I have to look away and will myself not to gag at the sound it makes. I hate vomit—but then I imagine everybody does. I enjoy any opportunity to see Jamie at his less-than-best, but this is a bit too much. He flicks on the tap to wash it away and then runs his face underneath to wash himself. I'm relieved there are no dishes on the drying rack. I'm going to bleach the hell out of that sink in a minute. Small mercies, though—I doubt he'd have made it to the bathroom. This is so gross.

After a little more dry-retching, Jamie's stomach is empty and he leans against the worktop to catch his breath. I take the opportunity to pull out the bleach and anti-bac spray, de-germing everything that could possibly be germy from stray flecks of vomit.

"Flo," Mum says, "take him up. I think he'll be all right for bed after that. I'll clean up."

"Jamie," I say, walking over to him. It's like he can't hear me—he doesn't move. "Jamie?"

I reach out a hand to his back, so finally he looks at me.

"Flo," he replies, openly happy to see me, only just realizing I'm there. Then a shadow crosses his face, and his tone darkens. "You didn't come to dinner," he goes on. "You went out with *him* instead, didn't you?"

I look at him, at the questions etched into his features, and let his words hit me. But then just as quickly I remember we're not alone. I make a show of looping his arm over my shoulders and say, "Left you? I left everyone! And look what's happened—you're all drunk as skunks."

My voice is bright and cheery. The men in the room might not be compos mentis, but Kate and Mum are, and the last thing I want is them sniffing around the truth. I mean, whatever the truth is. That Jamie is . . . jealous? When he has no right to be?

"Say good night," I instruct Jamie, not meeting anybody's eye. "Let's get you upstairs."

He doesn't say anything else as we manage the two staircases up to the eaves, but as I try to lower him down onto his bed, he pulls me with him so that I'm lying on top of him. He is solid and firm, even in his drunkenness, his skin warm, like the sun we've been enjoying every afternoon.

"Gotcha!" he says with a slur, maddeningly charming, even like this. He's grinning.

I study him. "What do you want from me?" I ask, knowing full well never to ask a question you aren't prepared to hear the answer to. I suppose I'm banking on *in vino veritas*—that a drunk man will tell the truth.

Jamie smiles with one side of his mouth, and paws the hair away from my face. For a man who was chucking his guts up mere moments ago, he's recovered handsomely.

"Hmmm," he says, his hand still at the side of my face. "Well," he goes on. "Not to hate me, Flo. I want you not to hate me. I mean, actually I mean, fuck it . . . I'm drunk, I don't care. Whatever. I'll say it. I want you to *want* me, Flo. Can't you tell?"

I can't believe what I'm hearing. He had the chance for all that, and he blew it!

I go to speak—to say what, I'm not sure—but Jamie carries on, "I want you to want me," he sings, approximating the Cheap Trick song. "I neeeeeeed you to neeeeeeed me." He pauses then, unsure. "I don't know the next words," he slurs. "But it doesn't matter. You don't want me . . ." His voice tails off, like he's on the verge of sleep. As if he's read my mind, he issues a massive yawn and lets his eyes flutter shut. "But I think you want the masseur," he says, talking more slowly. He yawns again. "We saw you. Me and . . . Jasmine." I'm not sure he even realizes I'm still there. It's like he's talking to himself, getting softer and softer. "Adonis. What a stupid name."

His eyes close properly, as if his main energy source has been turned off at the plug, and I pull back, moving to sit on the edge of his bed in case Jamie comes to again—but he doesn't.

I get him some water from the bathroom tap and put it on his bedside table. He's lying on his side, which is good for if he wants to be sick again. But I don't think he will be. His hands are under the side of his face, like he's playacting sleep—but I know he isn't. He inhales deeply and lets out a little snore. I let myself watch him and think of Christmas.

11

It's no surprise that Jamie is still sound asleep when I slip off for my morning jog, but when I get home he's coming down the stairs as I'm trying to go up. Neither of us stops to let the other by, so we get closer and closer, and with every step I take, my heart starts thumping louder. I still feel . . . *things*, about what he said last night. He wants me to want him? Was he joking, or being drunkenly truthful? I don't want to be a *pick me* girl, waiting for Jamie to change his mind and then flinging myself at him. I have far too much self-respect for that. And he probably doesn't even remember. It wouldn't be admissible in court, that's for sure.

I force myself not only to look up, but to hold his eye, too. I cannot be made bashful from *his* slurred half-confessions. He will not make me feel small! He's fresh from the shower, hair wet across his forehead, and the stubble chasing his jawline looks blond from the sun. I give him a hint of a smile—I surprise myself with how coy it feels—and Jamie relents, stepping aside to let me pass.

"Morning," I say brightly, and he winces for effect. I reward him with a laugh.

"Scale of one to ten," he begins, and there's only about six inches between his face and mine.

Anticipation gurgles in my hips. Hmmm, something has definitely shifted between us. It's almost imperceptible, but it's as if we've found the frequency that works. The energy between us is different this morning. I think it's been trying to find this frequency the whole time.

"How much did I embarrass myself last night?" he asks.

I take a dramatic in-breath and suck in my cheeks, looking to the ceiling like I'm weighing up all my evidence. "Put it this way," I say. "I've got enough ammo to lord over you for maybe a month? Possibly two?"

He shakes his head like he believes it. "Goddammit," he mutters. If he's going to say something else he stops himself and settles instead on: "Coffee. I'm going to go and find some coffee."

I feel like I've got the upper hand. And the notion of that—of Jamie feeling uncertain in *my* presence for once—makes me feel emboldened. And so I reach out to the collar of his T-shirt, a faded Ralph Lauren yellow thing that makes his tan look practically mahogany, and say, "You're crooked."

Jamie's jaw slackens and his lips part, and I can feel him holding his breath as I put my hands around his neck and smooth down the fabric. I focus on what I'm doing, but it's a challenge: His gaze is trained on me, and he tips his head to one side quizzically, making those six inches between us only five. I can feel his brain whirring. I finish fixing his T-shirt and tap a hand to the smooth muscle of his chest.

"There," I say, my voice low.

DOWNSTAIRS, BY THE pool, only Mum is up, and she says she's going to the market.

"Oh," I say, "you know I'd love to offer to come, but I was going to stretch out my hip flexors after my run. I'm not sure what I've done, but my right hip has been niggling me since we got here."

"Oh, gosh," Mum replies. "You know, it's different terrain here, isn't it? I had a similar thing when we were in Sicily, when you were about eleven, I think. I'll go, don't worry. Set the table once you're done?"

"Deal," I say. And then, because I'm all in my feelings this morning, I open my arms and give her a hug. She's visibly taken aback.

"I won't ask why," she says, with a squeeze. "I'll just take it."

When she's gone Jamie says, "I hope you've got your sun cream on." I hadn't realized he'd stopped swimming—I was totally in my head. He stands up in the pool, rivulets of water cascading down his lithe, tanned body. His collarbones jut out with pride, his pecs swell with satisfaction. He wipes his face with a colossal hand and shakes his hair back from his face. It's like being spoken to by a real-life model.

"I don't actually," I respond, from where I'm standing near the veranda. He looks at me, blinking. It's *that face* again, except whereas before it used to drive me mad that it was impassive and blank, impossible to read, now I see it for something else: a dare. Curiosity about what I'm going to do next. "You offering to help?" I add.

The right side of his full lips curls enough to let me know that he absolutely is. I mirror the gesture, and grab my bag from where it's hanging inside the kitchen door. I hold the sun cream in my hand, my invitation for him to climb out of the pool.

He puts a foot up to the edge—an easy feat for him, from the shallow end—and lunges upward. His walk is lazy, like a Southern drawl. He's in no rush. Like a panther in the forest keeping a steady eye on its prey, he gestures to the sun lounger where his towel is, and I go toward him.

"Such a gentleman." I don't know why I say it, but I do. When Adonis was here, I was struck by how smiley he was when he spoke to me, his features expressive and open. He didn't have any fear around owning his interest. It's different with Jamie. There's too much at stake, too much to lose. Every sentence is like a move on the chess board, careful and loaded and unclear. I'm playing with fire.

Jamie responds by wiping a finger at the side of his mouth, a bit like you would when an especially tasty-looking pasta is put down in front of you. He takes the bottle and uses a hand on my shoulder to spin me round.

I hear him open the lotion and squirt some into his hand.

"Good run this morning?" he asks, as his hands find my back. I am transported back to Christmas, the first time his hand lingered on my lower hip as he squeezed past me in the kitchen. There'd been plenty of room, no squeeze necessary. But that's where it had all started.

"Nice," I reply, as he reaches the back of my bikini. "Just ten K, down around town and up through the hills to get back."

"Do you want me to go under the strap?" he murmurs, the movement of his fingers slowing down. "Or . . . ?"

My voice sticks in my throat. I have to will myself to speak. I'd much rather close my eyes and let his hands do whatever they damned well please. I think of that first night playing volleyball, and of my disappearing bikini top. I tell him, "It's nothing you haven't seen before."

He lets out a gruff chuckle. "True," he replies. "But a gentleman never pervs and tells."

"I'd never pegged you for one of those," I shoot back, reaching behind to pull on the string of my top so that it comes undone. I put an arm over my chest in case anybody comes out, but then that is half the thrill.

"If you never had me pegged as a gentleman," Jamie says, and he works his way perilously close to my left boob, "that's your problem."

I don't know what to say to that.

"And yet here we are," he continues, voice low. He keeps his hands on me, running down the length of my torso so that his fingertips all but graze my nipple and I gasp. I am most definitely protected from the sun with the thorough job he has done. He's showing off now.

Jamie gently takes the string of my bikini from in front of me, leaning in so that I feel his breath on my skin. I move my neck, a silent invitation. But he doesn't take it. The agony of this is painful, and delicious. I'm buzzing at a cellular level. I'm thinking a million things and nothing, all at once. I close my eyes and take a breath.

When I turn round, I get to see those gray eyes and blank expression.

"We're doing a good job of being nice to each other today, aren't we?" I ask quietly.

"It's almost like we've declared a cease-fire."

"Almost," I retort.

He breaks into a huge grin, like he can't hold it back. It makes me smile, too, and we stand, in a kind of smile-off, something shifting between us yet again.

"Morning," Laurie yells from across the pool. It breaks our spell. Goddamn this family! Always interrupting things.

"Morning," Jamie shouts back.

"Morning," I say, quickly doing my top back up.

When I'm done, I hold out a hand.

"Friends?" I ask. "Officially?"

Jamie takes my hand and gives it a firm shake.

"Friends," he says, holding on to me for a second longer than a friend should.

"PRETTY LADY!"

The voice comes from around the side of the house, and it comes from Adonis. I'm in the middle of trying to list all the states in America quicker than Laurie can. Why? I have no idea. Somehow it came up, and then somehow it became a competition.

"Adonis!" Mum says, opening her arms to issue two air-kisses. "I'm so glad you could come. It's Flo's hip, you see . . ."

"You missed Hawaii," Jamie says, pointing at Laurie's sheet of paper. "And Missouri," he adds, forcing me to scream, "Adonis! Hi. Jamie—fucking stop it."

Jamie holds up his hands in surrender like he didn't realize meddling was such a big deal, and Adonis approaches with his brow furrowed, wondering what the hell is going on.

"Oh, New York *State*," I mutter to myself, going back over my list and forcing myself to remember what I'm missing.

"You didn't even get New York State?" Laurie teases, before obviously writing it down himself.

I am determined to beat him. Absolutely determined. Kate, Jamie, and Alex have gathered around us like we're playing a grand master chess final in fifties Soviet Russia, everyone with bated breath and narrowed eyes, trying to figure out who has the smarts to emerge victorious.

Mum and Dad wander over, Mum saying, "Adonis! Hello." She gives him a kiss on either cheek, and Alex points at my list and says, "You need to think about what others begin with *M* . . ."

I've got Maine, Massachusetts (which I don't think I've even spelled right), Michigan . . . Gah, this is so annoying! I know Americans all learn a song that helps them remember the states, but as a Brit I never have, and it turns out I might lose this stupid competition because I can only think of thirty-nine.

"You're seeing Florence at her most authentic right now," Mum explains to Adonis. "In competition with her brother, over something inconsequential but deadly serious . . ."

Adonis laughs. "I think she might have achieved her strength this way, no?" he offers, and Dad laughs.

"Oh no," he says. "That's from her mother. All of our children are incredibly pigheaded, and quite frankly, we've got no idea where that's from, have we, Vee?"

"None at all," Mum says with a laugh.

"Minnesota!" I blurt out, when I eventually think of an *M* state that's missing.

"Finally," Alex comments, and I give him the finger without looking up.

"I'm on forty-three," says Laurie.

"Bullshit," I hoot. "No way. Somebody check his working," I instruct. I hear Adonis say to Jamie, "So the game is . . . writing down places in America?"

"All the states, yeah." Jamie nods, not altogether warmly.

"I saw your friend Jasmine at the food market," Adonis tells him, and I pause my pen above my paper to listen.

Laurie has paused, too, though—we're both running out of steam.

"She's not really my friend . . ." Jamie says, and Adonis cocks an eyebrow.

"I understand," he replies, butting his shoulder against Jamie's arm.

Jamie sees me look up. "It's not like that," he presses on, telling Adonis but, oddly, looking at me.

I cast my eyes back down quickly. It's none of my business if Jamie's "friend" Jasmine says hi. Jamie said he wants to kiss me, but this is a mark in the "he must have just said it drunkenly without meaning it" column.

"Laurie has thirty-nine states," Dad announces, leaning over Laurie's shoulder and putting a line through his duplicates. "You're neck and neck."

"Siri," Alex says to his phone, "set a timer for ninety seconds."

Siri beeps confirmation and Kate stage-whispers to both of us, "Neither of you has the Dakotas!"

I scribble down *North Dakota* and *South Dakota*, and that triggers a mental map that means I suddenly remember Colorado, New Mexico, Wyoming, and Nebraska.

"Stop her from writing," Laurie yells, pointing at my moving pen. "She's cheating!"

"How can I be cheating?" I say, full of glee—Laurie hasn't written anything after the Dakotas.

"Five . . ." Alex says, holding up his phone. "Four . . ."

Everyone else joins in now. All of us, bar Laurie, shout: "Three . . . two . . . one . . ."

Siri sounds her alarm, and Laurie throws down his pad of paper and his pen petulantly.

"That's not very sportsmanlike," I point out. "Aren't you going to tell me: Congratulations, the best man won?"

Laurie rolls his eyes and holds out a hand. As I reach for it, he pulls it away and slicks his hand back through his hair, like an eight-year-old.

"Very cool," I tut. "Very mature."

I watch him walk away and dive-bomb into the pool, Mr. Moody Pants because his little sister is smarter than he is.

"Well," Mum says, "I'd rather Laurie lost than Florence. *Then* we'd know about it!"

"Oh, really?" Adonis says, laughing.

"Absolutely," says Mum. "When she was fifteen she once lost at Monopoly and she didn't speak to any of us for almost seventy-two hours."

"And when we went on that adventure holiday when we were about twelve and she lost at archery," offers Alex.

Even Kate offers her two pence's worth. "Flo once tipped over the Scrabble board at the pub because she was losing. Said it was an accident, but we all know it wasn't . . ."

I am aghast that my family would all pile on and assassinate my character in this way.

"Adonis won't want to play Dobble if you scare him with stories like this," I declare. "Shush, the lot of you!"

I didn't know Mum had asked Adonis to come and look at my hip, but it's feeling okay after a good post-run stretch. Instead of a massage, I motion for Adonis to sit and I take the seat next to him. Laurie sloshes about in the pool nosily.

"Who's in?" I say, reaching for the cards.

"Me," says Jamie, sitting opposite me.

"Anyone else?" I ask. Kate shakes her head, Mum and Dad pull a face that I take to mean *not on your nelly*, and Alex looks between us all and decides, "Nah. I'm going to challenge Laurie to an underwater handstand competition."

"Fine," I say. "Just us three, then." I look between Jamie and Adonis. "Ready?"

"As soon as you explain what I must do," Adonis says. "Yes."

I click my fingers and point at him. "Fair enough," I reply. "Right. Well, Dobble is a kids' game, really. There's a massive pile of cards, and you all have to race to match the symbols on them. See here? There's an ice cube, sunglasses, a knight . . ." Adonis nods. "I like it because it gets you properly thinking," I say. "And when you get into the rhythm of it, you feel really clever."

Jamie laughs. "And when everybody else is matching them really quickly and you get stuck in a rut, it's *horrible*," he says.

"Okay, then." Adonis smiles. "I'm ready."

Dad delivers a big jug of water and some glasses with his cursory pun. "Did you ever hear the joke about hydration?" he asks us, and on account of having heard this for my whole entire life, I don't answer.

"No," Jamie supplies. "Because it's no laughing matter."

Dad smacks him on the shoulder good-naturedly. "Good man," he says. "Now drink up!"

Jamie grabs the cards and starts dealing them out, and as he catches my eyes he . . . smirks. I quickly focus on the cards and on what he's doing, watching his big hands deftly flick between the three of us. I have to reach and get a glass of water, taking it down in big, deliberate gulps.

"Ready?" Jamie asks, to which Adonis and I say, "Ready!"

And we're off. Adonis does great, considering it's his first time, matching ice cubes to ice cubes and pencils to pencils.

"Dog!" shouts Jamie, matching a pair, and then I yell, "Treble clef!" and whack my card down, too.

"Treble clef?" says Adonis. "What is that?"

But we don't answer him, because now for every card I put down, Jamie puts one down, too. Adonis leans back in his chair, his beginner's luck no match for my and Jamie's determination, and I find myself leaping up out of my chair so that I can stand over the piles, all the easier to win.

"Yes!" I say, getting rid of three cards in a row, and then a fourth. Jamie gets two. We go at it quickly, Jamie leaping out of his seat to get a better angle for doling out his cards rapidly, too. Bam, another. Bam, another. Bam! Another!

When we're both left with a single card in our hands, we know we're so close it's painful and it suspends time for a moment. But then I see a small spider's web that matches the spider's web on my card and I throw it down with a force and shout, "DOBBLE! Yes!"

Jamie drops his jaw and looks at me like he can't believe it.

"*No way!*" he exclaims, and his expression is priceless.

"Oh my god," I say. "You look like you're about to cry. Are you okay?" I put on a silly voice. "Is Jamie-Wamie not very good at being a *loser*?"

He pulls a face, rising to my bait. "Two out of three," he says. "Because I guarantee you can't do that again."

I issue a hoot. "Ha!" It's not an attractive sound, but it's an authentic one. "I don't think I dare," I say. "Because when I do win again, you might *actually* cry, and then where would we be?"

"Right," Jamie retorts. "That's it!"

Before I realize what's happening, he's lunged at me, scooping me up and throwing me over his shoulder so that my butt is by his face and my legs are up in the air.

"You're getting dunked," he yells.

And I squeal, "No. I hate chlorine water on my face. NO!"

"Lies!" shouts Alex from the pool. "She says that all the time and it's not true. Don't believe her."

Jamie lingers at the edge of the pool. "Who is telling the truth?" he asks, his voice low and serious.

"Me," I yell, still kicking. "I promise."

"Lies! Lies! Lies!" Alex reiterates. "She was swimming underwater just this morning."

"I'm going to kill you, Alex," I holler.

And Jamie shifts me in his arms so that he's dangling me over the water, holding me like a kid under the arms, as if I weigh nothing. I close my eyes as Jamie counts, "Three, two . . ."

Before he gets to *one* he launches me into the pool, flinging me with incredible muscle power so that I hit the water hard and sink to the bottom, where I find the tiles with my feet and use them to launch myself up. I come to the surface fast, wiping my face with a hand and catching my breath, to see Jamie holding his arms aloft at the side of the pool—the champion personified.

Well, revenge is sweet, dear Jamie Kramer.

"I can't believe you!" I say, making a song and dance about being "upset." I need to throw him off the scent, because I've got a plan . . .

I swim to the edge and hoist myself out, walking round the side like I'm furious, convincingly enough that even Laurie issues an "Oooooh!" from the water.

"Are you all right, Flo?" Adonis asks, and I feel fleetingly guilty as I say, "No! Jamie is such an ass."

"Flo . . ." Jamie says, walking toward me. "I was just messing around! I'm sorry. I couldn't resist."

I dodge out of his path, in the direction of the water, so I'm closer to the edge of the pool. As Jamie comes near, I take my chance and grab his arm.

"Gotcha!" I cry, pulling him toward the water, and he yelps, "Flo!"

I give a pantomime laugh, and Laurie and Alex start to chant, "Dunk him. Dunk him!"

I pull and pull, sidestepping Jamie so that I'm behind and can give him a massively satisfying shove. But right at the last second, Jamie manages to grab me, so that as he falls over the edge I go with him and we hit the water together.

The force pushes my body into his, so that when we're underwater we're entwined. Everything slows down. When I was in the water alone, I came up for air so fast. But together, it's like being on the pause button. I open my eyes underwater and see that he is doing the same—and he's smiling. I give a small wave. Jamie waves back and then moves toward me, taking my hand so that we emerge at the top together. I take a gulp of oxygen and twist round to see where he's gone, and he throws himself at me.

It becomes all-out war. I lob myself toward him when I break the surface again, getting enough force to dunk him successfully in return. Squealing with delight, I let him splutter, and then push off the side of the pool directly toward his legs underwater, where I manage to grab both sides of his shorts and pull.

"Florence!" he yells, horrified, as he scrambles to pull them back up. "This will result in your punishment," he intones, and I swim to the steps to climb out, happy that if I haven't won the war, I have at least won this battle.

"We should do water games," Adonis announces, taking in the feral performance we've just given him. "You guys are crazy!"

I flop down on a chair with my towel, catching my breath. Alex and Laurie are seated at one end of the pool, out of the way of the commotion that has occurred, and Jamie swims to go and sit with them.

"Only if I'm on a team with these guys," Jamie says. "I want to whoop your asses!"

I slap my thigh, like what he's said is the funniest thing in the world.

"Me, Adonis, and Kate against you three losers?" I ask. "That's barely a competition."

"And Mum," Laurie says. "You have to have Mum on your side, too."

From her sun bed, Mum tuts, "I can actually hear you, Lawrence, thank you very much. I'm not that much of a handicap, am I?"

Laurie and I look at each other, and I make a zip-across-the-mouth motion. Mum is, actually, that much of a handicap when it comes to water games, as we have all learned through experience. On land? She's a beast. In the water? It's actually embarrassing.

"He's trying to get in your head, Mum," I say. "Don't fall for it. You can be our mascot if you want; even three against three, we'll win."

"Game. On," Jamie yells, standing up and swiping a finger across his neck, as if we're dead men walking already.

"RIGHT. A SIMPLE relay to start," Kate shouts, sitting in the shade with a whistle and a lemonade. She's assigned herself judge status, so it's two against three, with Dad prepared to help us out if we ask nicely enough.

"I'm in a very meaty bit in my book, you see," he says. "But I'll help if you need me to."

I could never tear him away from his reading, so Adonis and I are going to do our best as a two.

Kate continues, "Everyone has to swim to the end of the pool and back, with Adonis going twice."

"Pffft," yells Jamie. "Easy!"

"Now, now, Kramer," Kate warns him. "This is only a warm-up game. Don't get too cocky."

As she says *cocky*, Jamie looks at me and winks. I screw up my face, making a show of being unimpressed.

"Ready?" asks Kate, and we tell her we are. "Go!"

Adonis dives into the pool, swimming against Laurie in long, smooth strokes that put my brother to shame. Adonis gets the lead and keeps it, getting back to tag me in seconds, before Laurie can tag in Alex.

Alex is a good swimmer because he's strong, even if he's not the leanest man around. I'm trying my best to do big arms and measured breaths, but by the time I get to the other end of the pool and flip round to head back, Alex has the lead and I don't swim so much as flail to catch up.

But I do catch up. And Jamie and Adonis dive into the pool for the final lap in seamless synchronicity, absolutely neck and neck.

"Go on, Adonis," I cry as the boys yell their support for Jamie.

At the far end of the pool, Jamie and Adonis are perilously close to each other, like they could physically bump into one another.

"Did Jamie just hit Adonis?" Alex asks, as they reach the wall and push back.

"I don't know," I say, watching Jamie take the lead. "Surely not . . ."

Adonis drops back slightly, but suddenly Jamie lurches in the water, coming to a shuddering stop, where Adonis overtakes.

"Hey," yells Jamie, standing up in the pool. "You can't do that!"

Adonis reaches the wall, Kate shouts, "And we have a winner," and as he clambers out, he grins widely, happy and satisfied.

"We won!" I tell him, giving him a high five.

"We won," he repeats. He reaches over into the water to where Jamie is saying something about cheating—offering a hand that Jamie bats away.

"I've got it," Jamie grumbles, and Adonis steps back.

"Okay," declares Kate. "Let's do some dive games. Laurie, can you get those sinking pool toys from the kitchen table?"

Laurie gives her a salute and runs off to find them, with Kate explaining that there are four sinking toys that will sit on the pool bottom, and each person in the team has to collect all four before they're thrown back in for the next person.

"Easy," I tell Adonis. "I can collect all four in one breath—I'm good at diving."

"She's almost as good as me," stage-whispers Alex, and I shake my head like he's nuts.

"Have you always been like this?" Adonis asks. "Doing competitions all the time?"

Laurie, Alex, Kate, and I all answer at once. "Yes!" we say and then laugh, because you either love it or need to get out of our way.

Adonis looks afraid.

"You okay?" I ask him. I've never hung out with a boy in a family setting before, never had somebody who is "mine" (for lack of a better word) be in this situation. I quite like it. Alex has occasional boyfriends, but they don't tend to last long, and of course Laurie and Kate have been a pair for years. As the little sister, I've always been bottom of the pecking order, but having Adonis here gives me status—a gravitas that is messing with what my brothers must think is the natural order of things. Even Jamie seems surprised at whatever new dynamic is coming into play right now.

Laurie re-emerges with the goods and proceeds to lob four toys at one end of the pool and four at the other.

"It doesn't matter which you get," instructs Kate. "You just need four. Go!"

I launch in, breezily grabbing my loot and emerging victorious.

Kate throws them back in and sends in Adonis, as Laurie comes up with his.

"Dammit," he says, as he realizes we're already beating him.

Adonis goes in, followed by Jamie. I see Adonis get one, but then Jamie swims really near him and gets the toys closest to him, making it harder for Adonis. As tactics go, I get the general idea: Adonis now has to swim further to get his. But Jamie is wasting time by blocking him. Adonis comes up for air as Jamie does, and Jamie blocks him again as he tries to go down.

"Hey," I say. "Cheat!"

"He cheated first," Jamie yells back, but then Adonis has the four toys he needs and it's time for me to go again.

I have no idea what happens when I'm in the water, but by the time I get back up, I'm the only one who cares about my record-breaking and natural talent for underwater-toy accumulation, because everyone else is focused on Adonis and Jamie.

"You can't do that, man," Jamie is yelling, and Adonis is half laughing, half scared-looking as he says, "I apologize. I thought this was supposed to be fun. That's all."

"Yeah, well . . ." Jamie huffs, without finishing the sentence.

I swim to the edge and look up at them all. "What's going on?" I ask.

Nobody speaks; they all just look at each other as if they don't know where to start.

"Okay," I say. I climb out and drop my collected toys onto a nearby sun lounger. "So who won?"

"Urm . . ." Kate murmurs, like she's scared to say, in case we cause a riot over it. "It was a tie," she settles on. "Two points to each team."

I have no idea what's going on—everyone seems super-weird.

"You good?" I ask Adonis, because he's the guest, after all.

"Of course," he replies, giving me his adorable smile. "Although I do have to go soon. I have massages booked."

"Okay," I say to him, and then to the group at large, "This will have to be our last game, because I'm down to being a one-man team in a minute."

"Oh, Adonis, you can't stay for something to eat?" Mum asks, over the edge of her magazine.

Adonis shakes his head. "I must work," he says in his accented English, and Mum replies, "What a shame." To me he asks, "Can I see you later? Or tomorrow?"

I nod. "Sure," I say. "Just text me?"

"Okay," he replies, and the way he looks at me—it's hungry, and it makes my tummy do three somersaults in a row. Adonis wants me! With Jamie, it's all so conflicting. What he says and what he does are at odds, don't line up. Adonis and his intentions are crystal-clear. If Jamie doesn't want me to hate him, he could start by taking a leaf out of Adonis's book.

"LAST GAME," Kate yells, "is the Pink Swan game."

"Oh god," groans Laurie. "I know what this means . . ."

"Go on, then," Kate invites. "Be my guest."

"The Pink Swan game is where you have to take a run and jump onto one of the big inflatable pink swans, paddle to the other side, get out, run and jump onto it again, and get back to where you started, so that your teammate can have their turn. Am I right, or am I right?"

Kate rolls her eyes. "You're right," she says. "Boys! Assemble the swans."

Jamie hops into the pool with the swans, but they keep floating in all directions, so it's decided that Dad will hold one at one side, and Mum will have to hold the other.

"They're not level," yells Alex. "Dad! Come forward."

Dad inches forward and Alex reassesses.

"Okay," he says. "Fine. I'm happy."

I go first, against Laurie—Laurie is slightly in front, the jackass—and then Jamie and Adonis go.

"Funny how they always seem to race each other, isn't it?" Alex comments as they thrash about like two hungry hippos running rampage in the lake of a national park.

"Is it?" I say, realizing, as I speak, that it is, yeah.

They both climb out of the far side of the pool, and Mum and Dad grab the inflatables and hold them again. But before Adonis can run onto his, Jamie pushes him back so that he gets a head start. Adonis stumbles, but isn't fazed, and then instead of jumping onto his own inflatable, he lands on Jamie's, pushing him off into the water.

"Ah," says Alex, *loving* this turn of events. Are they doing this playfully? Or is it a fight? It seems pretty serious for two blokes who barely know each other . . . "Behold," he narrates, like he's David Attenborough, "the peacocking rituals of the straight male. The tall Adonis, local to the area, is asserting his dominance over visiting breed Jamie, using his height and tan to wow the rest of the flock and take his place as alpha. Notice how Jamie is scrambling to give him a challenge, but is ultimately failing, perhaps from underestimating Adonis's desire to show off to one Florence Greenberg."

"Shut up," I say, pulling a face. And although I do not approve of Adonis playing dirty, I scream for him to get to the finish line, so I can race Laurie. "Go on, Adonis," I yell, and Jamie looks up from where he's trying to get on the other swan, hurt etched across his angry features. But he's not on my team, is he? Why would I cheer *him* on?

I get on the swan, passing Jamie in the water, who hisses, "Your boyfriend is a dick."

I glide by, climb out, and am almost all the way back to the start as Laurie gets on his swan to complete the race.

"You all right there?" I ask, as I swim beside him in the opposite direction. "Not your finest hour, is it?" I say.

To which Laurie cries, "Fuck it!" then gets off his swan and pulls me off mine, with everyone launching into the water for a massive water fight that mostly involves dunking each other, until Adonis grabs my hand in the water and pulls me round.

Except, it isn't Adonis.

It's Jamie.

"Oh," I say, my lips parting in surprise. "Sorry," I continue, pulling quickly away. "I thought you were . . ."

Jamie sighs. "Isn't it time for him to go?" he says.

I don't know how to reply to that. "Be nice," I say, and Jamie shrugs.

"He just makes it so hard," he replies, and anger flares across my face. Why does Jamie get an opinion? I don't have an opinion on *Jasmine*. And even if I did, it's Jamie who told me he didn't want me; Jamie who asked to never speak of our *almost* again. And I've done that! Because of my massive embarrassment, I haven't uttered a word about it. But dear Lord, I could almost throw that back in his face now, if he thinks he can comment on who else I see. He's so . . . so . . . so *Jamie*.

I climb out of the pool and wrap myself in a towel, and when Adonis comes over, I open it so it wraps around us both. I don't care if it's inappropriate around my family, I want to make my position clear to the one person who I shouldn't even care about at all—but here we are.

"Thank you for having me," Adonis says. "I like your family very much. Although Jamie . . . I don't think he's my biggest fan. Is that how you say it?"

"That's how you say it," I say with a smile. "And Jamie isn't family," I explain. "He's Laurie's best friend."

"Oh." Adonis nods. "He's not your brother?"

"No." I shake my head.

"Ah." Adonis nods again.

"What?"

He shrugs. "Nothing," he says. "It's nothing. I have to go now, but later, yes? See me later."

"Okay," I reply, and as Adonis kisses my cheek and says good-bye to everyone else, I can't help but notice Jamie is shooting daggers at him—the only one not to say it was nice to see him.

12

We spend the rest of the afternoon soaking up the sun, and I flick through one of Mum's magazines, reading about celebrities and what clothes are hot right now. Jamie and Laurie are playing Ping-Pong on a table they found in one of the outbuildings, and Alex and Kate are . . . coloring.

"I don't understand," Dad says, peering over at them. "He has a whole book of drawings and carries that pencil case with him everywhere?"

"I believe so," Mum replies.

"I can hear you," Alex says, without looking up.

"I'm only curious, son," Dad replies. "That's all. You didn't even like coloring in when you were little. I'm just surprised."

"It's quite therapeutic actually," says Kate. "You should come and try it."

I look over at Dad and he shrugs.

"I'll do some," I say, wandering over to their setup across the table. Alex has an A4 page of three men engaging in various sexual acts

Laura Jane Williams

in front of him, one-third of it colored in. "Classy," I comment, pointing at it.

"It's whatever holds your interest, isn't it?" Alex shrugs. "Kate chose a woman getting oral sex off an octopus, a rip-off of that famous painting of the fisherman's wife or whatever it's called, but I don't hear you judging her."

"Is it porn, then?" Dad asks, suddenly more interested. He comes and stands beside me and picks up the pad of drawings that Kate and Alex have ripped their "art" from. "A *Kama Sutra Coloring Book*," he reads off the front. As he opens it up, he says, "Look, Vee! We know this one, don't we?"

"Dad!" I squeal, disgusted, as Alex says, "Ha ha. Just pick one and start coloring. Kate and I are crosshatching our lines, so it looks even better. Like this, see?" Alex demonstrates lightly running his pencil in one direction and then going over the top in another, so that all the lines are less visible.

"I remember learning crosshatching with Ms. Watts at school," I say. I feel like if I know what crosshatching is, I might be good at this—and being good at stuff is my kink. "Go on, then, I'll do it, too."

I leaf through the book and find a drawing of two people fully clothed and kissing passionately. They look happy, like the whole point of life is to enjoy each other. I like it.

Mum and Dad pick one each, too—I refuse to acknowledge which *Kama Sutra* positions they've chosen, and we work side by side for a while, the only noise coming from Jamie and Laurie playing Ping-Pong.

"Have it!" Laurie gleefully shouts after he sends the ball sailing past Jamie's head. As Jamie goes to retrieve it, he adds, "I feel like I'm playing a brick wall, to be honest with you. Where's your head at, Kramer? It's not like you not to put up a fight."

168

Jamie doesn't say anything, simply glances at me and then takes his serve.

"Gosh," says Mum after a while. "I see what you mean. Something about the strokes back and forth, concentrating on staying in the lines . . ."

"Yes," agrees Dad. "A moving meditation of sorts."

Mum points to the air in delight. "Yes, darling," she says. "You're so clever, that's it entirely!"

"I love how kind you two are to each other," says Kate. "My parents like each other, but I wouldn't say they champion each other as you do."

"Oh, Kate," says Mum, "that's a lovely compliment. Thank you."

Over at the Ping-Pong table, Jamie gives away another point.

"You're welcome," Kate replies, putting back the dark red I've been waiting ages for.

"And I will say, I think you and Laurie do a beautiful job of supporting and championing each other, too. That's all I want for my children: for them to live bold lives with partners who want the best for them."

"I'm working on it, Mum, I can promise you that much," says Alex, once again not looking up. I'm startled by the admission: Alex plays lovable rogue with a heart of gold, but has never outwardly said he'd like to settle down.

"Really?" I ask, not doing a very good job of hiding my shock.

"What, because I'm such a Lothario?" he bats back, and I can hear the edge in his tone.

"No judgment," I say, "I just didn't know. It's . . . nice. You deserve nice."

Alex looks up and crinkles his nose at me. I crinkle my nose back.

"Do you ever think about settling down, Florence?" Dad asks. "In the abstract, I mean. A husband, kids . . . ?"

"Dammit!" Jamie shouts, throwing down his Ping-Pong bat. "That's it, mate, I'm out. You won. I'll beat your arse tomorrow." He puts his hands behind his head and closes his eyes. We all watch him, and then the attention comes back to me.

I take a breath to decide how I feel about being asked about settling down. I don't think Dad is asking with any judgment, either, but I can sense Mum is holding her breath for my reply.

"In the abstract, yeah," I offer. "Of course. I mean, Kate's right about how you and Mum support each other. It's pretty rare."

"Hard-agree," says Alex. "It's a tough act to follow. Most men I date either don't want to 'settle down' or—and this is an awful thing to say, but it is my experience—see that I'm a doctor and think they can be the main homemaker while I go off to work. And I don't want either of those things! A proper fifty-fifty setup is—"

"Elusive," offers Kate. "I think so, too. Laurie and I have to work at being equal, to be fair, but I think that's half the battle: finding somebody who wants to figure that out with you. And, you know, it's not always fifty-fifty, is it? Sometimes it's twenty-eighty and sometimes it's ninety-five–five, depending on what's going on with everyone."

"But knowing it all works out in the end?" offers Mum.

"Exactly," says Kate. "God, we're getting a bit deep and meaningful, aren't we?"

"It's the pencils," says Alex sagely. "They're a gateway to emotional honesty and peace."

"Well," says Dad, "I wouldn't go that far. But I see where you're coming from."

———

"YOU LOOK NICE."

Jamie.

I'm in "our" room, putting the finishing touches to my makeup. Adonis texted and said to come down to the beach. Kate and Laurie are having a lovebirds' night and everyone else is chilling out here, but it feels like a waste of where we are to stay in again, since I stayed in last night, and the one before. Mum practically hit SEND on the text for me, she's that eager for me to *Go out and enjoy yourself, darling. You're only young once!*

"Thanks," I reply, looking at him in the reflection of the vanity mirror.

Neither of us speaks after that, but Jamie doesn't leave.

"Was there something you needed?" I ask when I can't take the silence any longer.

He shakes his head. "No," he replies.

I nod, slipping lipstick into my bag and spinning round on the chair to stand up.

Jamie looks me up and down and smiles softly. "You look *really* nice," he reiterates.

I can't quite find it in me to say something witty or self-deprecating even, so I give a shy smile and suddenly feel twenty levels of self-conscious. "Are you staying here?" I ask.

He shrugs. "Jasmine said to meet down in the town, but . . ."

I wait for him to give me his *but*. He doesn't.

"Oh," I offer. "Well, I'm sure that would be . . ."

Jamie waits for me to give him my verdict. I don't.

"Yeah," he says. "I dunno."

I nod—at what, I'm not sure.

"I'd better go," I say, slipping out of the door behind him.

———

171

AT THE BAR where Adonis told me to meet him, he's sitting at a table on the veranda with a group of people who are hanging on every word he says. But when he sees me, he interrupts himself and stands up to greet me, making me feel like the most special girl in the room.

"You came!" he says, kissing both of my cheeks.

"Yeah," I say. "I promised I would."

He shrugs as we settle in at his crowded table.

"Everyone, this is Flo," he says, going round the table and saying names as he points. The only name that sticks is Jasmine. It's Jamie's Jasmine. The hair, the silly laugh—I remember both, from the cave. I give her a quick smile and settle in beside Adonis.

"I played water games with Flo and her family at their villa today," Adonis tells them all. "I nearly drowned. They are *very* competitive."

Everyone laughs and I lightly throw up my hands as if to say, *What can I say? We can't help it!*

"I grew up with two brothers," I respond. "I've had to learn to hold my own."

Across the table Jasmine frowns. "I thought you had three brothers," she says.

I shake my head.

"At the beach BBQ," she presses on. "There was . . ."

"Oh," I say, understanding. "Jamie isn't my brother. He's my brother's best friend. Adonis got it mixed up, too."

"Ohhh," she says with a nod. "Well, he's very handsome."

I pull a face. "I couldn't possibly comment," I say. "I suppose I don't see him that way."

I feel myself burning at the cheeks and tuck my hair behind my ear, willing the conversation to move on.

"I thought he might be here," Jasmine persists. "I told him to come."

"He mentioned that, actually," I reply. "I think he might be staying at the villa, though."

Jasmine motions for Adonis to stand up and switch chairs with her.

"Girl talk," she commands, and Adonis does as he is told. When she's next to me, Jasmine leans in and whispers, "I don't want to seem needy—can you text him and encourage him to get down here? Not to kiss and tell, but I'm kinda into finishing what we started the other night, if you know what I mean." She gives an OTT wink, and I am gobsmacked. I do *not* want to be talking about Jamie with her.

"Urm," I say, staring at the table dead ahead of me.

"Pretty please?" she begs. "Girl code means you have to. Come on!"

There's no logical reason why I wouldn't help this girl out by texting Jamie, except for the fact that the thought of him with Jasmine makes me want to throw my cheap drink in her face.

I smile, forcing myself to seem more amenable than I feel. At the end of the day, I *am* here with Adonis. Should I care what Jamie does? Maybe he won't even come.

"Sure," I say, picking up my phone to fire off a missive.

JAMIE DOESN'T TEXT back, but as we all mosey on down to the beach to where there's a fire and somebody has a guitar, he appears like an apparition at the edge of the sand. I nod at him, but don't get up. Adonis has slipped his hand into mine and pulls me across onto his lap as we settle in around the fire. This is me, having fun, being young and wild and free, exactly like my mother tells me to be. And that Jamie has come to spend time with his *Jasmine* is absolutely fine. That's his prerogative. He doesn't owe me anything. In fact obviously we're supposed to be learning how to be friends, so this is what friends do: They go to the same parties, don't they, and they're happy for one another's holiday flings, or whatever. I don't even know if I still fancy Adonis. He is *gorgeous*, but is that enough?

"You're so beautiful," Adonis whispers in my ear. Objectively, he is very handsome, and he gets on with everyone and is charismatic and fun. But it's hard to ignore that he doesn't make my heart skip a beat. I like his attention, but I don't feel like I'd die without it. Is Holiday Flo trying too hard?

I look up just in time to see Jamie staring at us, but he glances away quickly, as if he wasn't staring at all. My heart skips a beat for him, merely from seeing him across the sand—but I shake my head, willing the thought away. Maybe this is part of the exposure therapy, that in order to transcend his rejection I need to acknowledge, if only to myself, that he bruised my heart last Christmas. It's untenable, hating being around him. This tender spot will not last. It can't. Adonis tightens his grip on me, and I give him a smile.

"I'm going to get another beer," I say. "Want anything?"

He shakes his head. "No thank you, pretty girl," he replies, and it gives me The Ick.

I wander over to the cooler and grab a beer, and Jamie appears at my side.

"Evening, Cupid," he says, and I cock an eyebrow at him.

"I prefer Facilitator of Young Love's Dream, actually," I bat back.

"Let's not get carried away," Jamie says, laughing. "I'm not sure I'll stay much longer."

"No?" I say. "Jasmine seems . . . hopeful."

"Hopeful?"

"Hopeful of getting in your pants," I say. "If I may be so blunt."

Jamie blinks slowly. "I don't know how I feel about *that*," he tells me. "But thanks for the heads-up."

We stand. We drink.

"Things going well with the Greek god?" Jamie asks, after a beat.

I search for my response by looking up at the dark sky.

"Sorry," he says before I can answer. "I don't know why I asked that. I don't actually want to know."

My eyes shoot to his. We look at each other.

"Why . . . wouldn't you want to know?" I ask, so quietly I'm not sure I have even spoken.

Jamie lowers his voice to be equally low.

"I think you know, Flo," he says, and my breath has become so shallow I could almost be hyperventilating.

I shake my head. "I don't . . ." I say, not understanding. Jamie doesn't want me. Why would he infer he doesn't want anybody else to have me?

"Pretty lady, I thought you had left!" Adonis slips his hand into mine and nods at Jamie.

"Evening," Jamie says petulantly, but when I try to catch his eye again, he's busy looking anywhere but at me.

"Jasmine is over there," Adonis says, pointing her out with a group of girls over by a windbreak. "Florence? Shall we walk?"

I don't give an answer, just start going in the direction Adonis is tugging me in, and it takes a lot not to look back to see if Jamie is going to stop us.

ADONIS DOESN'T SPEAK as we trudge through the sand to the exact same cave we went to last time. I don't know why I'm doing this. I don't want to be alone with him. I'm pretending.

He spins me round so that we're chest to chest and leans down to kiss me. He goes in hard and fast, not soft and tender, like I tend to prefer. It's like we're having two different conversations: He's on one topic and I'm on another. As I'm trying to figure out how I feel about his intensity, Adonis cups my face and runs his hands back through my hair, where he tugs.

"Oh!" I say, in a cross between surprise and pain.

"You like?" he asks, but I don't. He doesn't wait for an answer—his mouth is back on mine, swallowing all my words. This is a whole new side to the man. He's being rough and forceful. He either hasn't noticed that I'm not reciprocating or doesn't care.

I try to get into the mood, let myself be kissed and experiment with how it feels to submit to this dominance.

"You're mine, aren't you?" he says. "Nobody else can have you, because you are mine."

That seems too full-on, but I don't know how to pull back and ascertain the limits of what "mine" means. I'm not anybody's. No woman is a possession of any man. But obviously saying so would ruin the mood.

"Mmmm," I say, thinking, *I need to leave. I don't want this.*

"Show me," Adonis says, pulling away and pushing down on the top of my head, making it very clear that he wants me on my knees.

"Urm . . ." I say. "I don't think—"

"Go on," he presses. "I need you . . ." His hands fall to my wrists, where he holds on and grips tightly.

"Let go," I say, a growing sense of unease pulsing through me.

"Come on," he says. "Don't be a tease."

He moves his massive, commanding body in a way that almost makes me fall to the floor, but I'm just strong enough to resist.

"Stop," I reply, trying to get out from his grasp. It doesn't work. "Hey," I repeat. "Stop!"

"SHE SAID STOP!" comes Jamie's voice. "Get the hell off her."

Adonis lets go and pulls me toward him in a hug, so that my face is against his chest. "Fuck off, man," Adonis says. "This is private."

"Flo?" Jamie asks, and I push Adonis away and hate that I have tears in my eyes, that he could make me feel this way and that Jamie gets to bear witness.

With both hands I launch myself at Adonis's chest, hard, so that he stumbles back, and then I run as fast as I can out of there, leaving both men behind me.

I DON'T EVEN know where my shoes are. I run past the bonfire, up to the main road and let my bare feet hit the rough stones of it, and then the dirt path that leads back to the villa in darkness.

Fortunately I have my bag looped over my body, so I have my phone. I'm trembling as I fumble at the zip and struggle to get hold of it.

"Shit," I say, looking at my fingers wobble.

"It's adrenaline," Jamie says, from further down the hill. "That's all. You'll shake it off in a minute."

I look at him. "What the fuck?" I say. "That fucking . . . that horrible . . ."

Jamie comes closer and lingers opposite me.

"Do you want to be hugged?" he asks, and I nod miserably. When his arms are wrapped around me, I let the first tear fall, and then another, and then I am sobbing uncontrollably.

"I know," Jamie says, stroking my hair. "I know. That wasn't your fault."

I feel so ashamed. I should never have gone into the cave with

Adonis, never made him think that's what I wanted. I knew, on some level—even if I didn't want to admit it to myself—that I didn't want him, but I went with him, anyway.

"It's not your fault," Jamie keeps telling me, over and over again. "Okay? Just breathe, Flo. Do it with me: in . . . and out . . ."

He pulls back, so that he can hold my face between his hands and look me in the eye as he demonstrates extra-deep breaths. I follow him, and move a hand to rub over my heart.

"I'm okay," I say. "I'm okay, I'm okay, I'm okay . . ."

Jamie reaches out and puts his hand to mine and tells me, "You are."

We stand, with Jamie watching me like a hawk, I suppose to assess how traumatized I feel. The answer is: quite a lot.

"I don't know what would have happened if you hadn't been there," I say. "That's what really gets me. That's why I'm freaking out."

Jamie shakes his head *no*. "Flo, you would have kicked him in the balls, and Adonis would have deserved it. But I *was* there. So."

I digest this.

"Yeah," I say. And then, "Wait. But why were you there?"

Jamie blows out air with puffed-up cheeks, like it's the sixty-four-thousand-dollar question. Finally he says, "You know why, Flo."

I blink.

"No, I don't," I reply, and it comes out louder than I mean it to, because it's true: I don't. Not intellectually. My body hints that it might know something, but my brain understands the facts as clear as day: Jamie is a womanizer. I almost let him in, and he blew it. He doesn't think I'm worth it. We're not meant to be.

He sighs. "Not now," he says. "Come on. Let's get home, yeah?"

I nod. *Okay.*

I don't realize I'm holding on to his arm like a chaste Victorian aunt taking the air in the park until we're almost home, and when I do, I immediately feel super-weird about it. I let go.

"Sorry," I mumble. "I didn't even know I was doing that."

"No worries," Jamie says. "I don't mind."

I slip my arm back through his without saying anything. I feel calmer now. What just happened was horrible, and Adonis is an ass, but I'm away from it and all right, and holding on to Jamie makes me feel safe. *Jamie* makes me feel safe, like he looks out for me. Like he'll always look out for me . . .

"Nightcap?" he asks when we're back. "For your nerves? You don't have to. It's only an idea."

The house is dark, everyone already in bed. I've got no idea what time it is.

"Anything wet and in a glass," I reply, and Jamie smiles.

"Careful," he warns. "You almost said that with a grin."

It's my turn to sigh now, and I pull up a chair at the lamp-lit table.

"I don't want you to think badly of me," I say. "For . . . I don't know. Thinking Adonis was an okay dude in the first place? I feel like you knew he wasn't . . ."

"Don't do that," Jamie says, pouring a couple of glasses of wine and handing me one. "Don't blame yourself, or think anybody else had some big insight into where it would all lead. Your own mother encouraged it, remember? And it's no more her fault than yours or mine, or the moon's. This is all on Adonis, and he's lucky I didn't pummel him. But it was way more important to come and check on you than stay behind and give him a piece of my mind. I mean, I assume I don't have to warn you about second chances or anything like that?"

I screw up my face. "You do not," I say. "Most people deserve a second chance, but not Adonis—not for this. In fact I'll block and delete his number right now."

I half expect to see an apology text from him as I pick up my phone, but of course I don't. There's just a text from Dad saying he and Mum are going to bed and he'll see me in the morning.

"All done," I say, putting my phone back on the table. "God," I go on. "All I wanted was a bit of holiday fun—to be less like myself for a week or two, you know? And look where it got me."

Jamie reaches out a hand to mine.

"Stop it," he says. "There are men lining up to help you have a fun time, don't you worry about that."

I look down pointedly. He doesn't move. When I dare to look back up, Jamie's eyes are all crinkled and soft, his lips gently parted, his body still.

"Jamie," I say quietly. "Where did it all go wrong for us?"

He blinks slowly and chews his bottom lip. I swear he's leaning forward, like he could kiss me himself. It makes me lean in his direction, too, the gap between us closing.

"I don't know," he says. "I really don't know."

I try to search for answers in his face. His handsome, beautiful, melancholy face.

"Bed," he says with finality. "Come on."

I don't argue.

I LIE IN the dark, staring at the ceiling. Jamie hasn't moved in the bed across from me, but he's not breathing heavily, like a man who is asleep.

His voice cuts through the darkness. "Are you okay?"

I turn over. "I knew you were still awake!" I whisper. "Are *you* okay?"

"Yeah," he whispers back. "Just. Thinking things. Thoughts."

"Hmmm," I say. "Yes. Thinking thoughts. Same over here."

I can just about make out his profile in the hazy moonlight from outside.

"When I was little and I couldn't sleep, my mum used to climb into my bed and tell me a story," I say. "All these tales about a little girl called Flo who found a spaceship on the village green."

"Good old Vee," Jamie replies. "I'll bet she still got in to work early the next morning, too."

"You've heard the superwoman stories, then?" I ask.

"I've met the woman," Jamie quips. "I don't think I've ever met a more motivated and together person in all my life."

"Right," I whisper. "God, she intimidates me. Like I feel so . . . not up to scratch, you know?"

"Florence, no!" Jamie says. "Come here. Come here right now."

"What do you mean?" I ask.

He flings back his bedsheet. "Let me tell you a story," he says.

Heart pounding, I slip out of my bed and into his, fitting snugly around him like we're two commas. I feel his hand on my forehead from behind, where he pushes the hair off of my face tenderly and says, "There was once a girl called Florence, who found a spaceship on the village green . . ."

I smile and let him talk.

"Now Florence was a very clever girl. Woman, really, although because she was the youngest in her family, everyone treated her like a kid, which bugged her, but she was too classy to let on. She rose above it and set about dominating everything that crossed her path because she understood that actions speak louder than words."

I feel myself unwind, my shoulders loosen, and my breath regulates and deepens.

"Anyway, the spaceship scared Florence. She had dreamed of space her whole life, but actually riding in a spaceship was terrifying, because then her dream wouldn't be her dream anymore, it would be a reality; and if the reality wasn't as good as her dream, she'd feel sad and disappointed. The thing is, Florence also knew that being in space could be even better than anything she'd ever imagined. And she'd only know if she actually got on board and let it take off . . ."

"That sounds like a big decision," I say, keeping my eyes closed. "And being scared isn't to be underestimated."

"Hmmm," muses Jamie. "Good job she has somebody to help her along, then. Her friend Jamie."

I laugh. "Good old Jamie," I say. "Best-friend-for-life material?"

"Well," Jamie says, "it's been a rocky path for Florence and Jamie, because they've never been sure if they are supposed to be friends or not, but Jamie decided to seize the day and be a pal, because it was better to have Florence in his life than not, and he liked to believe Florence felt the same."

I open my eyes now, and shift my weight to look slightly back over my shoulder.

"Yeah," I whisper. "I think Florence does the feel the same . . ."

I can just about make out his smile in the darkness.

"Good," he says quietly.

"Keep going," I urge, letting my eyes flutter shut. Jamie's nose knocks against my shoulder. It tickles, in a nice way.

"So, Jamie stood beside his friend Florence and said, 'Come on, let's go for it. Let's launch off into space.' And Florence agreed, taking the lead before she could change her mind, dragging poor old Jamie by the hand until they're in the spaceship and strapped into the seats, ready for takeoff."

"That sounds good," I say. "Exciting."

"Agreed," says Jamie. He tightens his grip on me.

Softly I ask, "What happens in space?"

Jamie laughs lightly. "Oh," he says, "they have a great time."

13

We must have fallen asleep, because I wake up as the sun starts to peek through the blinds, opening my eyes to see Jamie looking at me.

"Sorry to stare," he says sleepily. "I was just trying to decide how to get up without waking you."

"I'm awake," I say, yawning. "I fell asleep in your bed, sorry."

He shakes his head. "Don't worry. I'm glad you slept. How are you feeling this morning?"

I stretch, inadvertently pushing myself into his chiseled body. "Okay." I yawn again, making a mental note of the firmness of him.

"I meant about what happened with Adonis?" he clarifies.

"Oh," I reply. I run through last night's events in my head, searching my brain and body for evidence as to how it's left me. "Honestly?" I settle on. "It was fucking awful, but you came at exactly the right time, and at least now I know what a pig he is, you know? I'm okay. At least I let myself loose a little bit, even if it was with totally the wrong person. I'm proud of myself for that. I know that's a bit of weird rationalizing going on, but . . . yeah. I'm grateful it wasn't any worse."

"You have trouble letting loose?" Jamie asks.

And there's no reason why anybody would be coming upstairs to our bedroom, especially not as early as this, but I suddenly wonder what it would look like if they did—if Mum "caught" us in bed together, or Laurie.

"You know I do," I say, with another stretch, and then I climb out of his bed. "That's why Holiday Flo was invented. Anyway, thanks for the help, again," I tell him. "And for the flight to the moon."

Jamie smiles. "You're welcome anytime," he replies, and we look at each other for so long after he says that, it's like we've slipped into screensaver mode. "You're cute when you've just woken up," he observes. "All puffy-eyed and red-cheeked."

I stick my tongue out at him and go to the bathroom.

"MORNING," JAMIE SAYS, as he joins us all at the breakfast table.

"Oi, oi," Laurie responds, reaching out a fist to bump Jamie's. "I thought you'd slept elsewhere last night! Were you here all night?"

Jamie's eyes flicker toward me and I look down at the table. I assumed I didn't have to brief him on not letting my family know what happened last night, but I suddenly get a stab of angst that I should have made him swear he wouldn't.

"I wasn't back too late," Jamie says. "Had two drinks and then left everybody to it."

"Oh," says Laurie, sounding disappointed. "I thought you and Jasmine were . . ."

He makes a circle with the forefinger and thumb of one hand, and then sticks the forefinger of his other hand into it.

Dad coughs. "Let the boy be, Lawrence."

"What?" Laurie squeaks. "Why is Florence allowed to hook up with Adonis, but we're not allowed to talk about Jamie and Jasmine?"

"Whoever is railing who is none of your business, young man—and certainly not at the breakfast table. Let people have their mystery, would you? Focus on your own . . . rails."

We all burst out laughing. Dad has totally misused that term on purpose, to give us something else to talk about.

"I'm envious they even have their rails asked about," Alex offers, buttering some toast. "Nobody asks me about my mystery."

"That would involve you actually having some," Kate says.

And Alex looks at her in surprise and shrieks, "Kate! You bitch! I'll take you off my Christmas-card list."

"You don't send Christmas cards," she shoots back.

"Well, no," agrees Alex. "I don't. Anyone I'd want to give a folded-over piece of paper to—a folded-over piece of paper they'll throw away in two weeks—I see every day at work, anyway."

I put on my doing-an-impression-of-Alex voice. "What's the point of hacking down trees to say 'Merry Christmas' to each other when we can all do it in person? Not to mention the price of stamps now. I could teach a family to fish, with the cost of a first-class book of stamps these days."

Dad chuckles. "You really are old before your time sometimes, Al," he comments. "You're far too young to be so grumpy."

"Which is where getting railed would help," points out Laurie. "People with a healthy sex life aren't as grumpy. It's biologically impossible."

"Hence why I am such a relaxed and sanguine man," Dad says with a smile.

And we all collectively gasp, "Stop!"

"I rest my case," says Dad. "Railing is off the agenda. Shall we talk about what we're all reading instead?"

Before I can launch into a TED Talk on the storytelling merits of Mum's airport thriller, Mum trills from the kitchen, "I'm baaaack!"

"Oh, wicked," Alex says, getting up. "She's done the food-roulette shop," he explains to us. "Today's the day!"

I pour more coffee and brace myself. Food roulette is something we do on every family holiday. It's a stupid tradition, but one of us has to go to the nearest grocery store or market and buy a handful of particularly interesting (and sometimes deliberately gross) local foods. We tend to put it all in the middle of the table and take turns trying to guess what each item is, discovering some terrible things, some so-so things, and some outrageously good things in the process. Whatever we like, we buy multiples of, to take home and keep in the cupboard for the rest of the year for when we're all together, as a tasty reminder of where we've been and what we got up to.

"I love food roulette," Laurie says, rubbing his hands together.

"Remember those chocolate-dipped crisps in Mexico?" Kate recalls.

"And basically any of the chocolate in Portugal," I remind her.

"Oh my god," Dad says. "But the saltwater crisps we had? In Cornwall? Urgh." He shudders. "I wanted to scrub my tongue after those. Foul, horrible things."

"I quite liked those," Mum says, delivering two tote bags stuffed with treats to the table.

Alex comes out behind her with extra napkins and a replenished water jug. We know, from experience, that both can be necessary.

"Right," Mum says, unpacking. "I don't want anyone smack-talking me! I get so nervous trying to please you lot, when at the end of the day I'm actually one of the better selectors of local foods.

Laurie, yes, I'm looking at you when I say some of you are downright terrible."

"Mum!" Laurie says, shocked. "How rude!"

They bicker, and I make them insist they can't start without me—I'm just nipping to the loo. Kate gives me a thumbs-up. At least she's heard me.

I pad barefoot through the kitchen and round the corner to the downstairs toilet. As I do so, I bump into Jamie.

"Oh," I say, surprised. "Sorry. I didn't realize you were in here."

I step one way, as Jamie steps in the same direction, too. We laugh.

"Sorry," he replies. He steps the other way, right as I do.

This time I stand still, so that Jamie can move around me. But he doesn't. One of us shifts—I'm not sure who—and the gap between us closes. Our bodies lightly touch. I think of last night, of being held by him as I slept. I can't look up. If I do, what will I say? I feel like somebody has hit the pause button on reality. The metaphorical ground between us isn't solid. It's shaky and uncertain, and I hate shaky and uncertain.

Jamie's chin is lowered so that his mouth is close to my ear as he exhales, tickling my neck with his breath.

Time suspends. It is just Jamie and me. Almost touching.

Almost picking up where we left off at Christmas.

Am I an idiot for letting myself feel excited for that? Is this what I wanted when I climbed into his bed last night?

I dare to lift my hand and put it to his chest. I can feel his heart beating, too, a steady thud that is almost as quick as mine. His chest is solid, carved from rock. Jamie grabs my waist, his fingers thick and firm on the curve above my hips. And the shock of it, or maybe even the *delight* of it, finally forces my chin up to look at him, a million questions in my eyes. But I don't get any answers. He's got as many questions in his own eyes—those deep-gray pools of unknowableness. We stand and stare, in a way that is far more open than it was this morning, or maybe ever has been. A genie is leaking out from the bottle, and in two more seconds we won't be able to get him back in.

Jamie shakes his head, almost imperceptibly, but doesn't let go of me. If anything, his grip tightens, like he's worried I might wriggle free. But I won't. I am glued to the spot. He closes his eyes then, taking a huge inhale, and it's like he's resolving himself, steeling himself, for what happens next.

"See you out there," he says, like it pains him to walk away.

I CAN'T LOOK at him when I go back outside to the others. I had to splash my face with water in the loo, rub my heart, and breathe deeply. I thought he was going to kiss me. I thought Jamie Kramer was going to land his lips on mine, right there outside the loo of our Greek holiday house. And I feel all kinds of things about it not happening. Mostly: disappointed. But also, relieved?

I've spent so long telling myself I hate him. But I don't. I never have. I'm scared he'll hurt me, like he did at Christmas. But I wanted the kiss more than I worried about what would come after it. It's good he didn't kiss me, though. Right? Yeah. Right.

I sit down gingerly, among everyone trying okra in tomato sauce, because they have indeed started without me, despite my asking them not to. Obviously, in this state, I don't mind. They're all too busy to notice my altered headspace, too wrapped up in acting like they're giving tasting notes on a high-end TV show about celebrity chefs to pay me any mind.

"I'm getting hints of ass crack and a texture of rubber," Alex is saying, his face screwed up.

I think I smile at him. I'm not sure.

"Okay!" Mum announces. "These are . . . oh, I think they're called carob rusks? I assume they're sweet."

She rips open a packet of small cookies and everyone grabs one. I sneak a look at Jamie, who is busy being handsome behind his sunglasses and pretending to be very interested in reading the back of the packet.

I grab my phone and surreptitiously text Hope.

ME
I ALMOST KISSED JAMIE
WELL, HE ALMOST KISSED ME ACTUALLY!!
ARE YOU IN PRAGUE YET?
I NEED TO TALK TO SOMEBODY ABOUT THIS!

HOPE
Yes, in Prague! No wi-fi on train for messaging, sorry!
YOU ALMOST KISSED?
ARE YOU DATING TWO MEN NOW?

ME
TL;DR. Adonis is a dick . . . so that's done
Jamie looked after me when I was a bit shaken up
I think I knew this was coming . . .
Something has been building. I can't decide if it's good or
bad, or if I should make a move or accept that he didn't or
WHAT

HOPE

Take a breath, babe!

Take several!

"Oh wow," Dad says, interrupting my thoughts. I lock my phone and put it away. He's dug deep into a bag of crisps. "Oregano flavor, I think. These are outstanding! Flo, try one."

I take a crisp and chomp on it. As we navigate some oatmeal cookies, cherry-filled chocolate-and-wafer rolls, I calm down a bit. I'm going to expect nothing with Jamie, because that's safest. There's not long left of the holiday, anyway. How much trouble can Jamie and I possibly get in? This is fine. It's all going to be fine.

IT'S A HAPPY coincidence that we're nominated to make dinner together. It puts us in close proximity in the tiny kitchen, and I find myself excited to spend time with Jamie, one-on-one.

"You gonna sous-chef?" he asks, looping an apron over my neck and reaching behind to tie it for me. His breath tickles my ear when he leans in, making every hair on my body stand to attention. I look at him, sideways on. He's so close, and then *poof*, the apron is knotted and he's stepped back, leaving only his cedary scent around me. I've replayed that moment we could have kissed over and over again in my head. I do it again now. I tingle with excitement.

"I'll do whatever is required of me," I tell him. "I am at your culinary mercy."

"Duly noted," he replies, one half of his mouth cocking up into a smirk. I smile, too.

A pot of boiling water threatens to overflow then, and Jamie catches it just in time.

"Damn," he says, moving it off the burner as he tries to figure out why the flame won't turn down. "I really thought I could impress you with how good a cook I am. Urgh. Why isn't this working?"

I peer past him and point to the dials.

"Try that one," I say, and he laughs.

"Right," he says with a nod. "So what you're telling me is that the knob with the little picture saying it's for the left *actually* controls the left and not the right?"

"Wild, isn't it?"

"It's a good job you're here."

"I'll say."

Jamie *winks* at me then. A grown man, looking right at me, *winking*. It's so cheeky and unexpected that I burst out with a surprised "Huh!" and splutter, "We're winking now, are we? We're bringing that back into style?"

He shrugs. "Let's make it *Vogue*," he says, using my dad's word.

I wink back at him, making Jamie chew his bottom lip in amusement.

"Yeah," he says. "We should *definitely* make that *Vogue*."

As we chop and slice and boil and fry, Jamie keeps telling me *good*. And *thank you*. And *well done*. I return the words of affirmation by saying *of course, chef*, and *you're welcome, chef*, and *anything else, chef?* When he comes up behind me to stir the sauce for his prawns, he puts a hand over mine gently. "You're being very helpful," he murmurs.

"Just doing my job, chef," I reply.

He lingers this time, his chin over my shoulder on one side, his hand grazing my hip on the other. *This*, I think, not really understanding what *this* means.

This.

I struggle opening a jar of capers and stand too close to him as I ask for help. He pops the lid off the jar and I hold eye contact as I say, "My hero." The way he looks at me—dear Lord, I will remember that look for as long as I live. Jamie inhales sharply and flares his nostrils as he lets out a long, slow breath.

"Flo," he says, like it's a warning, like he can't be held responsible for what he does next. His pupils are like saucers, big as planets. His tongue nips at his lip, and I realize then that every other single time he's done that, it has never—not once—not been on purpose. It has been for my benefit every single time. Goddammit.

"Sorry, guys," Alex's voice suddenly booms. Jamie and I leap apart like we've been caught with our hand in the cookie jar, but luckily Alex has his hands to his head, rubbing his temples, and hasn't noticed. "I'm gonna sack off dinner and call it a night," he tells us. "My head. Too much sun, I reckon."

I nod, as Jamie turns back to the stove and stirs a pot.

"Yeah, mate," Jamie says. "No worries at all. I won't be far behind you, I don't think. I'm pretty pooped, too."

"Cheers," Alex says, shuffling along the room to get to the far door. "Look after yourself."

"Yeah, you, too," Jamie says, and I watch Alex leave.

Jamie goes back to the table, but I linger when my phone beeps. Obviously it's Hope. Anyone else who might text me is here. She's sent a couple of photos from her day exploring Prague, including a selfie from outside a bar, where she's holding up a beer as big as her head. This was one pound fifty! she's written. Now tell me about Jamie whilst I drink it!

I tell her I can't—that he's here.

"I could take you sailing," Jamie announces when I've put my phone down.

"Sailing?" I say, confused.

"It would be good to . . . hang out," he says. "If you want."

I nod. "Okay," I reply. "Yeah."

"We could . . . chat," he offers.

"Chat," I repeat with a smirk. It doesn't sound like he's suggesting *chat*.

"Chat," he reiterates. "Jesus! Just say yes or no, Flo!"

"I already said yes," I shoot back as Kate yells from the veranda, "If you don't hurry up we're going to lose another one to an early bedtime. I'm starving!"

"Coming," I say, grabbing the rice with a tea towel for protection.

"Done and done, then," Jamie replies. "It's a date."

14

"Sailing?" Laurie says, the next morning at breakfast, incredulous at the suggestion.

"It's research," I reply. "For my next project."

"I think it sounds lovely," Dad says. "I've never got on with the sea myself. Remember when we took the ferry to France, Vee? God, it was awful."

"Yes, yes," Alex agrees mockingly. "We know. Four hours of vomiting so badly that you ended up bursting a blood vessel in your eye and calling yourself 'Popeye' for the whole of your honeymoon."

Dad looks round the group, like butter wouldn't melt. "Oh, have I mentioned that story before?" he asks innocently.

"Only forty-eight thousand times," chimes in Laurie. "And for the record, nobody believes you. We all know you have a fear of jellyfish and *that*'s why you don't like the sea."

Dad bats a hand. "They're unnatural," he cries. "Awful to look at, even worse if you get stung by one."

Everyone laughs, because it's true: Dad *is* scared of the ocean. That's why he skipped out on the snorkeling. But I'm not, and since

Jamie is qualified to take out a boat, I'm going to suddenly pretend it would be absolutely perfect help if he took me. Alone. For a whole day. Where we can figure out what's happening and what the rules are, and the boundaries—all out of the gaze of my bloody family.

"What project are you working on that means poor Jamie is stuck taking you out for the day?" Laurie asks. Then he turns to Jamie and says, "Mate, you don't have to take her, you know. Can't Adonis sort you out?"

I bristle at his name, but manage to say, "Adonis is persona non grata with me now. So."

Mum issues an *aww* sound. "But he's so nice!" she says, and I shake my head.

"He's not, actually," I insist, and Mum raises an eyebrow, but drops it.

It's Jamie's turn to wave a hand. "Anyway," he says, munching on his toast, "I'm quite missing sailing. And we'll be back by this afternoon."

"In my defense," I say, looking between my two brothers, "I'm not *horrible* company. I think Jamie might even enjoy himself."

If Jamie has a reaction to the thought of that, I don't see it, because he keeps his head down. Alex rolls his eyes, a sign that I'm too dramatic, and Laurie shrugs.

"Whatever," Laurie says. "Kate and I are going to get the local bus into the town a few miles away, if anyone wants to join. Enjoy your *research* trip," he adds, looking at me like he almost doesn't buy what I'm saying. But then, I can see him silently process, what reason would I have to lie?

At the side of me, Jamie moves to push back his chair, his arm brushing against mine for the tiniest of moments. My body practically hums with delight. He's already made the necessary arrangements—I heard him on the phone this morning, talking in Greek—and I'm going to prepare lunch, so we have supplies.

"You ready?" I say, once I've packed a basket with fruit and cheese, bread and olives and wine.

Jamie puts on his sunglasses and replies, "As I'll ever be."

Mum uses the rental car to drive us down to the marina—we were going to drive ourselves, but then nobody at the house would have had car access all day, and Mum said that wasn't fair. Not that they're going anywhere, but just in case.

"Gosh," she says, as we park up near the walkway that says BOAT HIRE. "This is magnificent."

She's not wrong. Row upon row of white boats cover the marina as far as we can see, all of different sizes. The sun seems especially potent today, spilling into the sky with abandon, making the blues bluer and the whites whiter. My tummy does a flip.

"Thanks so much, Veronica," Jamie says, pulling on his door to climb out of the passenger side. "I promise I'll take good care of her."

"Oh, I have no doubt," Mum coos. "I almost wish I was coming with the pair of you."

Jamie smiles and says—before I can think of how to reply—that she can come next time. "We'll think of this as a recce," he explains. "If today goes well, and we find some nice spots."

"Oh," Mum replies, "are you beach-hopping? I thought you needed to know about sailing, Flo?"

I haven't had to explain the specifics of why I need to know about boats for my imaginary project. I've had it in the back of my mind that if I simply say enough words, it might confuse people and they'll press me no further. Here goes nothing.

"I'm building on the PhD, my specialism. It's still the sea and water that I'm interested in, Mum. I want to take it further, because I think there could be a novel in it, maybe . . ."

Mum nods. "Oh, how exciting. A novel!" she exclaims. "Well, how very good of you to be thinking about all that on holiday. I'll have a lunchtime vino for you."

I laugh. "Love you, Mum."

"Darling?" she says, before I climb out of the back seat. I glance at Jamie, who has already walked ahead to the kiosk. "I just wondered . . ."

"Yes?"

"If you might need this?"

She's holding up my notebook. My heart stops. How could I have been so stupid not to at least *pretend* I needed it?

"Oh," I say. "Urm—"

She hoots out a laugh. "I'm joking, darling. Giving you shit, as your brothers like to say." She flings it at me, and I catch it. "Go on. Have fun."

I sigh with relief. Although—no, it's not possible she's figured out what's going on, is it? I mean, to be honest, I'm not entirely sure I know what's going on, so how she could is beyond me.

"Go!" she urges.

I climb out of the car and wave her off.

WE'RE HALFWAY THROUGH a sailing lesson when Jamie drops the knot he has been showing me and says, "Flo. It's just hit me. You didn't actually want to learn about sailing, did you?"

When we climbed aboard, Jamie got right down to business, showing me how to move this and wrap that, and talking about wind speeds and direction of travel. It was disorientating, not least because he is obviously *very* passionate about being out on a boat. It's kind of a turn-on to see him excited about something. But also his words have been crashing into each other and he's not stopped talking for about forty-five minutes. The way he looks at me now, color flushing up his neck, makes me understand that he's nervous. And I'm nervous. So we're two nervous people scrambling to figure out what happens next.

I bite my lip, hiding a smile.

"I mean . . ." I start, and Jamie begins to laugh.

His laugh makes me laugh and it goes on and on, every time one of us catches a breath, the other laughing harder and pulling them back in. This is ludicrous. Absolutely ludicrous. I'd have *pushed* Jamie off a boat less than a week ago. I don't have words for what I want. I'm not even sure I really know. But the closer we get, the more I like it, even knowing all the reasons I shouldn't.

"Let's swim," I suggest. "Can we do that?"

Jamie nods slowly. "Yes," he says. "Let's."

We lower the anchor and make sure everything is secure, and then Jamie flings himself off the edge of the boat, screaming, "Wayyyyyy!" on his way down. He lands with a splash and I look overboard to make sure he comes back up. It takes a minute—he's a good swimmer, and I can see him cutting through the water with strong legs and even stronger arms, pushing alongside the boat with impressive speed. He comes up for air dramatically, flinging back his head, water spraying everywhere.

"Get in!" he cries up at me, where I suddenly feel a lot less adventurous, now it's my turn.

"I'm scared," I yell back.

He shakes his head like he doesn't believe me. "No, you're not," he shouts back, with the kind of Harry Styles grin that means we're not talking about the jumping.

I launch myself in like a pencil, arms crossed over my body and one hand holding my nose. I slice through the water and am startled by the cold. I hadn't thought it would be this chilly out here, when it's so warm at the shore. I push up to get to the surface, feeling like Ariel in *The Little Mermaid*. I like the weightlessness of being underwater, with the weird combination of strength that it takes to swim up.

I feel the warmth of the sun before I can take a breath, but once I've made it to the surface, I do exactly what Jamie did and flick back my hair and wipe the water from my eyes. I search for him, but can't immediately see him. I look left and then right, and spin round with difficulty to locate him. And then I feel a tug on my ankle and he pops up beside me to make me scream. He loves that he's got a reaction—this smarmy smirk of satisfaction bleeding across his features—so I splash him and cry, "Arsehole! You're supposed to be nice to me now."

He doesn't retaliate, but instead considers what I've said.

"You're right," he replies, his voice serious, and we tread water opposite one another, staying where we are.

When we get out, I pull my hair over one shoulder and wrap it around itself to get out the excess water, and then fling it back. My skin glistens with droplets from the sea, like tiny jewels all over my body. I've got a bit of color now, and the way Jamie looks at me has never made me feel more beautiful.

"What?" he asks, back on the boat.

"That look you give me," I tell him. "I've never understood it."

"What look?"

"You have a look."

He continues to give me said look, while claiming to have no idea what I'm on about.

"Let me up," Jamie says then, tipping his chin to mean *climb up those stairs*. I follow his command, letting him follow, and we get our towels and dry off. When we're done, we place them flat on the double sun bed in the shade, our torsos covered, legs out in the sun. I grab the picnic and lay out a few of the things, and in our silence we let the air between us settle into something that feels more comfortable.

"Hey, do you ever think about Christmas?" Jamie says, when we've eaten a little and skipped the wine and hydrated with water instead. We're side by side, both looking at the water, and there's something about that configuration that feels easy. Looking out onto the horizon together, the boat gently swaying—it's like being rocked to sleep and letting all your thoughts tumble out of your head so that you can sleep soundly.

"Yes," I say, because obviously I do.

"Me, too," he says softly, and I swallow hard. It had all been so strange but had also felt so inevitable. I couldn't put my finger on why. I was feeling better than I had in ages, Jamie was jovial and fun, and there was a spark that caught with in-jokes and staying up talking, after everyone had gone to bed. And one night he told me he was going to knock on my bedroom door, after lights out, but never did. I just got his stupid note instead, and then the next morning he left.

Jamie reaches out a finger and traces it along my leg idly. He runs it up and down, sending delicious shivers down my spine. "What, exactly, have you been thinking about?" he asks me, voice low and serious. I part my lips and run my tongue over them—they're dry. My whole throat is dry. Jamie watches me, assessing me.

"I want you to kiss me," I whisper, because it's all I can think about.

Something flashes in his eyes—desire, I think, like flames burning brightly where his pupils should be. In one swift move he reaches out to my waist and pulls me toward him, so that I'm straddling him and we're nose-to-nose. He runs a hand down my back—those damned ticklish fingertips again—and I let a moan of pleasure escape, closing my eyes and exhaling deeply. I feel him swell beneath me, and I instinctively arch my back to grind against him lightly. It makes him gasp, and the sound of it is the hottest thing I've ever heard. I want to make him utter that noise again, and again, and again.

We pause that way—me straddling him, Jamie hard against the fabric of his swim shorts—and I lower my forehead to his, waiting for the kiss. He uses a hand to pin my wrists behind me and shifts his weight, pushing into me even more, so that I grind against him, once, twice, then a third time, and that noise emits again from between his full lips.

"Flo," he says. "I need to tell you . . ."

"Yes?" I ask, continuing to move rhythmically against him.

"Fuck," he intones, and he sounds exactly like I feel. Like he's about to explode. He says to me, "I once promised your brother I'd stay away from you."

"Hmmm," I reply. "How's that working out for you?"

"Not great . . ." he says.

"No," I agree. "I can see that."

Our lips are so close you couldn't get a sheet of paper between them if you tried. We're talking quietly, in between breaths—me focused on what I'm doing, Jamie struggling to both talk and enjoy it. It's here. It's happening. We're going to kiss.

"Flo," Jamie murmurs. "God . . ."

"Kiss me," I tell him again, because I want his mouth on mine.

He lifts me up and flips me over so that I'm pinned down under his weight. "I'm serious," he says. "Laurie—your whole family . . ."

"We are *not* talking about my whole family right now, are we?" I ask, trying to sound more outraged than I feel. We could be talking about quantum physics right now and I wouldn't care, as long as his hand keeps pawing at me this way. "You're part of the family," I say. "You're basically Mum's adopted son."

"Exactly," he says, loosening his grip. "This can't happen."

"Do you want to stop?" I ask, but I don't mean it. I part my lips and bat my eyes and sigh again.

"Jesus, Flo. You're making this really hard," he says, and he gives his cute half smile, marveling at the effect he's had on me.

"Is that a yes or a no?" I say, and I swear to god, if this man keeps touching me, I'm going to have an orgasm in about thirty seconds—kiss or not.

"Aren't you worried?" he asks.

"Worried?" I repeat.

And then he sighs.

And his smile falls.

And my heart sinks.

"Seriously?" I say, exasperated. I don't even feel embarrassed. I feel mad, and I know the blame is squarely on his shoulders. Jamie is the one with the issues, not me. That much is crystal-clear.

"Shit," he mutters, burying his head in his hands. "Oh, Flo, fuck!"

That's when his tears come.

"I'm so sorry," he says. "I don't want you to think I'm awful for doing this, that I've led you on, on purpose, or anything like that. I haven't, I swear. Honestly, Flo, I really do respect you. And I want this. I've wanted it for ages! You know that! But even knowing you want it now, too, I can't upset Laurie . . ."

He holds a hand to the bridge of his nose, fingers splaying to blot at his eyes.

"Hey," I say, my madness dissipating because, god, I'd be a real cow if I got mad at Jamie's loyalty to my brother—even if I wish he'd engaged that loyalty *before* I tried to dry-hump him. "Hey," I reiterate, so he listens to me.

"Sorry," Jamie says again, the crying slowing.

"Stop apologizing!" I say, and he laughs.

"Sorry," he repeats, but he's doing it tongue in cheek.

I grab a tissue from my bag for him and he wipes his eyes, blows his nose. He drinks more water and looks at the ocean, and I resume my position sitting at the side of him. Hope is going to have a field day with this, I swear. But I don't feel mad. The man is crying, for god's sake. I remember what Mum said about him being more sensitive than we think, sometimes.

"When did you promise Laurie anything about me?" I ask.

"Years ago," Jamie replies. "I think he knew I was sniffing around a bit, not long after he first brought me home, and then he saw us dancing at your parents' wedding anniversary. When they had the marquee tent?"

"That was, like, eight years ago," I say. "Seriously?"

He shrugs. "He's my best friend," he goes on. "And after my parents, especially . . ."

I nod. "Is that why you've ignored me all these years? Because of Laurie?"

"I suppose so," he says. "Just easier that way, isn't it? And I don't think I've *ignored you*—I've been perfectly friendly."

"I'd hate to see how you treat your enemies, then," I quip.

"Says she! You've been the ice queen since I got here."

"Until I wasn't," I point out. "I was gyrating on your crotch, after all. I think it's safe to say I've somewhat thawed out."

Jamie looks at me wistfully. "Have you any idea how hard it was to ask you to stop?"

"Are you making a dick-joke? It was *hard*?" I say, and Jamie shakes his head in dismay.

"See," he says. "This is why I like you. You're just . . . you."

I nod. "I am indeed me," I agree.

"Look," Jamie continues. "If you and I—if that were to be a proper thing, I'd man up and tell your brother, okay? Not even ask permission. I would *tell him*."

I digest what he's saying. The unsaid is: *But it isn't. It would be sex, and I cannot tell Laurie we are shagging.*

I hold up my hands. "Say no more," I insist. "I should have been more understanding. I didn't know . . . well, anything. I didn't think Laurie would be a consideration. Of course he would be, though. I wouldn't hook up with Hope's brother lightly, either." I think of Jamie's note at Christmas. It makes sense now. He must have had the same crisis of confidence then, too.

"Hope?" he asks.

"My best friend. Met her outside the therapist's office, so for a while she was actually in my phone as 'Despair.'"

"That's funny."

"So's your face."

"Ha ha."

Jamie groans, putting his face into his hands.

"I can't believe we almost . . ." he says. "God, Flo. I really do want you to know that you are *hot*. Like, it's-hard-to-concentrate-around-you *hot*."

"Shut up," I squeal, getting self-conscious. "You're teasing me."

"I am one hundred percent not," he insists. "Your face, your laugh, those absolutely incredible tits . . ."

I smack his arm. "All right, smooth talker. That's enough of that. Let's take this boat back to the marina and get home. If I can't fix my needs with you here, maybe there's a deckhand who can help me out up on the shore."

Jamie laughs.

"Don't let me stand in your way," he says. "Away we go . . ."

15

___

Jamie and I don't talk much as we sail back to the marina, but when we dock and walk to find a cab we stay close to one another in a way that feels . . . intimate. We've forged a new understanding of each other out there on the water. I feel for him. I don't know if that's wasted sympathy or makes me a mug, but the crying, the way he's prioritizing being part of my family instead of having his way with me? I respect that. So much makes sense now. Jamie's showing obvious gratitude that I'm not flying off the handle or anything. I suppose he's mugged me off twice now—if I wanted to tell him to shove it, I'd be well within my rights. But this past week or so has definitely illuminated how keeping a froideur between us hurts more than it helps. Life is short, and I enjoy family time far too much to let Jamie get in the way. So, c'est la vie. Holiday Flo isn't going to hold a grudge, and hopefully Ordinary Flo won't, either. I can move on. I *can*. We're better as friends, and shagging would ruin that. I get it. I mean, I wish he'd explained it better back at Christmas, but better late than never.

I smile at him as we wait at the taxi rank, aware of the nearness of him. Jamie smiles back. See? We can be friendly! Somehow his fingers end up curled around mine, and that's how the cab driver finds us: fixed to the spot, holding hands but not holding hands, wanting to be near to each other, but knowing this is the exact kind of nearness we've agreed not to actually entertain. I don't hold hands with my brothers when I'm waiting for taxis, after all. When we look at each other this time, the smile is more of a regretful grimace.

In the cab Jamie gives directions to the driver in Greek, and we both sit close enough to the middle of the back seat that our bare thighs touch. I look out of my window and he looks out of his, and the ride is a rocky one. So much so that it's easier to cushion my body into his, pressing against Jamie to steady myself, than it is to resist. Jamie loops an arm over my shoulder to hold on. To the driver, we undoubtedly look like a couple.

"Well," Jamie says, once we're home. He doesn't finish his sentence. The taxi drives off and we watch it, and then I open up my arms to welcome a hug.

"Thanks for a lovely day," I say. "Even though it panned out differently to how I thought it might."

Jamie steps toward me and receives the hug, and I rest against his rock-hard form. He gives good hugs. I briefly close my eyes and inhale the manly scent of him, exhaling deeply, too. Jamie cradles the back of my head, lightly caressing my hair.

"You give great cuddles," he says.

"You do, too," I say back.

We stay like that for a while.

LATER WE GO out for dinner, to a lovely place Mum found a review of online, and even though I try to navigate away from Jamie as we choose seats at the table, something happens where Mum moves me to her right, so she can sit near Dad, and then Kate goes to the toilet, and bam, Jamie and I are side by side. I smile at him, feeling oddly nervous. There's nothing to hide from our day together, but it feels as though we have a secret.

"And so I said to him, '*No*, I don't want two for twenty euros,'" Kate is saying. "'Give me four for fifty euros!'" She's regaling us with what happened at yet another market today.

"And the guy," adds Laurie, already laughing at the recollection of Kate's negligible haggling skills, "is so obviously confused at this crazy English lady bartering him *up* . . ."

Kate shakes her head good-naturedly.

"I just couldn't get it right in my brain that two for twenty should have been four for forty," she's saying. "I thought I'd managed to get money off, not add money!"

I can see the rise and fall of Jamie's chest in my peripheral vision. His arm is between us on the table, fiddling with a water glass. I can't even look at his fingers as they trail along the rim for too long—it's making me blush. But why? *Nothing has happened.* We've had one almost-kiss and agreed to drop it.

"I've honestly never known her like this," Laurie says, chuckling. He's got tears in his eyes, he finds it so funny. "Kate, you're so smart and switched on, and this baby . . . it's already sent your head gaga!"

"I know," Kate says and winces, taking a swig of water. "I can't believe it's going to be this way until *next year*. It's inhumane, really, to make pregnancy go on so long."

"Could be worse," Alex points out. "You could be an elephant. That's nearly two years of baby-brain right there."

"God. Not to mention what happens afterward . . ." Kate pouts.

Mum holds up a finger.

"Oh!" Alex points, noticing she's about to contribute, and I look up to demonstrate I am following along, listening intently. "Here she goes: Superwoman Veronica Greenberg is about to remind you that she went back to work two weeks after giving birth—"

"Yes, Alexander," Mum says. "A fact I am very proud of, thank you, because it was resilience personified." She focuses on Kate. "It was a different time back then, you see. I couldn't be seen to be weak, or different, after having children. The men didn't have that problem, of course. It's good that your generation has it different. Even in law, I'm sure there's a lot more understanding."

"And shared parental leave." Kate nods. "But I can't lie, I am nervous about that . . ."

I wonder if I seem distracted, because Alex gives me a look. I stay in neutral, as if there's nothing for him to comment on at all. Then I realize that he's not looking *at* me, but past me. It's Adonis. He's here with a pale-skinned and freckled blonde, who has the unmistakable air of tourist about her—her shoulders have sunburnt bikini-strap marks, just like mine did after day one. He waves at the table from where he is seated across the room, and Laurie says, "Are we okay with this?"

"With what?" I ask, since he's looking directly at me.

"I thought you and the Greek god were—"

I shake my head. "No, no," I say. "He's not"—I struggle to find the word—"my type," I settle on.

"I'd have thought he was everybody's type," Mum says with a giggle, and Kate leans across with her palm out. She says, "Veronica! Yes!" and Mum gives her a high five.

"I'm ready for a subject change whenever you guys are," I say, keeping my voice bright so that I don't accidentally lull my brothers into pushing the issue.

"Oooh," Alex says. "Touché, little sister! His loss—that's what I say." He wrinkles his nose at me.

I wrinkle mine back. Should I warn that girl what Adonis is really like? If somebody had warned me, would I have listened?

"How about we decide on a plan for tomorrow?" Dad interjects, and I am grateful. "I'd say we're about due some culture, don't you think? I'm a bit sick of all this relaxing. I need to *do something*."

"I second that motion." Mum smiles, with a nod. "We should at least do the ruins."

"I'm in," says Kate.

"Same," says Laurie.

"We might need to do two trips in the car, then," Dad considers. "Or call a cab."

"Great!" Mum says. "So—to bed now? It's already gone eleven ..."

"I'll get the bill," Dad says, and Laurie pipes up, "Let us, Dad. It's the least we can do."

Dad issues a raspberry noise in Laurie's direction. "Nonsense," he says. "Save your money for the baby. It's my pleasure."

"Drinks, anyone?" Alex asks. "I *really* want to go into town ..." He claps his hands together and rubs them, but his face quickly falls. Nobody wants a drink. He scowls. "Aww, man, come on! Somebody must want to come out?" he begs. He looks round the table once more, mentally assessing which person would be most ripe for convincing. You can see him write off Mum and Dad for being too old, and then Kate and Laurie for being too coupled-up.

"Flo? Jamie? Apparently things get really popping after midnight. Just a few drinks? I am *begging* you. This holiday is *marveloso*"—here he looks at Mum with a flattering smile—"but I am a young man in his prime. I should be out there. Doing questionable things! What happens on holiday stays on holiday!"

"I'm still trying to get over your use of 'popping,'" I tease. I feel Jamie smile next to me.

Alex fixes me with comically narrowed eyes, which makes me giggle, and then switches tack to sweet and innocent. "Please?" he says in a baby voice. "Pretty please?"

I could *almost* be tempted by drinks. If Jamie comes . . .

"Jamie, mate? You must go mad out there on the boats. Don't you wanna have a little drink? A dance? A little flirty-flirt?"

"I could be persuaded," Jamie says, and both men look at me.

"Okay, fine," I say. "Let's go and get fucked up in town!"

Mum tuts. "Not 'fucked up,'" she says. "That's unladylike, and unsafe, for all of you."

Alex pulls me out of my chair and turns me round to face my mother.

"I think she was joking, Mother. Indulging my fantasy of a raucous night out, when in all likelihood we'll do two drinks and then head back, disappointed by our lack of stamina."

I smile at Mum with my lips pressed together, so that it lands sarcastically. She sighs.

"I worry about you two together—you're a bad influence on each other." She looks at Jamie. "Look after them for me, won't you?" she asks.

And Jamie puts a hand to his heart and says, "Scout's honor, I will."

SPOILER ALERT: JAMIE does *not* look after us. Three shots in, and Alex is on *fire*. I've had one shot, just to be sociable, and am sipping my Jack and Coke *very* slowly. Alex is totally on one, and it's a relief when he pops off to the bathroom. He's been talking a mile a minute and eyeing up every guy in the place.

"A minute to breathe!" I laugh, as Alex pootles off.

Jamie laughs, too. "I can't blame him," he says. "Poor guy works so much, hardly ever gets to date, and in his time off his family wants to go to bed before midnight, when there's a whole world out here."

I pretend to be offended. "Are you calling us boring?" I ask.

"Only in the best possible way," Jamie replies. "It's a family holiday, and that's fair enough. But I get why he's been sneaking out every night to come here."

"WHAT?" I shriek. "He's been coming here every night?"

Jamie pulls a serious face. "I thought you knew," he says. "I thought you and Alex told each other everything?"

I shake my head. "Not really," I reply, hoisting myself up onto a bar stool that's just become free. Jamie turns and looks for another spare, finds one, and drags it beside me.

"You and Alex aren't BFFs?" Jamie asks.

"I mean, we get on," I say. "And I love his company. But we don't, like, trade secrets."

"Huh," Jamie says, confused. "To hear Laurie talk, you'd think you and Alex were joined at the hip."

"Really?" I ask. "He said that?"

"Maybe I misunderstood," Jamie offers. "But yeah, I always got the impression you and Alex hung out, and Laurie is the outsider a bit."

I arch an eyebrow. "He's so lame," I say. "Not to bad-mouth your pal there, but Lawrence Greenberg is *very* good at inventing a narrative to suit him. He and Alex gang up on me all the time!"

Jamie mimes zipping his lips shut and throwing away the key.

"So you've noticed it!" I shriek. He shrugs, like he couldn't possibly say any more. I scowl at him.

"You hold your own," Jamie says. "And aren't bad at giving what you get . . ."

"How diplomatic of you."

"I'm an only child. I know enough about siblings to know you gotta stay out of their shit. You guys can hate on each other all you want, but I know for a fact you'd gang up on an enemy outsider, like the Avengers finally coming together after Agent Coulson gets it."

"Ahhh," I say. "An Avengers fan!"

"Do you fuck with the MCU?" he asks, looking like he's expecting a no.

"Captain Marvel is my homegirl," I say. "Me and Hope watched every film in timeline order before the last *Guardians of the Galaxy* came out."

"No way!" Jamie says. "Me, too. Except I did it with Laurie and Kate."

"I think he got the idea from me," I say. "I'm kind of a thought leader that way."

"I've heard that about you, yes," Jamie smirks.

The bar person interrupts to ask if we want anything else, and I look at my half-empty glass and then at Jamie.

"I actually don't," I say, and Jamie tells the bar person we're good. "Not to be a party pooper, but that shot isn't sitting well on my stomach. I'm more of a chilled-white-wine girl."

"They have wine here," Jamie offers, and I scrunch up my nose.

"The Greenbergs don't order wine in pubs and clubs," I explain. "Our gastronomic snobbery cannot have passed you by."

Jamie shakes his head. "I've never met a family less able to just eat a sandwich. It has to be the best sandwich, with the nicest bread and the ingredients arranged exactly so. You guys love food like Loki loves mischief."

"Guilty!" I laugh.

And Jamie tips his head and looks at me, fondness in his eyes. I look straight back at him. "You're beautiful," he says, making me blush. "Really, properly beautiful."

I look around in case Alex is coming back. I can't see him anywhere. "Stop," I say, but I don't mean it.

"Are we idiots?" he asks, and I shrug.

"Probably," I reply. "But at least we have each other."

Jamie looks round. "I think Alex has abandoned us," he decides. "Shall we go? We'll be sitting here until tomorrow if we think he's coming back to us."

"Oh!" I say. "Did he meet somebody?"

Jamie nods. "I think so," he says. "He was a man on a mission, after all."

I shake my head good-naturedly. Well, good for Alex.

We walk the beach way back to the house, and it's quiet and calm. It is deserted, on account of it being midnight and semi-private. By Christ—the moon! It is comically massive, low in the sky, and the size of it means the whole ocean is lit up, like it's been tasked with putting on a dazzling light show solely for us. There's the gentlest of breezes, which I'm aware of because it tickles my skin—but I'm not cold. I'm very much the opposite. Blood courses through my veins, pumping hot and fast, a life force. The bushes against the hillside sway back and forth in slow motion, and the sand stretches in a sheet of blond to what feels like either edge of the earth. We are totally alone, shipwrecked on a slice of paradise, and I forget to breathe for a moment. I'm suspended in time, in place.

"Shall we sit?" Jamie says, pointing to an abandoned blanket looped over a washed-up tree trunk. It's beside the bushes, a tiny little enclave for two.

"This feels so . . . not natural," Jamie says, after a while.

"Not hooking up?" I say, and he chuckles. I'd been thinking it, too.

"And the rest."

He's right. To think we can fight whatever is between us is madness, especially if we're always going to have to spend time together in the end. It's Christmas all over again, with the magnetic pull strong. Only this time, I know him better—and I know myself even better, too. Once bitten, twice shy: Isn't that what they say? Fool me once, shame on you; fool me twice, shame on me? At Christmas I was willing to give Jamie my heart, but I won't make that mistake again. Still. He's a good man, and I will gladly give him my body. If I don't, I think I might go mad from desire.

"I really want you," I say.

"Yeah?" he replies.

"Yeah," I whisper.

Maybe he won't make the first move because of his stupid pledge to Laurie, but I maintain that it's none of Laurie's business and, what's more, nobody has to know. I *know* Jamie understands that, too. He's a loyal friend—he's proved that. Laurie is lucky to have him, and Jamie is lucky to have Laurie. Jamie and me, though: It's separate. It's doesn't matter. We're allowed to give in to this temptation.

"Come here," I intone, pulling at his face so that he looks at me.

And then he surrenders. Our lips meet, hard and meaningful. His tongue slips past my teeth and into my mouth, probing and exploring with grace and ease. Jamie's a *fantastic* kisser. I lace my hands behind his head, tugging at his hair. He gives me a light moan—one that means he likes it, and he wants more.

The kiss lasts a long time and eventually I am on my back, Jamie on top of me, and I realize that he's drawing this out, making it last. His mouth moves slowly, lazily, like he wants to appreciate every second of what we're doing. He holds my face with one hand, pulling me into him, so that his breath is my breath—we are one person. I've never been kissed this way. Never been kissed like I am the most special, beautiful, desired woman in the world. I let myself melt into him. I'm in no rush, either.

"You're fucking gorgeous," Jamie whispers eventually. "Sitting next to you at that dinner tonight . . ."

I smile. "Ditto," I say. "I thought about dragging you off to the bathroom with me."

He laughs. "I would have gone," he tells me. "I've wanted you for such a long time."

The kissing resumes, but now I can't stand it. I want him inside me. I want to be on this beach, my legs wrapped around him, pulling him in, in, in.

I roll over, so that I'm on top, and then pull him up to sitting, so I can take off his T-shirt. In return, he takes off my blouse and then pulls off my bra. He takes my nipple in his mouth, sucking so hard that I yelp.

"Was that too hard?"

"Yes," I whisper. "Except, no. . . . Do it again."

He runs his tongue around my other nipple before putting it in his mouth, and this time I decide I like it.

I wriggle off him to take off my shorts, watching Jamie as he does the same. I want to be naked. I don't care that we're outside—nobody is here, nobody is going to be here. I feel wild and free, unconstrained by what I *should* do and emboldened by doing exactly what I want: which, in this moment, is lowering my naked body onto Jamie's to feel the length of him curve up inside me.

He shudders as he enters me, and I claw at his back to take him deeper. My legs are knitted behind him, my arms wrapped over his shoulders, my head tipped back so that he can kiss my neck. We move in time, slowly, until it is impossible to bear any more and we give way to haste, to friction. I push my pelvis against him, his hands on my arse encouraging my speed, and I can hear the lap of the waves against the shore, my eyes fluttering open just enough to see Jamie illuminated by the moon, rock-solid and smooth as butter. I can't stop touching him, luxuriating in him. He says my name, and I writhe in ecstatic release. Jamie bites down onto my shoulder, following my lead, and we lie there, panting, spent, Jamie's cheek to my bare breast.

AFTERWARD, AS WE sit there, entangled in one another, suddenly there's the sound of voices.

"Somebody's coming," Jamie whispers, and I push up off him quickly, noticing how close the voices actually are.

"The bushes!" I sputter, launching myself, stark naked, into the shrubbery.

Jamie doesn't follow, I realize too late—he's out there, and whoever else is out there too has found him.

"Jamie." It's Alex. Alex has found us. But who is he with? At least this solves the mystery of where he went—he's pulled! "What are you doing here?" he presses.

"Alex," Jamie says, and he sounds winded. Out of breath. "We wondered where you'd gone."

"I bumped into a friend," says Alex.

"Cool," Jamie replies. Then I hear him say, "All right, mate. I'm Jamie."

"We'll leave you to it," Alex says. "Sorry to interrupt. Did Flo go to bed?"

Jamie begins to say that Alex and his mystery pal aren't interrupting, but Alex is having none of it.

"Jamie, mate. I don't know what exactly you're up to, but I know it isn't kosher. However, I'm a discreet man. So, I won't tell if you don't?"

Jamie must nod, or wink, or *something*, because then Alex's footsteps retreat, seemingly up toward the house.

"It's safe," Jamie whispers. "Flo?"

I crawl out. "Did he know it was me?" I ask.

Jamie shakes his head. "I don't think so."

"Who was he with?"

"No idea. Some guy."

I nod. "Whoa," I say. "We almost got caught!"

"Alex seemed as surprised to see me as I did to see him," he reasons. "He seemed sheepish at being caught taking somebody up to the house. I think he was more bothered about himself than about me and whoever I was with . . ."

Jamie holds out a hand and I take it, pressing my naked body against his boxer-shorts-wearing one. He clasps me to him, runs his hands up and down my arms.

"That was amazing," he whispers into my hair, and I tell him he wasn't so bad himself. I feel him stir in his underwear, standing to attention, despite having nearly been caught.

"Are you . . . ?" I ask, and he nods.

"I am," he says and laughs. It makes me laugh, too.

I snuggle into him, looping my body around his. The waves crashing against the shore lull me into closing my eyes, so when Jamie says, "I'll tell Laurie as soon as we get home. I don't want to spoil the holiday," I don't hear him, because the edges of sleep have already pulled me in.

16

It feels illicit to wake up in the same room as Jamie this morning, knowing what we did last night. We snuck back in as the sun was coming up, giggling like teenagers.

He must feel my gaze on him, because he opens one eye halfway and mumbles, "Morning."

"Morning," I whisper with a smile. It was a bold move to share a bed, but we did it last night and things were fine. I really don't think anybody is going to come up here. The crucial point is that we cannot have *sex* in the bed: The thin walls and wooden floors wouldn't allow for that. But who cares if we spoon as everyone else sleeps? We've got mere days until this holiday is over, and nobody has come up here first thing in the morning, ever.

I daren't risk lying here whispering sweet nothings, though.

"I'm going to get up," I say, "whilst I have the willpower."

Jamie smiles, and I scramble out of bed to start the day. As I climb over him, though, he grabs my arm and grins. When he plants a kiss on my hand, my heart does a double-beat leap in my chest, before plummeting to my stomach and back up again. I roll my eyes at him playfully and head to the bathroom. I've finally had the kind of sex I've only ever seen onscreen. I didn't know real people could have it. I ache between my thighs, but it's a nice ache, like a reminder he was there.

There's a light knock on the bathroom door as I brush my teeth, and Jamie stands there in his boxers, all disheveled and more handsome than ever.

"Room for a little one?"

I smile, careful not to let toothpaste spill onto my chin, and watch in the mirror as he wets his brush, pops on some toothpaste, wets it again, and then puts the brush in his mouth. I wonder how many women have seen this side of him. The off-guard, first-thing-in-the-morning side. Jamie looks up and we hold eye contact through our reflections, brushing our teeth like the domesticity of it is the most normal thing in the world between us. I feel something inside my chest swell, but I spit into the sink instead of acknowledging it, rinsing my mouth and then washing my face. I have four more days to enjoy this, and I'm not going to start self-monitoring about what every little butterfly means, so that I'm back in my head and end up diminishing the passion. I'm getting him out of my system, giving in to the physical, so that it no longer has to be this weird "almost" thing between us.

"Whatcha thinking?" Jamie asks, rinsing off his toothbrush and wiping his face clean.

I get in an eyeful of his body, openly appraising him, because I can.

"Wondering how we might get a moment alone today," I say, lips pursed in playfulness.

"Are you now?" he asks, and we're both whispering, knowing we can't get caught.

"Damned right I am," I say, slapping his butt.

———

DOWNSTAIRS THERE'S A note on the table: *Gone to the ruins*. Fair play—it's mid-morning already. Our late night meant we both slept in, so no wonder nobody hung around. I wonder if Alex got up with them, despite his own adventures last night. He's never been able to sleep in, even as a teenager. They will have gone quite early, I reckon, to beat the heat, and Mum likes it when I get my rest. She will have told everyone to let me sleep. I stick my head out of the kitchen door, to look around the pool. Nobody is there.

"Where is everyone?" asks Jamie, pulling on his shirt as he rounds the corner to where I'm standing. When he sees me admiring him, he pauses and then doesn't do up the rest of the buttons. I wink. My way of saying: *You understand. Good. Let me see.*

"They've left for the day," I tell him, and my cheeks could fall off from smiling so wide.

Jamie arches an eyebrow. "Interesting," he ponders.

"That's what I thought," I reply.

He sidles over to me and says, voice low, "Is it safe for me to give you a morning kiss, then?"

I push my face closer to his.

"It might well be . . ." I say. And then I think, *Wait. I really should check for Alex.*

Jamie puts his face between my hands and holds it there for a beat, like he can't believe our luck. We're nose-to-nose and then he gently puts his mouth on mine, and it is delicate, like this second alone is a treat to be savored—which it is. He's absolutely right.

"Hold that thought," I whisper, slipping from his grasp and doing a quick sweep of the rooms downstairs and then upstairs. Nobody is here. I hotfoot it back to him.

"Coast is clear," I say. "Now. Where were we?"

We kiss, and it's cute. But I can feel myself getting heated if I'm not careful, so as hard as it is, I pull away. We stand there, not know-ing what to do next, my pelvis aching, between my legs hot already. I look down. Jamie clearly has a boner. The thin fabric of his swim shorts is held up like a tent.

"Can't help it," he says, his palms in the air in surrender. "I hon-estly could take you here and now. *That* is what you do to me."

I feel that way, too. It's like our bodies are designed to slot to-gether seamlessly. Having sex with Jamie feels like the reason I *have* a body. Most of the time I'm just a brain in a meat suit, but when his hands were on me last night, when he was pressed up against me and then inside me . . . nothing else mattered.

"Sod it," I say, pulling at the fabric of his shirt. His body slams into mine with such force that my bum bangs into the kitchen table, but Jamie treats it as an invitation. He scoops me up so I'm sitting, and we paw at each other hungrily, like one of us is on day-release from prison, like we've not seen each other in years, like we not only want this, but *need* this.

I end up on my back, Jamie climbing onto the table. He lies down on top of me, kissing and touching and running his hand be-low the waistband of my denim shorts, which at some point in the last thirty seconds have come undone.

"Yes," I tell him, as his fingers find my most alive spot. "Yes."

I writhe underneath him, his breath hot in my ear, and I must kick something, because there's a crash, the noise of pottery hitting the floor.

"Don't stop!" I implore, as Jamie freezes above me. He's looking over at the doorway, face in a weird expression, a bit like he might be sick. I crane my neck, Jamie's hand still between my thighs, to see . . . Kate. My whole body tenses, and I swear every ounce of air leaves my lungs.

"Kate!" I say. "This isn't—"

"I didn't see anything!" she interrupts, spinning round so that her back is to us.

Jamie moves his hand and I button up my shorts as he clambers off. I swing my legs over the side of the table and say, with as much authority as I can muster, "This is the first time anything like this has happened."

I don't know why I lie. It just slips out.

Kate half turns her head, but not fully. She's already scarred by what she's seen.

"It's none of my business," she tells us. "I didn't feel well, so I didn't go with the others . . . I've been for a walk . . ." She shakes her head. She's giving us too much information. "I'm going to the super-market now. I said I'd have a late lunch ready. Bye." And she disappears.

I scrunch up my face at Jamie, noting that he is adorably flushed.

"At least it wasn't Laurie," he says. "Although if she tells him . . . Well, it should come from me."

I shake my head. "She won't tell him," I promise Jamie. "Not if I ask Kate not to. She said it herself: It's none of her business."

"Okay." He sounds unsure. "I need to find the right words, the right time . . ."

"Ssssh. Come here," I command him, and he steps toward me. I tilt my chin up and he gets the hint. He lowers his lips to mine and we share a chaste kiss.

"I *have* rather lost my hard-on now, though," I say, my face apologetic. "For lack of a better term. Nothing to do with you, it's just . . ."

"Yeah." Jamie nods. "Close call."

He swallows, finally catching his breath, and I hop up to kiss his cheek.

"Breakfast?" I ask, and he nods.

"WHAT'S IT LIKE?" I ask Jamie, as we sit among a small feast that we've made for ourselves. This holiday basically revolves around meals.

"What's what like?" Jamie replies, peeling an orange. It's scandalous to me, how he can walk around with hands as skilled as those, peeling fruit so that his forearm muscles flex and he gets juice all over his fingers.

"Sailing," I say, buttering my toast. It's very civilized of us to be sitting here, but with Kate due back any minute, it's for the best. Plus . . . I suppose Jamie and I don't actually know much about each other, because there's always been this weird distance. I mean, if Laurie told him to stay away from me, I guess I know why. "I couldn't tell if everyone was teasing me when they said how much money you made."

Jamie laughs. "Yeah, I fell on my feet there, to be honest. Although, well, there's no way to say this without sounding like an idiot, but I don't really need to work. My parents . . ." He trails off, and it takes me a second to understand what he's getting at.

"That doesn't make you sound like an idiot," I tell him. "Christ, I'm sure you'd rather have them here than have their money."

"Yes," he says and nods. "Exactly." There's a silence then, but I get the sense the worst thing to do would be to change the subject.

"What were they like?" I say. "If you don't mind me asking."

He's wearing his sunglasses, so I can't see his full reaction, but he lets air out through his nose and half smiles, so I think he appreciates being asked. I'd want to be asked, if the unthinkable happened; *when* it does, I suppose. It doesn't bear imagining, a world without my mum and dad.

"Mental," he says, and then he laughs. It makes me smile. "They were absolutely mental. Just . . . I was so lucky, really. Most people's parents were so serious to me, you know? Everything was about doing well at school and getting into a top uni, and shaping yourself to be a good working man with a good salary. But they never put value on those things. They really gave me their time, you know? Really wanted to *see* me, and encouraged me to be the most *me* I could be. Mum would get on the floor and play Lego with me for hours, and Dad took me to the local reservoir for outdoor swimming as soon as I was old enough to get in. And they had all these routines and rituals. If anyone had to go away for work, or even when I had a sleepover or away-camp or whatever, we'd all sit down for Mum's lasagna and garlic bread, first chance we were all back together."

"You don't have siblings?" I ask, although I already know the answer. It's just that most of the stuff I know about Jamie is secondhand, from Laurie or Mum and Dad.

He shakes his head. "It was only the three of us. I still have Mum's dad—my grandad—and my dad's stepmother is still alive, and there's some aunties and uncles and cousins who we'd see a few times a year. But under our roof, in our house, it was simply us. And I didn't need any more, I never longed for a brother or anything like that. I was just so, so loved."

"I wish I could have met them," I say. "They sound like they knew what life was all about."

"Yeah," Jamie says, nodding. "I keep trying to find that feeling somewhere else, you know? That feeling of being safe. You asked what it's like—sailing—and it's amazing. I love the physicality of it, and obviously all the different places I get to see. It's awesome to see your brother and Kate doing so well, but after Mum and Dad had their accident, I couldn't see the point of giving my life to the law. I have the opposite problem that most people in their twenties have, I think. I don't need to prove to my parents what a great job they've done, by being a good workhorse. I know what they'd want for me is to be free. To follow what feels good for as long as I enjoy it. But I want both: freedom and safety."

I nod, contemplating that.

"I'm envious," I tell him. "My world is the two square miles from my flat to campus. I don't do much adventuring. I think I'm *too* safe."

Jamie pours us both more coffee. "You'll get there," he says. "I believe in you."

"Thanks," I reply. "I'm a very anxious person. I feel like you don't have all the answers, but at least you know how to switch your brain off and be in your body. The only time I've done that lately is—" I pause. I cannot believe I nearly said: *The only time I did that lately is when I had sex with you.*

"What?" he asks.

I shake my head. "When I'm running," I lie, and he accepts my conclusion.

"A lot of people think the opposite of anxiety is calm," Jamie says. "But I don't think it is. I think the opposite of anxiety is trust."

"Trust sounds a lot like 'safety' to me . . ." I comment.

He nods. "I think you're right. Tomahto, tomayto."

"And so that's what you meant the other morning when we went for a run? That you thought I—out of everyone—would understand how you feel?"

"Yes," Jamie says. "It's weird. The safest I've felt lately has been—" He stops himself. I swear to god, I get a flash that he might allude to feeling safe when he's with me, but exactly like I did, he reins it in.

"Yes?" I say, throat dry.

"When I'm running," he settles on, and I feel like there's an elephant in the room with us, but neither of us is going to acknowledge it.

"Here's to running, then," I say, holding my coffee cup aloft in cheers.

He holds his cup up, too.

"To how good it feels to run," he says.

We sit in companionable silence then, drinking our coffees and looking at the sun shimmering off the pool, and I think: *God!* My preconceptions about Jamie really have been all wrong. I made myself think he was an arse, a womanizer, and unserious about anything that matters, off on his boats and never settling down. And then the second I gave him a chance, he blew it—confirming that my instinct was right. But it wasn't. That isn't who he is. Jamie is thoughtful and loyal, and is just trying to get through a day as best he can, like the rest of us. He's reassuringly human. I don't know how I missed that.

Kate comes home then, and we become a three. I don't mind the interruption actually. If Jamie and I were alone for much longer, I get the feeling we'd have started to say things that really would be best left unsaid. He's got me all up in my feelings, now that I see the real him.

"OKAY," KATE WHISPERS to me as we float on matching swans next to each other in the pool, shopping unloaded and more coffee consumed. Jamie is inside, washing the breakfast plates. "I'm going nuts over here, babe. You're going to have to fill in at least a few details. I beg you."

"Kate," I say, my voice low. I don't want Jamie to hear, but obviously I don't want anyone else in my family to hear, either, should they arrive back earlier than planned. "I cannot emphasize this enough: It was a moment of madness. I don't know what we were thinking, and I'm sorry you had to see it."

I scoop up a bit of water with my hand and pour it over my tummy to cool me down. It is *hot* today.

"An eleven A.M. hump-sesh in the middle of a family holiday home?" Kate whispers back, her voice incredulous. I have to note that her whisper is more of a stage whisper, so is not very discreet at all. It's a good reminder not to tell her everything.

"Like I said: madness."

"I don't buy it." She lowers her sunglasses and peers over their rims. "Jamie has fancied you for *years*, Flo."

I look in the opposite direction to where she's floating, because my face will give too much away. "Hmmm . . ." I say, knowing anything else is too dangerous.

Kate keeps talking. Nothing will deter her. "Something happened at Christmas, didn't it? More than you've told me?"

I keep examining the trees over at the far side of the garden, near the steps to the beach. I know I'm blushing, a hot rash of embarrassment creeping up my neck to my cheeks.

"Flo," she implores. "*Did* something happen at Christmas?"

"No," I tell her, because it's more or less the truth. "No more than an almost."

"But something is happening now?"

I shake my head. "Kind of," I end up saying, and as soon as the words leave my lips, Kate launches on them.

"Really!" she squeals. And Jamie is no idiot: He's going to know full well we're talking about him. I wish he'd come and rescue me from this Spanish Inquisition, but he's probably giving us a wide berth so that I can convince Kate to keep our secret, like I promised she would.

"Sssssh!" I tell her. "Jesus, look. Just promise me you won't tell Laurie, okay? Jamie is really worried he'll be mad, and although I personally think Laurie can go screw himself, Jamie actually cares what Laurie thinks and doesn't want to jeopardize their friendship, or whatever."

Kate furrows her brow. "But . . . if this is happening, Laurie is going to find out eventually? You have my word I won't say anything, because I understand it's none of my business, but starting a relationship in secret doesn't seem smart to me. At least not if the secret goes on for too long. And you don't want Laurie finding out by walking in on you, like I did . . ."

"No, no, no." I wave an arm about, batting away her commentary. "It's not that deep. There's no 'relationship.'" I put air quotes around that, with my two bunny ears. I can tell Kate isn't impressed. Maybe I've misread her. I thought she'd find it exciting and exotic. She's looks concerned.

"He travels the world for a living, I live in Scotland. He's Laurie's best friend—there's no future or whatever . . . We both know that."

I bite my lip. I can't believe she's managing to get all of this out of me.

"We hooked up," I tell her. "Finally. Yesterday. After the bar. And I want it to happen again, and it's all quite a relief, because my dislike of Jamie—or whatever it was—took too much effort to maintain. But it won't happen again after this holiday. Okay? That's why Laurie doesn't need to know. It's a short-term fling that means, in the long term, we'll be able to actually get on, because we've got it out of our systems."

Kate laughs. "The plan is to shag each other, so that you eventually don't want to shag anymore?"

I don't know what to say to that. It sounded better in my head.

"Just . . . don't tell Laurie. You promised, okay?"

"I did," Kate tells me. "You're going to have hot sex with hot Jamie, and in a few days you'll forget it ever happened."

"Exactly." I nod.

"Flo?" Kate says after a while.

"Yes?"

"You're living in a dream world. You know that, don't you?"

I float away from her, not dignifying the comment with a response. Does she mean that we won't stop shagging? Or that I'm dreaming to think Laurie won't find out?

Either way, she's wrong.

17

Dad asks me to go for a walk before dinner, because he says we've had no one-on-one time all holiday and I'm his favorite.

"Dad," I say with a smile, "I know you say that to all of us."

He chuckles and gives a shrug. "It's true, though," he counters, somehow both proving my point and still upholding the integrity of the statement. "Anyway," he says, "let's go and do a few laps of the beach. Make the most of this magical twilight hour, shall we?"

He's not wrong about it being magical. Not only is the sky swirling shades of pink and orange, but it's like the air has been infused with the same somehow. Everything feels softer at this hour, more delicate. When the heat subsides and the air settles, it makes me want to whisper to preserve whatever delightful thing is happening.

"Okay, sold," I say, putting down my empty beer bottle and taking one last handful of crisps. I haven't been the first one down to predinner drinks all holiday, and I'm glad I am tonight. I've made a decision to trust that Kate won't tell Laurie anything, and another decision to believe I deserve this little holiday . . . thing. Fling! Non-fling?

Whatever Jamie and I are and have, or don't have, it's making me happy. I can't remember when I last felt this way, to be honest.

Dad and I meander down the winding steps and onto the sand, turning left toward the end of the bay, where the water edges out the sand and we're blocked off by a massive rock formation. We talk about what they saw at the ruins that day, and that Kate and I caught up, once I'd woken up. Jamie is not mentioned in any capacity, and I certainly will not bring him up. It's easy to be with Dad. He's amazing, too—as accomplished and competent and able as Mum is. But as much as I hate to admit it, he's a man, so I don't compare myself to him (and come up short) in the way I do to Mum. The friction is taken out of the relationship, then.

"You seem to be enjoying this trip, anyway," Dad says, as we stand at the edge of the sea and let the water lap up onto our bare toes. He picks up a stone and skims it over the water.

"I think we all are, aren't we?" I reply, picking up a stone of my own. It skims twice and then plops into the sea. Dad skims another one and it glides once, twice, three times, then a fourth, before succumbing to the same fate.

"Yes," he says with a nod. "I feel very lucky that my grown-up children will still come willingly to spend time with me. It's not the case in every family."

"No," I say, knowing it's true. "Good job you and Mum are so awesome really, isn't it? And that you raised awesome kids."

"We certainly did," Dad says with a grin, and then he loops an arm round my shoulders and pulls me in for a sideways hug, landing a kiss on my temple.

"What was that for?" I say.

"I love you, that's what it's for," he tells me, letting go. "And you seem good now, Flo. I feel like I've got my daughter back."

I don't know what to say to that. *Sorry my breakdown made you sad?* My therapist said I can acknowledge that the breakdown affected the people around me without assuming responsibility for it. I think of that now, to remind me not to shoulder Dad's feelings about what happened to me.

"Somebody told me recently that the opposite of anxiety isn't calm, but trust," I say. "And that makes a lot of sense to me."

"You're feeling more trust lately?" Dad clarifies. "In yourself or the world or . . . ?"

We stop throwing stones and turn to head back the way we've just come.

"It's a work in progress," I tell him, "but I think in myself, and that kind of affects my trust that everything will work out. I've never felt that before. Like I really might be okay, you know?"

"Yeah," he says. "I know that." He pulls a leaf off a nearby tree branch and shreds it with his fingers, contemplatively. "I thought it might be a romance making you happy," he goes on. "That Adonis bloke. But you said it didn't work out?"

I laugh. "It was the man-bun," I tell him. Dad furrows his brow. I make a ball shape with my fist and rest it on the top of my head. "The hair? Never trust a dude with a man-bun, that's what I say."

He considers this. "I see what you mean," he says and smiles. "No hipsters allowed?"

I shrug, the responsibility not mine—I don't make the rules.

"Are you doing okay?" I ask him then. "Are you having a good holiday?"

"I am," he says, dropping the last of the leaf to the ground. It flutters down slowly, like a ballerina's pirouette.

His tone catches me off guard. "You don't sound sure," I tease, but instead of him reiterating his joy, pain crosses his face.

"I worry about your mother," he continues, and we're at the bottom of the steps to the house, but instead of going up, he leans against the handrail post and looks up at the sky. I wait for him to speak. I don't think I have ever heard of anyone being worried about my mother. "It's hard, you know, becoming retired. She's still got thirty or forty years in front of her to fill, and it can be overwhelming."

I cock my head. "I don't think Mum has ever been overwhelmed in her life, has she?" I offer.

Dad tuts. "Flo," he says. "You know better than that. Everyone goes through stuff, even if we can't see it or necessarily tell from the outside."

I nod, thinking of what Jamie said about assuming that I, out of everyone, could feel sympathy for somebody going through it.

"You're right," I tell him. "I'll check in with her. Sorry. You're worried about her, and I'm glad you told me, so that I can share half of that worry, okay?"

"Okay." Dad nods. "You're a good girl, Flo. I'm proud of you."

"Thanks, Dad," I reply, and we head back up to the house, every step I take making me realize that I'm proud of me, too.

MUM, KATE, LAURIE, and Alex are all having *aperitivo*s on the veranda when we reach the house. They're laughing and joking about who knows what, pouring wine and opening beers, and the playlist I've come to think of as *The Holiday Playlist* is reverberating from the Bluetooth speaker. I desperately want to ask where Jamie is, but I daren't. I have another beer and listen to the details of another restaurant Alex has found for us, and it's only when we start getting our things together to leave that I begin to feel really confused. Are we going without him? If we are, then why? I'm eager for clarification, but truly do not trust myself to speak his name out loud. I think if I do, it won't sound like, *Oh hey, where's Jamie?* It will sound like, *Oh hey, I'm hoping to hook up with Jamie again and thought you should all know. Is he about?*

"He left this for you," a voice whispers in my ear. Kate. I turn round, alarmed that she'd allude to him—to me—with everyone around, even though nobody can really hear.

She stuffs a piece of paper in my hand, and my heart sinks. I know what this will say. It will say, *I can't do this. I'm sorry.* I scurry off to the kitchen and round the corner to the living room while everyone else shuts the doors and locks up. I take a breath.

Up the hill, where we went running. From the house, walk for about ten minutes. Ten P.M. I'll be waiting.

I put the note into my bag and pull out my phone.

ME
I had sex with Jamie
Last night
It was really good
And we almost got caught doing it again this morning, too
By Kate!

HOPE
What?
Jesus! I cannot keep up with you two!
This has more will-they-won't-they than Ross and Rachel!

ME

I know. But. Exposure therapy, right?

HOPE

The extreme version, yeah!

ME

I'm not crazy, am I? Have I been a "pick me" girl?

HOPE

Are you having fun?

ME

So much fun

HOPE

Fuck it then! Go forth and bump uglies!

ME

He's not out with us tonight, he's gone off somewhere, but he's
left a note to meet him later

HOPE

Sexy!

ME

Feels kinda romantic, tbh

HOPE

And that's . . . bad?

ME

I don't know!

You tell me!

HOPE

I think . . .

Follow your heart

And if she's busy

Follow your va-jay-jay.

JAMIE SCARES ME half to death when I get up there after dinner. It's dark, there are no streetlights, and I'm using my iPhone torch to see.

"Sorry," he whispers, when I let out a *Gah!* "There is no way to loiter in the dark for a woman without it being innately creepy." I hit his arm and tell him he's an idiot, and in the beam of my phone light I see him smirk and say, "Fright as an aphrodisiac? Maybe?"

"Spoken like a true psychopath." I laugh, rubbing at my chest to catch my breath. "What are we even doing here?" I ask. "Have you *actually* planned to murder me?"

"I feel like if I tell you the French for orgasm is 'the little death' you'll accuse me of being off-topic," Jamie offers, to which I nod.

"It feels like you're stalling for time," I reply. "Which is inherently suspicious."

"Noted," he replies. "Take my hand then, and come this way."

Jamie laces his fingers through mine, and I relish the touch of his skin; how easy it feels, how natural, to walk this way with him. I'm aware that's a bit OTT for a fling, but I figure it's okay to enjoy the bits of this that I do enjoy—if I withhold the pleasure of the small things from myself, what's the point of doing this?

We trudge up to an old outbuilding and Jamie positions himself behind me, hands on my hips, to face me at the door.

"Okay, now I'm really worried," I joke, noting the pressure of Jamie's pelvis in my back, how excited he already is.

A guy passes us then, making us jump, but it's nobody we know or anything—simply a bloke smoking a cigarette, passing through.

"Ουγγνώμη," he says apologetically, and Jamie replies in Greek. I assume he's saying, *Don't worry.*

"Go on, then," Jamie says, and I reach out to push the crumbling old door to the crumbling old barn, only to be confronted with the most romantic setup I have ever seen in real life. In fact this could come straight from a big-screen movie.

Inside this derelict barn are hundreds of tea-lights in glass jars. They're on the floor, on upturned crates, in the rafters: everywhere. On the floor is a throw and some pillows, with a small vase that has a single rose peeking out of it. It's a cozy love den, just for the two of us.

"Jamie!" I say, amazed. "What did you do? How did you get all of this stuff?"

He pulls a face. "I know a guy who knows a guy," he tells me.

"Is this why you weren't at dinner?" I marvel. "You were doing all this?"

Jamie steps inside and gently closes the door. He puts his arms around me from behind and rests his chin on my shoulder. He whispers, "I thought you deserved a little more than the great outdoors." I turn my head and we kiss, slow and deep and surprisingly gentle. "Not that you aren't fantastic alfresco," he adds.

"Thanks," I say, laughing. "I think."

There's a cooler that I recognize from the house, and inside it a bottle of champagne. Jamie pops the cork and pours us both a glass, and we toast.

"To doing . . . *this*," I say, and Jamie smiles.

"To this," he echoes. "It's probably warm by now," he goes on. "But, I don't know. I've thought about us doing this for so long, and I know it would be easy to just have sex and not talk, but for what it's worth: I want you to know I'm so happy about this."

"Me, too," I say.

Jamie eyes me, and I can see his fondness for me. He makes me feel safe. And I trust him. I do.

"I like talking to you, too," I continue. "In fact I actually quoted you to my dad earlier, so I think you're making quite the impression on my brain."

"Aww, that's nice. I wonder what he'll say when he finds out . . ."

"Oh my god, don't!" I squeal. "It doesn't bear thinking about."

We have this weird moment then, champagne flutes suspended halfway to our mouths, staring at each other—the air between us doing that thing it did on the boat, getting all still and loaded and . . . complicated. I briefly wonder how many women he's been with in his life, how many have felt this special.

"What?" I say, when I can't take it anymore.

And Jamie blinks and tells me, "I don't think you understand how beautiful you are, do you?"

"Put your drink down," I reply, because I've decided to do something. I'm not the most experienced woman on the planet—I haven't ever actually given anyone a blow job before. And I feel like I want to, with Jamie. He's not asking for it, and I don't feel any pressure or anything like that. It's just that suddenly I want to give him pleasure. And I want to be in charge of that pleasure.

Jamie lingers with his glass, as if he doesn't understand what I've asked him, so I take it from him and find a wooden beam on which to put it. I kiss him, reveling in the fact that I can. I don't have to worry about rejection or mixed signals because we have our agreement—it's all out in the open that we both want to do this. I rub my lips from his mouth to his neck to his firm shoulders, my tongue on chiseled pecs, and I only pause once I have to kneel, my face looking up to the waistband of his trousers. I look up at him, and Jamie stares down with an earnestness I've never seen before. He reaches out a hand, rubs a thumb over my lips, and then I tug down his shorts to see that he is ready—*very ready*—for what comes next.

He lolls back his head and says my name, and the power of it, of being the one to make him lose control in this way, is heady.

I start slow but get faster, following the lead of his moans to figure out what to do next. He rests a hand lightly on the back of my head, and I suddenly realize I'm going to have to make a choice between spitting and swallowing, but then I hear, "I want to finish inside you."

I decide I want that, too. I'm more turned on than I've been in my life.

I stand up and we end up stumbling backward as we embrace, so that somehow we tumble down to the blankets that he'd laid out earlier. I straddle him, grabbing a nearby condom and sliding it on as Jamie half lies and half sits, taking my nipple in his mouth in that way he is so good at. I push against him, and then his mouth is on my earlobe and my chin is over his shoulder, and I find myself saying his name over and over. We're slick with sweat and our rhythm gets faster and faster. I can't imagine it ever feeling this good with anybody else, not if I practiced with somebody for a million years.

"I want to do you from behind," Jamie instructs, and so I hop off, turn round, and feel him enter me, pawing at my stomach, my boobs, panting once more as he doubles over to lay his front across my back. "God, you feel so good, Flo. So, so, good . . ."

It's enough to make me climax, feeling him that way, feeling *myself* that way: empowered, desired, desiring. Jamie follows not long afterward. It seems we're pretty good at the mutual-pleasure thing.

WE STAY STILL once we've finished, collapsing so that Jamie holds me from behind and the moment sustains itself for as long as we can make it last.

"That was . . ." Jamie murmurs.

"It was," I agree.

We lie side by side, stomach to stomach and chest to chest. He holds me gently. I take in his gray eyes and angelic eyelashes, the single bead of sweat still lingering at his temple. It hits me that I really, *really* like being looked at by Jamie in this way. And that's not the plan. Realizing this makes me feel claustrophobic with my own heart, my own feelings. If he keeps looking at me like this, any crush or fondness or hotness I feel for him won't quell, it will swell. I thought, by getting to know Jamie better, I could get him out of my system, like the poem said. Exposure therapy. But I might be getting in over my head here.

I move away from him, wrapping myself in one of the blankets. The privacy in the barn means we're almost like bedfellows, which is a new level of intimacy. I reach over to the cooler and am grateful to see some water in there. I grab a bottle and drink half of it in one gulp.

"Four more nights of the holiday left, anyway," I say. "So what do you reckon? Eight to ten more spectacular shags?"

I mean it to sound light, to steer us into jovial, cheeky territory. But Jamie doesn't laugh. He just says, "Well, four nights and then . . . everything after."

"Everything after?" I say.

"Yeah," he replies. "Obviously, once Laurie knows . . ."

"You're telling Laurie?" I say, surprised.

"I kind of have to?" Jamie says. "Like we agreed."

I'm confused. "So we *are* going to tell Laurie we're—you know—fooling around?"

Jamie narrows his eyes. "Fooling around," he repeats.

"Wait," I say. "I don't get what's going on here. This is a fling, right? A holiday fling?"

Jamie opens his mouth and then closes it again, choosing not to speak. He moves to cover himself up, reaching for his boxers and pulling them on. He's beautiful, in the candlelight. A feeling swells in my chest, and it reminds me of what I felt at Christmas, when I thought something was happening and it wasn't. Except it actually was. And I don't know what made him change his mind, or why he has changed his mind again on this trip, but I start to pull at the thread of a thought I've been pushing away ever since we talked about trust. It's actually a thought that's been growing all year. Anger. I am angry at Jamie, for never saying sorry for what he did. And if I thought I could level the playing field by having some quick hookup and walking away, I was wrong, because . . . because . . . Well, I don't know why. Only that I can't.

"Why did you leave me hanging at Christmas?" I say suddenly. I've done it. I've said the *C*-word, the thing we've danced around this whole trip.

Jamie narrows his eyes. "I could ask you the same thing," he replies coolly.

I don't understand what he means. He was the one who led *me* on; he led me down the garden path and then changed his mind.

"Urm . . ." I say, remembering how terrible I am at confrontation. I wish I could take back the last ten minutes. Neither of us speaks. This has gone horribly wrong. We look at the floor, the walls, the ceiling—anything but at each other. Anger brews.

And then Jamie is furious: red-faced and manic eyes, his voice raised.

"Do you know what, Flo? I don't know in what world you think I wronged you last Christmas, but it's all adding up to me now. You just do what you want, don't you? You think because you had your breakdown, you're the only one who can hurt, and you hide behind it. You do whatever you goddamn choose: You lead people on, dump them when it suits, treat them coldly and horribly and make them feel *unwelcome* . . . Did you decide you'd use me to pass the time again, because we're on holiday and it didn't work out with Adonis?"

He says *Adonis* like he's spitting it out, like it pains him.

I shake my head. "You've got this wrong," I say. "This is all backward."

"No," he says, pulling on his shorts and grabbing his T-shirt. "I've got this exactly right. I see this for what it is now, crystal-clear. I've been a grade-A idiot."

"Please don't go," I say as he walks to the door. "None of this makes any sense . . ."

"Hard-agree," Jamie replies. "I don't know how you dare accuse me of shitting on your heart, when if you ask me it's quite the opposite."

And then he is gone, and I am lying naked under my blanket, looking at the barn wall, wondering what the hell just happened.

18

I sit on the beach, on my own, in the dark. It's not nearly as romantic out here by myself. I'm dressed, but have schlepped the blanket from the barn down here, for extra warmth. It's actually quite cold at this hour. When I was here with Jamie, I didn't notice. Without him, it's freezing.

There's a gentle sway to the ocean under the moonlight. I'm biding my time. I assume Jamie stalked off to our shared bedroom, and I can't face going up there. I've been replaying our argument over and over again in my mind, trying to pinpoint the moment it went wrong. All I can conclude is that he's mad this is purely physical, but that's what we agreed. Not out loud maybe, but . . . this is Jamie Kramer. Even if he did commitment—which he doesn't—I live in Scotland, and he lives on the sea. It would never work. I feel kind of insane, not being able to understand. I think I'm probably better off out of it; that it's better it's over now. I wonder if we'll go back to being enemies. That would be such a shame when we've been getting on so well. And god, the sex! I've never known sex like it.

I've not been with many men. I didn't lose my virginity until university, in Freshers' Week, and it had been terribly disappointing. In my second year I let a bloke in my Gothic Literature class finger me twice, but again: not great. There was a guy during my master's, but after the breakdown nobody would come near me, take all that on—it was hard enough to keep friends, let alone think about boyfriends. And then last Christmas it was such a surprise to discover something between Jamie and me . . . But I know our lives are just so different.

I DRAG MYSELF up the steps to the villa, deciding on the way there that I'll take the sofa tonight, to give Jamie some space. I can't lie awake watching him sleep. I'm almost at the top when I realize I can smell smoke, and immediately panic that something is wrong with the house—that somebody left the stove on or something. As I approach, it feels warmer, and for a split second I think, *Should I even go in there?* But then obviously I should, because my family needs to get out if there's a problem. Which there obviously is, because it *stinks* of smoke, except it isn't coming from the villa—it's coming from behind it.

I slip round the side of the villa and see the barn, where Jamie and I were not an hour ago. It's up in flames, with thick, angry fire licking at the roof.

"No," I mutter, panicked, trying to understand what I'm seeing. "No, no, no . . ."

Jamie wouldn't have gone back there, would he? He can't be in there?

"Fire!" I shout, but it comes out like a squeak. I'm closer to the front of the house than the back, so I bang a flat palm against the front door, over and over again. I hit so hard and fast that my hand begins to sting. When nobody comes, I bolt round to the back, because I know for sure it's open. I need help.

As I rush through the kitchen I see that Jamie is on the sofa in the living room, so I dash in there and shake him awake. I don't have time to think about him being mad at me, and what has happened—that's beside the point. He needs to wake up, and fast.

"Jamie," I say loudly. "Jamie! There's a fire!"

His eyes open, startled, and for a beat we look directly at each other and don't speak. Those big gray eyes, framed by eyelashes longer than any human deserves . . . I'm struck, all over again, by how much he can convey with so little expression.

And then I remember why I'm here.

"Get up," I say, shaking myself of any other thoughts. I'm already backing away to go and wake everyone upstairs. "There's a fire at the barn. We have to do something!"

I take the stairs two at a time, banging on everyone's door, one after the other, before circling back to Laurie and Kate's room, where Laurie is up now, in his boxers, asking me what the hell is going on. It's only when I see Kate sitting up in bed behind him, absentmindedly rubbing her tummy, that I remember she's pregnant. She should head down to the beach, out of the way of the smoke. She can't stay here and she certainly can't go up there, toward the danger.

"There's a fire outside, at the old barn opposite. It's huge. But, Kate—the smoke . . . don't risk it, okay? Laurie, we have to do something."

I don't hear what he says, because now Mum is up, standing at her door listening to what I'm saying.

"Michael," she says to my dad, "there's a fire. Where's your mobile?"

There's no sign of movement from Alex's room, which we both register at the same time.

"Get him," I say, gesturing to his room. Mum tries his door, but it's locked.

"Alex, get up," Mum shouts through the door. "There's a fire! Alex!"

I'm halfway down the stairs when Alex's door opens ajar and a man who is not Alex says to my mother, "We're coming. I just need to untie him."

Mum turns puce and then deathly pale, and she says nothing as the door is closed in her face, then follows me. I hear her mutter, "Jesus. My bloody kids."

Collectively we race up the hill, where a small fire truck has already arrived, thank the Lord. It's only when I see the thing that it occurs to me I had no idea what I was going to do when I got there. It's not like I can fight a fire on my own. I don't even know the number for the emergency services here. But I couldn't do nothing, could I? I was in there only an hour ago.

Laurie, Jamie, Dad and Mum and I stand, watching the fire roar and two fire officers survey what's happening while two more fix a massive hose to something near a drain. Alex jogs up behind us and says, "What happened?"

"Fire," Dad says.

"Obviously," adds Laurie drily.

Panic rises in my chest: Is this our fault? Did we leave a candle burning? More than that, since I was the last one out of there: Is it *my* fault?

"What can we do?" I shout, desperate, in the direction of the firefighters and a concerned local couple in their nightwear. The couple blink at me and give a small shrug. Their faces are bathed in the eerie glow from the fire. Is it their barn or are they neighbors? I hope they're insured. This is awful.

"Is anybody hurt?" Kate asks, appearing at the side of us all, with a scarf over her nose and mouth. Laurie looks at her with a frown. "I know," she says, reading his mind. "But I couldn't just stay at the house, Laurie. And the wind is blowing that way." She gestures away from us. We're lucky that Mother Nature is doing us a solid: The smoke is being carried off up the hill and far away, instead of toward the villa.

Laurie puts his arm around her protectively. "Okay," he says quietly.

I look at Jamie, wanting reassurance from him that this is all going to be okay: the fire, and him and me. He's watching the flames, but I know he feels my eyes on him. His face flickers enough for me to know that he's trying his best not to give me his attention. My heart sinks. The feeling I was wallowing in on the beach rises to the surface—thoughts of how I was foolish to think I deserve anything good leaking back into my consciousness. I look back at the fire. It's pretty bad. Not only have I ruined things for me and Jamie, but I've ruined somebody's actual property, too.

I look at Jamie again and the words leave my mouth before I can register what I'm saying out loud. "I thought I blew out all of the candles. I'm sure I did . . ."

Jamie looks at me this time and I stare at him, hard, willing him to tell me this isn't my fault. His eyes dart away from me, to my left. To where Laurie is. He quickly looks back, but I can't help it: I look at Laurie, too. It's a rookie mistake, because Laurie whips his head back and forth, following the imaginary tennis ball between me and Jamie, busily connecting the dots. His sixth sense has been piqued.

"Candles?" Mum asks, trying to catch up. I look at her, then at the ground. Dear Lord, what I wouldn't do to rewind the last sixty seconds. There's self-sabotage, and then there's this: leaking our secret to the very people we agreed would never find out. Fuck!

"Oh," I hear Mum say then. In my peripheral vision I see Kate give a small nod of the head.

Alex—whose friend, I suddenly realize, is nowhere to be seen—hits Jamie's arm and says, "Seriously?" Jamie rubs at the site of impact. "Is that who you were with at the beach the other night?"

The floor continues to be the most interesting thing I've ever come across. The fire is relenting now, the firefighters having done their job. But the heat is still in the air. I feel its pressure against my face, making my skin slick and clammy.

"Veronica," Jamie says, "Michael, I'm sorry . . ."

"Nonsense," says my mum, right as Dad asks innocently, "What for, Jamie?"

Before he can respond, it feels like Laurie grows six inches in height as he pulls back his shoulders, lifts his chin, and steps toward his best friend. "He's apologizing," Laurie says, and his tone is so strained in its civility that we all instinctively understand he's about to blow, "for FUCKING Florence."

It all happens fast after that. Laurie launches himself at Jamie like a bullet from a gun, tackling him to the ground, where Jamie pushes him off and tries to get back up. But Laurie is angrier than I've ever seen him, and all the stronger for it, so he reaches up and grabs Jamie's leg, pulling backward until Jamie is on the floor with him once again.

They tussle, not really landing punches so much as wrestling in the dirt, and it feels like the rest of us are all screaming and shouting for them to stop—except Kate, who has taken a step back and is rubbing her stomach, eyes wide, like she cannot believe what she is seeing. Laurie gets a punch in—not a big one. He hits Jamie's jaw, but it sounds soft almost, not like the massive thwack that punches make on TV. It's violent enough to make Dad launch himself on top of them, as if he's a father separating six-year-olds, not thirty-somethings. He issues a booming command of: *Enough!*

There's a bit more scuffling, but with Dad between them now. I can practically see the red mist in Laurie's eyes, and the shame in Jamie's. This is the exact thing he feared, and seeing him so sad breaks my heart. Laurie has no right to get involved in any of this, but I can tell Jamie *feels* terrible that he broke whatever promise he made. And it was me—*I* made him do that. Kate was right: What did I think was going to happen? It hits me: I've messed up, and messed up badly. I've put Jamie in a horrible position.

Laurie looks up from the ground and says to us, "Jamie's been messing around with Flo, and it's like you lot don't even care! Let me fucking *have him*."

Dad stands, brushing the dust from his knees, and as he straightens up he says, "No, Lawrence, I don't care. Grow up!"

"I don't, either," declares Mum, taking Dad's arm and giving him a squeeze. They look at each other, and it's a look that says a million things: *I love you for breaking that up. Are you okay? What the hell is going on? I'm glad you're my partner in all this.*

"I'd encourage it actually, Laurie," says Kate, and I can tell by her face that she's livid at him for fighting. She shoots him a look that I take to mean, *We'll talk about this later.* And if Laurie is going to argue against everyone's calm reactions, that single glance stops him. It's like the wind has been stolen from his sails. He looks quickly from one face to the next, disbelief etched across his features—and,

I'd dare say, a level of betrayal, too. He thought *everyone* would be mad, that he'd done the right thing in "protecting" my "honor," and he's shocked nobody is backing him up here.

"I'd say it was pretty inevitable, to be honest, bro," Alex says to Laurie.

And Laurie frowns, then nods, understanding the unsaid. I see the look between them. I feel like there's something I don't know, something I'm missing. "I don't believe this," he mutters. "I can't believe nobody cares."

Jamie clears his throat. We turn to him expectantly, but when he opens his mouth, he just looks sad all over again, and instead gets up, holds a hand out for Laurie, and looks broken once more when Laurie smacks it away and gets up without help. It makes me feel dreadful for him—for Jamie.

"It's all over now, anyway," I announce, trying to smooth things over in any way I can. The manner in which Jamie stormed away from me made it clear we won't be hooking up again. If that can go any way toward appeasing Laurie and making sure he forgives Jamie quickly, it's better to spell it out. "It was a mistake. We got carried away, is all. It was that holiday feeling, but we both agree it's stupid. Don't hold anything against him—it was all me, okay?"

"Oh, Flo . . ." says Mum.

I give her a weak smile, trying to reassure her I'm all right. Because I should be, really. Laurie has no choice except to forgive me, but I am worried about him and Jamie. I never took seriously that "pledge" Jamie made, because I don't take Laurie seriously. That was a mistake.

"Sorry again, everyone," Jamie utters, still in the dirt, smoke from the embers of the barn smoldering behind him. But before the

words fully leave his mouth, both Mum and Dad tell him it's fine—
there's nothing to be sorry for.

Laurie gives a massive tut. "Yes, there is," he says petulantly.
"That's my *little sister*, dude. I fucking told you to stay away from
her . . ."

Jamie looks at the ground, shamed.

"Don't be an idiot," Alex tells Laurie, hitting his shoulder. Laurie
scowls. "This isn't the 1600s. She's my little sister, too, and I couldn't
give a shit."

"Come on, lad," Dad says to Jamie, putting an arm round him.
"Let's find you some ice for that cheek, shall we?"

"Yes," Mum agrees, rounding us all up with open arms. "Let's get
out of everyone's way. It's all under control now."

We all start to schlep back down the hill to the villa, but are
quickly stopped by the sound of the old man who had been watching
the barn burn alongside us, with his wife. He yells in Greek, so I automatically look at Jamie to translate. I think the man's asking if we
have a cigarette.

Jamie listens, nods, and then translates. "It was a cigarette butt,
they think," he says. "The fire started behind the barn. The grass is so
dry, it made its way to the building."

"It wasn't a candle?" I ask, making sure I understand.

Jamie shakes his head. Goddammit, I'm relieved it wasn't my
fault, but I've just outed us to my family for no reason at all, then. I let
my anxious thoughts become blurted-out words, and now . . . *this.*

Jamie and I end up falling behind the group as we walk. I think
everyone is giving us our space. Kate has taken Laurie's arm and is
practically frog-marching him to the villa, and Mum is sandwiched
between Dad on her left and Alex on her right, linking arms with both

of them. I loiter, letting everyone's good nights wash over me in the darkness, and I hope Jamie will stay behind to talk to me. There's so much to say—starting with a proper apology from me, for everything, including the stuff I don't even understand.

But he doesn't linger. Jamie heads right inside, straight to the front room. And before I can ask him to stay, the door is shut in my face.

19

A lot of people think the opposite of anxiety is calm . . . I think the opposite of anxiety is trust. That's what Jamie said to me. Well, I certainly don't trust him. I have woken up so, so angry. Fool me once, shame on you; fool me twice, shame on me. This has all exploded in my face. But now I've had time to think about it, I'm furious. How dare Jamie yell at me that way? He thinks *I've* used *him*? What about him? I can't help feeling that the seeds for tonight were all sown last Christmas, and it would have been better to leave it well alone. Nobody cares about me and Jamie, except for Laurie. But like Alex says, why does he get a say? It's all so toxic.

HOPE
You okay, pal?

ME
I guess
I just . . . well, it's embarrassing
I feel embarrassed

HOPE

What have you got to be embarrassed by?

ME

I don't know—having this stupid "exposure therapy" plan in the first place? Look where it got me! There's a burned-down building and Jamie isn't speaking to me

HOPE

The fire wasn't your fault, and the arsehole didn't talk to you to begin with
You've not lost anything

ME

So why do I feel so shitty?
Jamie wasn't at breakfast
The mood in the family is an unreadable one: Mum, Dad, and Alex are being extra-bright and chatty, as if compensating for the dourness of Laurie, who is doing a very dramatic sulk whilst professing "everything is fine" . . .
And Kate and Laurie have obviously fallen out, but aren't declaring that out loud, and so we're all ignoring it until they get it together

HOPE

I think you'll be fine by this afternoon!

Kate drags me off to the market. I've got an anxious tummy, which is quite the kick-me-whilst-I'm-down move from my body.

Like it isn't enough to have my brain going haywire, but I could also poop my pants if I don't stay close to a toilet. I've had way more than my fair share of bad days in my life, but this is a first for me, to feel so sad and untethered that even my tummy is upset. Even during my breakdown I didn't get freaking *diarrhea*.

"Thanks for sharing," observes Kate when I tell her what's going on. We're climbing off the bus for the market stop, but I had to say something. She surveys the shopping kingdom laid out before her, and with a happy glint in her eye slips on her sunglasses. I didn't have a choice about coming this morning—Kate has been threatening it for ten days, since she first discovered the market with Laurie; but also, after the very awkward breakfast with all these unsaid things floating in the ether, she all but kidnapped me. She'll be wanting the gossip, of course, the full story of me and Jamie. And do you know what? When it comes up, I'm going to tell her. I slept like a log last night, which surprised me when I woke up. It was a thick and dream-less sleep, and in a weird way I think the relief of everything being out in the open worked in my favor. Jamie was nowhere to be seen, though—he didn't come to the room, his bed didn't look slept in.

"Right," Kate says, with a snap of her fingers. "The market is ba-sically over three streets, and we found a really nice bakery with good coffee and an outdoor courtyard, which will be great for a break later. I don't know which hormone means I get tired now after twenty minutes' walking, but it has kicked in and the only way not to be mad about it is pastries."

"Duly noted," I say. "They'll have a toilet, too, so that makes both of us happy."

"God, how glamorous we are!" jokes Kate, linking her arm through mine. "I used to be all dancing-all-night and working-all-day, thinking I'd sleep when I was dead! And now I need rest breaks scheduled in, and regular snacks to stop my blood sugar getting too low."

"To be fair, I've always needed to know where my next meal is coming from."

"Ah," says Kate, getting my point. "You're a Greenberg. Of course you do."

"Glad you understand," I quip, and she laughs.

"God, when I first started seeing Laurie, I'd never known somebody so committed to not only knowing where their next meal was coming from, but also knowing what they were going to eat for the entire day."

I shrug—like, *What can you do?* "We were raised around the dinner table," I say, not sounding one bit sorry. "It's how we measure time."

Kate laughs again, the sound of somebody hearing something they know to be absolutely true. Then she gestures for me to walk ahead of her, toward the hustle and bustle of people.

The streets are wide and cobbled, with huge ornate buildings towering on either side and a faded old-school vibe, like they're past their best, but challenge you to find anything more majestic in *your* hometown. The shops underneath them are cavernous and dark, filled to the brim with whatever wares they specialize in—although a few shops have guitars next to pots and pans, next to braided bracelets, next to cat food, so I suppose their specialty is *everything*.

The fruit-and-veg shops are glorious: mounds of bright yellow lemons the size of fists spilling out onto the pavement, bunches of green beans and bags of wild garlic. There's a dried-food store, too, with piles of spices and herbs, buckets of olives in twenty different shades, sizes, and flavors: spiced, spicier, pitted, stuffed with cheese, stuffed with peppers, stuffed with garlic . . . And then linens. Shops filled with starched white tablecloths with blue embellishments, and baby clothes, too—which Kate makes a beeline for.

"I know they stay in these for about ten minutes," she admires, picking up a tiny cotton onesie. "But I want to spend every penny I have on all of them. I thought I'd be a practical, sensible mum . . . but oh, dear Lord, these things!"

It hits me all over again that I'm going to be an aunt. Kate is an only child, so I will be the only aunt. That's *huge*.

"I always thought I'd be the cool, fun aunt," I say, running a hand over a wicker basket full of napkins and making the woman behind the counter tut. I pull my hand away quickly and give her a sheepish smile. "But I think I'll take it all very seriously, you know. Buying her books on feminism and gender theory, and making sure she's got a good knowledge of the classics, but an appetite for contemporary stories, too . . ."

"I think we'll be relying on you and Alex," she says, smiling. "Imagine being born to two lawyers? Boring dot-com. You and Alex will have to show her the arts, broaden her horizons. Well, I expect you will. Alex can be the silly uncle, giving her sweets and fizzy pop and offering to babysit, but then forgetting to show up."

I smile at her. This is a whole other side to Kate: She's gone all soft!

"And Jamie, of course," she says, but her back is to me, already leaving the shop and meandering to the next one. I follow wordlessly. "If Laurie gets his act together and grovels an apology," she adds. "I don't know what came over him last night . . ."

I look at the imaginary watch on my wrist. "Right on time," I say, and Kate turns back to give me a butter-wouldn't-melt look. "That's ten minutes you've waited to bring him up."

"We can change the subject if you want," she offers, but she knows perfectly well I won't.

"Is it time for that coffee break yet?" I ask.

"Of course it is," she replies, checking her own imaginary watch. "I couldn't care less about the shopping. Tell me *everything*, Flo. I've been desperate to find out the facts."

"Now why doesn't that surprise me?" I say, although I can already feel the relief coursing through me that I finally get to tell somebody the beginning, the middle, and the end. I'd like to try to make sense of it all myself.

AT A PRETTY place on the corner with a small courtyard and lots of shaded seating, we order drinks and water and pastries, and take turns to use the loo. By the time we're settled, I'm breathing more deeply than I have all morning. I think one of my favorite things in the world is being somewhere new, at a café, people-watching. It feels like anything could happen, like everything is a possibility. How funny that I am happiest this way, but spend my time doing the same old thing, day in and day out, never going anywhere. Maybe my big lesson for this trip is that I need to get out more, take more chances. I don't think there's a single person in my life who would disagree. *Take the plastic off.* I heard that on the radio once. They were talking about their Italian grandparents, who always kept a plastic cover over their furniture so it didn't get ruined. But that made the furniture uncomfortable. The radio guest said it's a metaphor for life: Take the plastic off—things are designed to get messy. I remember siding with the Italian grandparents in my head when I heard it. I'm starting to get it now, though.

"So," Kate begins, ripping a croissant apart. "Start at the beginning."

I nod. "I think the beginning might be before this holiday started," I say, and Kate waves a hand and rolls her eyes.

"You think?" she teases. I take a breath. There's no hiding from Kate.

"You know most of it. It's hard to say what had changed last December. My studying was going really well, and I'd turned a corner after the breakdown. I always think of it as having been ill for a year, and now I've been recovering for a year. Soon it will be a longer amount of time I've been well again than I was ever bad, you know? But I suppose it was only six months at that point. I knew I was different, stronger, more capable—" I say, and Kate interjects.

"But the rest of us were too scared to believe it?" she supplies.

"Exactly," I reply. "And last Christmas . . . I don't know. I've had so much therapy and done so much 'inner work.'" I put quotation marks around this with my fingers, embarrassed to be using such a phrase.

"Don't worry," says Kate, sensing my mortification. "This is a safe space."

I shake my head, but it's a shake of appreciation, not annoyance.

"I came home and Jamie was there and it hit me, almost for the first time, that he's handsome, and easy to talk to."

Kate laughs. "If you go in for that muscly, thoughtful, chiseled-jaw, and heart-of-gold thing," she says. "Sure. I guess he's *okay* . . ."

"Exactly." I giggle. "Like what was I ever doing, thinking I could deny that?"

"No idea," Kate says, chuckling. "You *were* busy struggling to get through the day. That probably helped."

"Well, yes," I say. "There is that. I know I was bad, because I don't even remember his parents dying. Like, I was so in the throes of my own stuff that I have fuzzy recollections of just . . . now there's more of us at home at Easter, or August bank holiday, or birthdays, or whatever."

"But Christmas was a turning point?"

"I'd thought it was. We seemed to gravitate toward each other a lot, and I felt like Jamie saw me in a way the rest of you didn't. Well, maybe you did. But you and Laurie are a unit, if that makes sense."

Kate nods. "It does," she says. "Getting married will do that to ya."

"But the thing is . . . Jamie and I almost kissed one night. And then the night after that he was supposed to come and meet me in my room, but as you know he bailed on me. Left a note that said he'd led me on, and then the next morning he told Laurie he'd got a month-long gig on a boat. He took the job, and I didn't see him again until now."

"He's the reason you skipped your dad's birthday, and Easter?"

"And Mum's birthday," I say. "I couldn't take the fact that Jamie had rejected me, but my family still accepted him as if nothing had happened. I mean, not that they knew, because I couldn't tell anybody . . ."

"Oh, mate—I thought your excuses were a bit paper-thin."

I shrug. "I didn't even know Jamie was going to be here. I don't think I would have come, you know. Is that why nobody told me? Did they all know more than I thought they did?"

"Ah, the e-mail," Kate says. "I checked the family e-mail thread. You're definitely on it. So I think you need to check your spam filters, darling. Alex has the word 'ass' in his personal e-mail address, so I think the filters try to block it."

"Oh," I reply. "Thanks. Still. I regret coming. I love my family, but being around Jamie is so . . . loaded. But then he doesn't have anybody else. So maybe this is *my* problem?"

Kate sits back in her chair, chewing over what I've told her.

"Why do you think, honestly and truly, Jamie did that? Left you a note saying he'd led you on?"

"Just, like, cold feet or whatever. Couldn't do it to His Lordship King Laurie."

"And you still haven't asked Jamie about it?" she presses. "Even though you've been sleeping together? How did it not come up?"

"The note?" I ask.

Kate flags down the waiter again. "Hi," she says, with a big smile. "Could we get another croissant, please? In fact two more? Thanks." She turns her attention back to me. "Okay, so you didn't know he would be here because Alex's stupid e-mail address means you didn't see the family thread . . ." I shrug, assuming this sounds reasonable. "So Jamie gets here, with his tan and his abs and his heart of gold, and you're mad at him for doing a runner."

"Exactly," I respond. "But *he* seemed mad at me, which made me even *more* mad. Like so what: You flirt with me all Christmas, you say you want me to stay up and to come and see me one night, and then . . . you pie me off with a note under the door? And *you're* mad at *me*? No. No, no, no."

"I knew it was weird between you," Kate says, eyes alight with confirmation. "You wouldn't even look at Jamie. But, babe, I don't think he was mad at you—he kept staring at you, watching you, I even overheard him trying to make conversation with you . . ."

"I think it was for appearance's sake," I counter. "Invited here by Mum and Dad, their surrogate son, and all that—he was an arse to me, but fair play: He's got manners."

"Hmmm," Kate says, mulling over my point.

"So, okay, long story short."

"This is definitely long story long," Kate says, laughing. "But I am *here* for it."

"Long story long," I correct myself. "I'm mad, he's mad, there's all this unsaid stuff between us, all this tension, and then things change . . . I don't know. Like, we weren't very good at hating each other."

"That morning you said all those horrible things about him," Kate says. "And he heard . . ."

"Yeah." I nod. "I meant them, but I didn't mean them. He was *really* under my skin. So I had this idea."

Kate cocks an eyebrow, an invitation to go on.

"I read this poem about how if you get to know a man, you cease to be bothered by him."

"Okay . . ."

"So I thought: 'Okay, I'll be friendly, I can move past this. He might be gorgeous to look at, but he's an arse.'"

"Okay . . ."

"And that became this notion of, like, *exposure therapy.* That if we *did it*—got to know each other properly—it could cure us of this janky energy; we could get it out of our systems, and then we could all live happily ever after." I screw up my face when I've said this, because out loud it doesn't sound as sophisticated as it had in my head. "And as I'm saying all this, it probably sounds immature, but it made sense. At the time. We really did try *not* to do it . . . but it just happened."

Kate shakes her head, knits her eyebrows together. "I can't get over this note he left you," she says. "It doesn't seem like Jamie at all. And if he did that, why come on this trip when you'd be here?"

I shrug. "Like I say, I didn't ask."

"I've always thought he's in love with you," she presses on. "I can't comprehend this leading-you-on nonsense. I'm so good at reading people! But this . . ."

"Well," I say with finality, "it's over now. Laurie needs to forgive him, and we all need to forget it," I say. "It was incredible sex, but that's all it was. Until it wasn't."

Kate lowers her sunglasses and fixes me with a stare. "That's all it was for you?" she clarifies. "Sex?"

I nod slowly. "Yes . . ." I reply, because I feel like the question is a trick. She doesn't say anything, just pushes her glasses back up her nose and sighs deeply.

"What?" I ask.

"One last thing," she says. "Last night, it didn't all end because we found out—you said it had ended *before* we found out?"

"We had an argument," I say. "I . . . called Jamie a 'holiday fling' and it really hurt him. So he stormed out."

That's enough to make Kate take her sunglasses off properly and lean forward in her chair.

"Flo," she says, and it's not mean, but it is firm, "if you ask me, one way or another you've known Jamie is in love with you, and whether you can admit you love him, too, you willingly slept with him, knowing it wouldn't ever be enough. You're kidding yourself if you thought it would be."

"No." I shake my head. "It was just sex. And he hit on me first, for the record . . ."

"Not the actions of a man who leaves notes and runs away," she points out.

"Well, he did," I counter. "He left a note, ran away, and then hit on me again. And instead of letting my heart get broken once more, I let him in while drawing very firm boundaries that I thought you—of all people—would appreciate. It was just sex. I have done *nothing* wrong," I say. I'm shouting, and people are looking, but I can't stand what she's insinuating. "He's a big boy. Nobody had a gun to his head."

Kate sighs. We sit there, words exchanged, angry, and neither one of us wanting to speak first. Finally Kate says, "You're right. Nobody had a gun to Jamie's head that *made* him sleep with you. But if you think he could be in love with you like he is—as he has been for years—and turn down the chance to be with you, even for only a few days, you're delusional. That's not how love works. You knew he loved you, and you took advantage of it," she goes on, and I feel like I've been punched in the gut, her words are landing with such force.

I shake my head, willing the tears away. He doesn't *love* me. No way.

"Babe," she says, reaching out a hand to my arm. "The good news is, you can fix this. You need to find him and tell him how you really feel."

I look at her, and when I blink, it forces a tear to roll down my face. I push it away, devastated that I've behaved this way.

"I don't know what to do . . ." I tell her, my voice breaking.

"You do," she reassures me. "I promise you. You do."

KATE AND I leave the market in silence, barely speaking a word as we navigate the bus system to get down to the harbor, where we're meeting my family for lunch. I don't feel like eating or being social, because Kate's accusations are rattling around my head like loose change.

Do I like Jamie? Want-to-make-it-work like *Jamie?*

My head is swimming.

All I know for sure is that I will pull Jamie away from the group before we eat and apologize, straight up, like a grown-up. I'll start there. Clear the air. I will own my responsibility and say I will smooth things over with everyone, even though it's only Laurie who really cares. I'll promise Jamie he still has us.

"Oh," I say as we approach, because it is immediately apparent Jamie isn't there. It's a beautiful white wooden building over the marina, built on stilts, so it looks like our table is hanging out over the water. Kate must know what I mean because she touches my arm and tells me, "He'll be giving Laurie his space, that's all. I'll make sure they sort it out."

I think the reason I've been so quiet is because I know Kate sees things clearly. So she's held up a mirror to my own actions; but also, when she says she'll help Laurie and Jamie, I know she means it, and I know she'll be successful. That makes me breathe at least a little bit deeper.

"Thank you," I reply with a grateful smile. "And thanks for giving me the hard truths, too."

She knocks her shoulder into mine. "Sure thing," she says, "Auntie Flo."

As soon as she calls me that, we both turn and stare at each other in horror. "Aunt Flo!" I squeal. "No! That can't be my name. I can't be synonymous with having your period."

Kate shakes her head. "It's hilarious we didn't think of that. Oh my gosh! We'll have to drop the 'Aunt' bit, or else call you 'Auntie Florence'?"

"That makes me sound ninety years old," I say, as we weave through the other diners to our table right at the far edge. "We'll need to workshop it."

"Workshop what, darling?" Mum asks, craning her neck to signal she'd like a kiss on the cheek. I oblige, and then give one to Dad for good measure.

Kate kisses Laurie and takes a seat next to him, leaving me to sit opposite, where I clock the edges of a bruise spilling out from under his sunglasses. I hadn't realized Jamie had landed a punch. It serves Laurie right. Alex watches me assess Laurie, who studiously avoids my gaze. If he's embarrassed, then I am pleased. I want an apology from him for acting like the viscount from *Bridgerton*, as if my marital prospects are his concern, and his concern alone. But god, if I have to explain to him *why* I want an apology, I'll scream. If he doesn't get that by now, he's more of an idiot than I thought.

Luckily for Laurie, he seems contrite, so I shall bide my time and let him come to me. Though if anyone gets through this lunch without bringing Jamie up, I'll eat my napkin in shock. He's the elephant in the room. If he's skipped lunch to give us space, his absence actually means we feel his *lack* of presence even more.

We order lunch, because that's what the Greenbergs do best, going back and forth with *if Alex gets this, then I'll get that*, and *if we order extra for the table, we can always take it home*. All the guys order beer, and Mum and I split a bottle of wine, with Kate taking a small splash in the bottom of her glass, just to be sociable. The wine goes down effortlessly and quickly, doing exactly what I need it to: un-know the tension in my jaw and melt away the incessant chatter of my brain that otherwise would go *JamieJamieJamieJamieJamie*.

"I'm so pleased we did this," Mum says, raising a glass to toast. She looks around the table at each of us, giving a nod of appreciation. "I'm so pleased you all came. I love you all, so very much." Uncharacteristically, her voice swells with emotion, and I can see her eyes threaten to overrun with tears.

"Mum!" Alex exclaims, sounding as unnerved as I feel. "It's a happy thing we're all together. Don't cry. Christ!"

She waves a hand, then uses the corner of her starched white napkin to dab at her eyes.

"Sorry," she says. "I don't know why I feel like this. I've been a bit wobbly the whole time we've been here, to be honest. It's just nice, isn't it? I never want to take it for granted."

Dad puts an arm around her. "It is lovely," he tells her. "You're absolutely right."

Nobody really knows what to say after that: Yes, it's been a lovely holiday; yes, one of us is missing; no, nobody is going to bring up the fire or the big reveal or the fistfight or the delicate feelings of the morning-after-the-night-before. So instead Kate says how delicious the wine is; and I say I don't normally go in for something so fruity, but I quite like this; and Alex says, "Oh, go on then, let me try some" and sloshes a bit into his water glass before agreeing that yes, it's un-usual, but it's the perfect pairing with the seafood. We cheers again, to family and good health, and on it goes—everyone except Laurie being peppy and chatty and a little too bright.

"You're not saying much," I finally accuse him, halfway through our main courses. He doesn't look up, but freezes, his knife and fork held aloft. He was obviously hoping to fly under the radar all after-noon.

"I think," Dad offers, "that we're all feeling a bit tender today, aren't we?"

"*All* of us?" I clarify, and Dad shrugs, like he doesn't make the rules and so I shouldn't shoot the messenger.

"Nobody knows what to say, Florence," Mum says. "It's very strange not to have Jamie here with us, and of course we all know *why*. But we don't want you upset, darling. We don't want to upset any of the family."

"I'm a big girl," I reply in the exact opposite way someone who is a big girl would say it. Grown-ups don't need to assert that they are, indeed, grown up. "We can talk about Jamie. Of course we can. We can talk about *everything*!"

"Why? What else is there?" Alex says, wrinkling his brow in confusion.

I exhale dramatically. "I suppose," I say, because it's been brewing inside me all holiday—all year; for many years, in fact, "what I have been wanting to talk about for ages is my breakdown. Because a lot of how I feel about the whole Jamie-thing actually stems back to that."

"Okay . . ." says Mum carefully, and I can hear the *dot-dot-dot* in her voice, like she's worried where this might go and is bracing for impact.

"I am very sorry I had a breakdown, you know."

I pause after saying that. Dad has a fork halfway to his mouth and pauses like I've cast a spell. I wasn't intending to bring any of this up, but apparently I've decided this is the right time, when Mum is teary and Laurie is actually quiet for once.

"And I'm very sorry that it made you all scared for me. But I am not *still* broken. In fact I am very much mended. And so if everyone could go back to how they treated me before, instead of me being like a delicate doll . . ."

I'm rambling, and I know that sometimes the less said, the better, but on this occasion there's so much to get out of my system.

"It was scary, Flo, when you weren't very well," Alex offers in a small voice. "We thought . . . you know. That we might lose you."

His honesty steals the breath from my throat.

"Lose me?" I say. "No, I would never—"

Dad coughs and says, "We know that, darling. It is just our worst fear that anything could ever happen to you. You can't be mad at us for that."

I nod, picking apart what he's told me. I knew they'd been worried, but not *that* worried. "No," I say slowly, "I'm not. But I'm better, and all the stronger for what happened. I'm okay. Okay? And, you know, maybe I started to spend more time with Jamie because he's the only person who seems to know that about me."

At the sound of Jamie's name, Laurie looks up. Is this the thing that will finally make him contribute? He looks down again. Apparently not.

"Well," says Mum, "I, for one, wish the opposite. I wish that instead of everyone thinking I'm so strong and capable and ready for anything, sometimes everyone knew that I'm scared and vulnerable, and that I worry so much that sometimes I think I *gave* you all my anxiety—especially you, Flo."

Dad grabs her hand from where it lies by her wineglass. I suddenly realize that none of us have finished the food on our plates—with varying degrees of leftovers, we've all ceased to feel hungry.

"I'm as petrified of the next thirty years of my life as the rest of you, you know. If we're going to play the truth game, that's mine. You want us to give you *more* credit, Flo, but maybe I get too much. Maybe I want to be worried about just as much as we've worried about you. I know I'm the parent and I'm supposed to be strong, but I think you're all adult enough now to understand that there's really no such thing as figuring it all out. Anyone who says they've figured it out is imbecilic and not to be trusted. Anyone who isn't *scared* is a fool, too. Life is terrifying! At least sometimes."

Nobody speaks. I steal a look at Alex, whose facial expression tells me he had no idea Mum felt this way. I feel a pang of guilt that I didn't follow up with her, after Dad basically told me all this.

"Mum," I say, "I'm sorry. I didn't . . ." I falter at the lie. I *did* know. "I should have thought to ask you how you're doing. Any transition, at any age, must be scary."

"Correct," she says, sitting up straighter now she's said her piece. "Everyone has something they're afraid of. So I'll accept you're less afraid than ever, Florence, if everyone can accept that I'm . . . well, shitting myself about the future, quite frankly."

"I'm shitting myself about this baby," quips Kate, and we giggle, because it's funny to hear Mum swear and it feels like Kate is acknowledging that—but Kate doesn't laugh along with us. She means it. From everything she's said about the pregnancy, I thought she was thrilled. She was so bubbly and funny about it all back at the market, looking at baby clothes. God, if even Kate puts on a bit of a front, that must mean everybody does. She's normally the most truthful person I know.

"You'll be a wonderful mother, Kate," Dad tells her.

And Kate looks to the sky and says, "And yet you saying that doesn't help me at all."

A tear falls down her cheek, and Laurie reaches out an arm around her and pulls her in. He kisses her temple.

"I'm scared, too," he says quietly, mostly to her, but we all hear it. The waiters must think we've gone mad—this massive family who over-ordered on the lunchtime booze and is now in varying degrees of distress, crying on each other and giving impassioned speeches, as if we've just found out one of us is dying. They do not come to clear our plates, even though the distraction might be nice. We are left alone, with our wine and our monologues.

"Well," Alex declares, smacking a hand lightly on the table, "I'm bloody terrified that I will only ever be a good shag for somebody and never actually fall in love. Because that's all I want. True love. And it's a lot harder to get than the fairy tales would have you believe. Since everyone else has shared, that's my dirty little secret. I work sixty-hour weeks and sleep for all of my days off, and then go and find a man at a gay bar on the one night a month I actually go out. I love my work, but I need more."

"Everyone needs more than just their work," Kate says. "Of course they do!"

"Any man would be lucky to have you," I whisper to him, touched that he'd share that. Alex isn't that way inclined: He'll joke, but he's slippery with his feelings. It's about the truest thing he's ever said to us as an adult. He scrunches up his nose at me. I scrunch mine up in return, a silent *I love you.*

"And *I* am afraid," Dad says, so that we complete the impromptu circle of trust, "that I've let you all down somehow, because I can tell all my kids are scared in different ways, and I wondered if I could have taught you differently than that."

"No," Kate says quickly. "If I raise my kids to be even half as re-markable as yours, Michael . . ."

Dad gives her a smile. "You're kind to say that," he tells her. "And yet, you saying that doesn't help me at all."

Kate chews on her lip and holds up her hands. "Touché," she says, laughing. "Touché."

"Look what you started, Flo." Alex chuckles. "Jesus! Pass the bloomin' tissues."

"Sorry," I say, pulling a face. "Except also, not sorry."

Mum takes a big sip of water and says, "See, this is what getting together as a family is like. It's why it is important. When else would we have talked like this? It's always so quick, grabbing birthday meals at a weekend before you all go back to your lives; or there's always so much going on at the house when we're all there, scattered everywhere."

"We do a good job, though, Mum," I say. "Or rather, you and Dad do. Kate is right—you've raised a very good family indeed. I never would have managed these past few years without you. So, thank you. I don't think I've said that, so it's overdue. Thank you."

I raise a glass, and everyone follows suit.

"To the pain-in-the-arse Greenbergs," I say, and everyone giggles.

"To the pain-in-the-arse Greenbergs!" they reply.

At the sound of our laughter, the waiter comes to finally clear our dishes. We make a collective display of helping him, putting stray cutlery on plates and telling him how fantastic the food was—though from what we've left, you couldn't fault him for not believing us. I feel like this is the second time this holiday that I've had a reminder that it isn't only me who hurts. First Jamie, and now this, with my whole family. It's obviously awful if anyone feels wobbly, but it's reassuring that if even these gobshites have their "thing," I'm doing okay, after all. The atmosphere is emotional now, but full of catharsis. We're self-conscious with it, getting back to the business of pudding menus and coffees and teas, but once the waiter takes our order, silence falls.

"I don't know what I'm going to do about Jamie," I say, because I figure, *Sod it. Be the one to say his name.* "If anyone is wondering."

"We are," Mum says with a laugh. "He's a good boy, darling. I hope you don't think you can't be with him because of us. I've always thought he's a lovely boy. Well, *man,* I suppose. And I can see what you mean about him *seeing* you. He certainly looks at you like he's got a lot of love for you . . ."

"That's sweet of you to say," I tell her. "But it wasn't ever supposed to become this big thing. It's definitely not *love*. I do need to apologize to him, though." I look pointedly at Kate. "I've been counseled accordingly," I say, and she winks at me.

"We won't ask what you did," says Dad. "Since, if you're going to say sorry, it's none of our business."

"Ha!" I hoot. "You lot saying something isn't your business? Alert the press! Note the date and time."

Dad puts a hand to his chest, feigning shock.

Laurie issues a little cough. "You'll need to get a move on," he says, and because it's directly to me—his first face-to-face missive to me all day—everyone else is startled into sudden noiselessness.

"Sorry?" I say. "What do you mean?" I look around the table. Mum, Dad, Alex, and Kate all seem as curious as I do. Why would there be a time limit on apologizing, when we've got three and a half more days of holiday? I actually thought giving Jamie time to cool off wasn't a bad thing.

Laurie takes off his sunglasses and rubs at the bridge of his nose, wincing as he grabs between his eyes: The bruise is apparently *very* sore. He looks like absolute shit: bloodshot eyes, purple-and-yellow bruising, stubbled, and unslept.

"Laurie?" I press. "Did you . . . you didn't ask Jamie to leave, did you?" I say.

He ruffles his hair and stares at his lap. "I saw him after breakfast and Jamie said he thinks it's best to give you your space—to give us all our space. He feels he's let everyone down, so he's going early, I think."

"You think or you know?" I try to clarify, catching Kate's eye. She gives me a look as if to say, *Fair question, babe*. Why do I get the feeling Laurie *told* him to go?

"Know," Laurie says. "It was Jamie's idea, but I didn't stop him."

"Laurie!" I shout, louder than I mean to. "Jesus Christ! Why wouldn't you stop him? You can't hate him *that* much? This is a massive overreaction." I feel shaky and panicked—there's a pounding in my ears, and my throat feels tight. The person I really want to yell at is Jamie, because he's doing a runner . . . *again*? I swear to god, I hate confrontation, but that man consistently disappears instead of facing the music, and it's not bloody fair. Because as much as I owe him an apology, Kate is right: I need to get to the bottom of what happened at Christmas. Jamie should have offered an explanation, too. Did Laurie say something to him? Why wouldn't Jamie tell me that at the time? And what changed for him between then and now? I've quashed all these questions as best as I can, but now there's nowhere for them to go except out into the open.

If Jamie goes before I have the chance to talk to him, he might stay away from the whole family for longer than he needs to. If he goes, is his plan to miss every meet-up we have, every bank holiday . . . and what about next Christmas? He doesn't have anybody else! Somebody needs to make sure he's there. I want him there.

No.

Shit.

It's more than that.

I *need* him there. The way that I feel, this isn't just about making sure he knows he is welcome in our family, forever and always. It is that I want him to be my family, forever and always.

"Oh my god," I say, hand flying to my mouth. I can't believe this. I can't believe I didn't know this before now.

"What?" says Alex, looking worried. "What's happened?"

"I . . . I like Jamie," I say. It's as simple and easy as that.

I.

Like.

Him.

Laurie's eyes fly up to me, and I blink back tears. "Exposure therapy was never going to be enough," I mutter, as much to myself as to them. I'm reasoning out loud, trying to figure out when this happened. "I wanted to break down his walls," I say, and Kate nods. I think I'm finally catching up with her. "I called it 'exposure therapy.' I thought we could be friends. But I fell for him. I think I fell for him at Christmas actually, and have kidded myself that I got over what he did—whilst being *desperate* to know why he turned his back on me."

"Christmas?" asks Dad. "Oh yeah. I remember seeing you kiss his cheek, when we were doing the jigsaw. I thought something might be happening . . ."

"It was," Mum says. "You were so kind with him, when he was outside with me. Do you remember? He was upset about his parents."

I nod. "I remember," I say. "Bless him."

"So it was a lovers' tiff—why he left so quickly?" Mum clarifies. "The day after Boxing Day?"

I shake my head. "No. Not exactly. I feel like something happened, that I'm missing a vital piece of the puzzle. I'm sure he fell for me, too, at Christmas. I can't have made that feeling up. I can't have! We spent all Christmas getting closer and closer, and right before he suddenly left, he wrote me a note saying he'd led me on."

"He what?" says Dad, and he looks at Mum, who is similarly troubled by this revelation. "Jamie?" he clarifies. "What a bloody idiot."

"I've spent months feeling like I made it all up, that it was some one-sided infatuation that I could only handle if I decided to hate him. But it wasn't, I'm sure of it. It wasn't a one-sided infatuation."

"It wasn't," Laurie says then.

"What?" I ask.

"I need to tell you what I did, Flo," Laurie says. "But before I do, I want you to know that I am really, really sorry."

20

Last Christmas

I'm so sorry, he writes on the blank piece of paper. It's more of a scrawl than legible handwriting—he's always been told he writes like a doctor, all pinched and slanted and jumbled, like he has better things to be doing than scribing longhand. But who writes by hand anymore? It's an unnecessary skill, penmanship. He's trying his best, though, to make it look thoughtful. He knows that much is important.

He pauses. Pinches the bridge of his nose. He has a headache. This doesn't feel good, to be doing this.

But he must.

It's for the best.

I have led you on, he continues. *I am not good for you. Please forgive me, and let's not speak of this again . . .*

He sighs, staring at what he has done.

"You'll regret this, you know."

He looks up. He didn't realize he was being watched.

"Maybe," he replies, and his headache gets worse as he folds the paper and writes her name on one side.

"It's none of our business," Alex insists. "And he's not a bad guy, is he? He's your best friend—surely if he's good enough for you, he's good enough for Flo?"

Laurie looks at him, but quickly averts his eyes.

"It's not that," Laurie insists, pulling out another piece of paper from the notebook. On it, he writes exactly the same thing: *I'm so sorry. I have led you on. I am not good for you. Please forgive me, and let's not speak of this again . . .*

He signs it, *Flo*, and after it is folded, he puts Jamie's name on the front.

"So he thinks she's bailed, and she's going to think he's bailed?" Alex asks.

"I'm not a bad person," Laurie says. "It's just . . . he's still in a bad way, you know? After his parents? And Flo is still healing. At one point or another these past few years I thought I was going to lose both of them. It's been awful. So fucking *horrible*. You can't let two broken people get together and expect them to make one another whole. This isn't a fairy tale, Al. It's real life! I'm trying to live as a married man, trying to become a father. I can't look after Jamie, and after Flo, when it doesn't work out. They could *destroy* each other, surely you see that. And then what? Jamie is *family* now. It will ruin everything. And they'll get over it. He's got a lead on a sailing job, and Flo lives in Scotland. They need time to fall for other people and forget about each other."

"I see your point," says Alex. "But I'm backing away now. I'm going to pretend I've seen nothing, if I can't stop you."

"You can't," replies Laurie.

Alex steps out of the living room and creaks away upstairs, and Laurie holds the letters in his hand, the fire blazing wildly at his side. He could burn the things, let it all unfold as it may. But he can't. *It's better this way*, he thinks. He's not a bad person. He's doing this because he loves them.

21

"You did that?" I say when Laurie has finished speaking. He nods, ashamed. He looks like he knows he's messed up, realizes this is so far beyond crossing the line that the line is now merely a dot on the horizon. "What the hell is wrong with you?" I ask. I can barely process what he's admitted. He forged the note I got from Jamie, and he gave Jamie one and signed it from me? "Laurie, seriously, oh my god. That is *psycho*. Actually psychopathic. Are you KIDDING me? Jesus Christ! I egged Jamie's freaking car because of you."

Nobody else speaks. What is there to say? Actually, there's *plenty* for me to say. I let everybody else look down at their laps and play with their drink glasses. They can listen as I make Laurie understand how insane he is.

"Why would you interfere that way?" I ask.

And I'm shouting loudly enough that Mum says, "Flo. By all means go ape on him, but can you turn the volume down to three instead of ten, please? You're ruining other people's lunches."

I look around us—customers at a few tables are craning their necks to see what's going on, but they snap back to their own lunch companions when I catch their eyes.

I take a breath. I can't go and find Jamie with half the story: I want to know it *all*.

"Jamie said he once promised you he wouldn't go near me," I say. "When was that?"

Laurie shakes his head, opening his mouth to speak and then snapping it shut again like a fish.

"I deserve answers," I warn him. "When?"

"A couple of times," Laurie answers. "Maybe when he first came home with me, when you initially met. And then after Mum and Dad's big anniversary party. I thought I was doing the right thing," he goes on. "I'm your big brother, and you don't know Jamie like I do. He used to be a player. He slept with *everyone*. And so I told him you'd better not be one of them."

I nod my head. "Well, that's one thing," I say. "But making us both think the other wasn't interested when we had already . . ."

Laurie looks up. "What?" he says.

"Started falling," I tell him.

Laurie considers this and—fair play to him—does look distraught. "I didn't know you felt that way, that deeply," he says.

"It's none of your business, either way," I tell him. "I need to hear you say you understand that, Laurie. You can't interfere in other people's lives this way. Not in my life, not in Jamie's. And whatever happens next, Jamie needs to know that you're there for him." Laurie nods. "Although, god knows, if he decides not to forgive you, nobody could blame him."

I can tell that stings, because Laurie winces like it hurts to hear.

"We are supposed to be his family, and we've let him down.

You've let him down by doing this, and I've let him down by . . . Well," I settle on, "I've let him down in my own way, too."

"I'm sure you haven't, darling," Dad says. "You'll make it right."

"And we can all rally around, ask Jamie to stay for the last few nights of the holiday," Mum says, nodding. "We *are* a family—Jamie included—and family messes up sometimes. Family also has to forgive sometimes . . ."

Alex squeezes my arm. "I think Laurie's sorrier than he looks," he says in a stage whisper, and I'm too mad to laugh at him, but I give him a look that lets him know I get it, I can lay off Laurie now.

"You can shut up," I say. "You could have told me what he'd done."

"I understand now that I shouldn't have interfered," Laurie says. He looks sheepishly at Kate, who shakes her head at him and rolls her eyes, her way of saying he's an idiot and she forgives him and that they'll talk about it later.

"Do we know where Jamie is?" I ask. "I need to go and find him. Laurie?"

"When we were at the house this morning, he disappeared. Now he knows we're out for the afternoon, my money is that he's packing. I don't know. He could even have left already."

I stand up and it's only when I'm on my feet that my confidence wavers.

"Go," says Kate. "Go get your guy."

I nod.

And then I run.

22

I speed out of the restaurant and onto the main road that connects the harbor to the town further up. The villa is about twenty minutes on foot from here and I could wait for the bus, but I have no idea when it comes, where it picks up from, where it stops. I simply followed Kate this morning. The only thing I know how to do is run. I'm in cotton shorts and sneakers, so at least my feet are properly supported. I make a break for it, pacing down the side of the road, arms at right angles, feet one in front of the other, focused on the path ahead. It's only when I get to the town and think I should buy a bottle of water that I realize I don't have my bag. I've left it at the restaurant. It's hot, being the middle of the day, and I had that wine, but I've got no choice: I push on ahead.

I feel like I'm in a movie, but by the time I get to the villa I'm so hot and sweaty and out of breath that I'm obviously no leading lady. I go round the back, hoping to find it open, and I do. That must mean he's here.

"Jamie?" I call out, not caring how desperate I sound. "Jamie!" I yell again, louder. My voice is hoarse, and as eager as I am to see him, I also need a drink, immediately.

I head straight to the sink and stick my head under the tap, drinking right from it. I let it spill onto my face, cooling me down. When I'm done, I stand in the shade of the room and catch up with myself.

"Jamie?" I shout, one more time.

Nothing.

He's not in the living room, not outside by the pool or on the veranda. I run up the stairs to the first floor and shout up to the eaves. Still nothing. In case he's ignoring me, I go up and pop my head round our bedroom door. His bags are there, a backpack and a smaller rucksack, full of his stuff and ready to go. That's not encouraging—he really is leaving—but he hasn't left yet. Good. I head back downstairs and out of the back door, to the only other place he could possibly be.

I STAND AT the bottom of the stairs that lead down to the beach and watch Jamie. Marvel at him, really. He's standing at the water's edge, throwing stones into the sea. He's wearing his ratty white vest, the one that shows his nipples, and a pair of baggy surfboarder shorts. He's beautiful. Not handsome—beautiful. Tall and broad and strong and manly, but he moves elegantly, softly. There's a grace to the way he bends to pick up a stone, brings back his thick masculine arm, the flex of the muscles in his shoulders as he pings it back and flings it toward the water. He does it, over and over again, until he stops suddenly, like he can sense me. Without turning round he yells, "It's rude to stare."

I take that as an olive branch, a signal that it's okay for me to approach. I pad down across the sand and stand beside him.

"How could you tell I was there?" I say.

He doesn't look at me, just tips his head and replies, "I always know where you are." Jamie picks up another pebble and lobs it at the ocean. "I hate it," he says. I don't know what he means. "I hate always knowing where you are, but I do." *Ah*. "It makes me feel pathetic and needy. I don't want to be this aware of you. I don't want to be this in . . . *awe* of you. But it won't go away."

"Jamie . . ." I say. He still isn't looking at me. I reach out a hand to his, but he pulls away, like my touch causes him physical pain.

"It won't go away," he repeats. "And it hasn't gone away since the day I first met you. I remember it so clearly, out on your back lawn. You were still at school. Sixteen or seventeen?"

"Eighteen," I say.

"Well, at twenty-three I was too old for you. Not that my age mattered. You were always out of reach, never interested."

I watch him as he speaks, all of this pouring out of him toward the horizon like it's a relief finally to be able to say it.

"Will you sit with me?" I ask. "Can we sit and talk?"

I gesture to the sand and Jamie nods, lowering himself to the ground and burying his toes. It's not as hot down here—the sea breeze keeps it cool, the promises of secrets safe in the wind. I flop down next to him, hugging my knees to my chest.

"I've always thought *you* thought I was just Laurie's annoying little sister. I didn't know he'd warned you to stay away . . ."

"Yes, he did," Jamie says slowly, chewing over the fact like a Brussels sprout he doesn't want, but feels he should have, for balance.

"He's got a black eye, you know."

I wait for him to smile, or laugh, or say something to cut the tension, but he doesn't. He pulls his own knees to his chest and looks up to the sky. Sadly he says, "I've fucked it."

"No, you haven't," I say. "Jamie . . ."

"I have," he insists. "Everything I was worried about has come to pass, all because I followed my bloody *pecker*."

"Nobody says 'pecker,'" I tell him.

"I'm trying to be polite," Jamie counters.

I bash my shoulder gently into his. "There's no airs and graces with me," I say.

"I know." Jamie nods. "That's why I . . ."

I hold my breath. Is he going to say it? But no, he doesn't. He doesn't finish his sentence, just leaves it to hang between us. But it's unfair of me to expect him to properly get into his feelings when I haven't. I need to lay out my feelings for him first. And tell him what happened.

"I didn't write that note to you at Christmas. Laurie did. And he sent me the same thing. So I've spent this whole time thinking *you* changed your mind at Christmas, but I assume you thought the same about me?"

"I did," he says, nodding. "I can't believe Laurie would do that. That's . . . awful, for both of us. To make me think you were playing with me, blowing hot and cold."

"Laurie's mission was well and truly accomplished."

"But why would Laurie do that?" Jamie asks. "I'm his *friend*."

"You can talk to Laurie about that," I say. "But for now, Jamie, can *I* say some things?"

"You can," he replies. "I'm listening."

"Can I tell you some things from under the shade of that tree?" I press on. "Because I don't have lotion on and I am burning up right now."

And that's it—that's the thing that makes him laugh. He chuckles and gets up, holding out a hand to pull me up, too. Even when I'm upright, he doesn't let go, and it feels promising that we can walk hand in hand to the shade in this way. It makes me think that I want this. I always want to be holding Jamie Kramer's hand. It fits so well.

We settle down on a big piece of driftwood, in the shade of a tree. And it's then that I begin my speech.

"I remember the first day we met, too," I say. "Nobody in the world had ever asked me questions and actually listened to the answers. You smiled when you talked to me, and made eye contact like you couldn't believe what you were looking at. And I was an idiot, because I was eighteen and I didn't know how rare that look is. How special. I should have fought for it, not listened to the banter of my brothers."

Jamie looks at me, and because we're seated side by side, it means our faces are close. Not close enough to kiss, but closer than a friend's face should be. His eyes roam my face, and it's that exact look I am talking about. He glances at me like he's worried it might be the last time, so he has to drink in every detail.

"Over the years I think I convinced myself I hated you. It just became easier to say that because I could tell you were keeping your distance. And I couldn't bear to think I might have these feelings that you didn't. That would have been humiliating—especially if my family found out. And then at Christmas I suddenly realized I had no idea why I'd ever tried to stay out of your way, or deny what I think has always, for me, been there. It's made me feel insane. Truly bonkers. And then after I thought you pied me off . . . I egged your car."

"Wait. *You* egged my car? I thought that was kids from the village!"

"I was mad—it just sort of happened."

"Well, I was too busy being upset that I thought you'd pied me off to care."

"I would never. No! And I'm glad you weren't upset by the car—I was humiliated and tipsy. Not my finest hour."

"Nothing a car wash couldn't fix," he says.

"And then you showed up on my family holiday," I continue. "And I was determined not to feel a thing. But I do. And I thank god you kissed me that night, because it turns out everyone has known this for a while and I am only just catching on."

"To what?" Jamie says and he's closer now—an inch, max, between our noses—and his gaze flickers to my mouth, and I want to launch myself onto him, right here, right now. But first I have to say the thing I am no longer terrified of being true.

"That I am head-over-heels for you, Jamie Kramer, and it's been that way for a very, very long time."

Tears fill his eyes. He says, "Really?"

"Yes! I had to tell you before you left," I whisper, tears filling my own eyes now. "I've never felt this way about anyone before. And I can't hold it in anymore."

Jamie doesn't say anything for a minute, and I feel every second ticking by. I can't rush him—it wouldn't be fair. But I do watch him process what I've said, turning over my admission in his mind. He looks out to sea, down at his hands, then swiftly at me, with his trademark half-unreadable stare. Then he smiles.

Shaking his head, he says, "I'm head-over-heels for you, too."

I don't know how I thought it might feel to hear a wonderful, handsome, kind, and funny man tell me that, but it feels a hundred times better than any song I've ever heard or any movie I've ever seen. I let out a small *squee*-like sound of happiness, and Jamie laughs.

"It was like freaking lightning striking when we met. You were wearing the denim shorts and red tank top . . ."

He remembers what I was wearing? That's funny. Because I remember what he was wearing, too.

"You had on cargo shorts," I say. "And a Ramones T-shirt."

He looks at me, his tongue darting out over those full lips, happy that I have these memories, too.

"I'm sorry for everything," I tell him.

He holds out a hand, which, seated so closely, is hard to do. It means his palm is very close to his stomach, so when I reach out to take it, my knuckles brush his T-shirt.

"Truce?" he says.

"Truce," I reply.

We shake hands, grinning like idiots, and neither of us wants to be the one to let go first. He gives a gentle tug, so that our hands are entwined in his lap and I'm leaning closer to him.

I release my hand from his and cup his face, a hand up either cheek. I pull his mouth to mine, softly and with care, kissing him with every feeling I have in my body, slowly, slowly, slowly, admiring every inch of his chin, his stubble, his chiseled cheekbones, the way he tastes like oranges and smells like spice. He pulls on the back of my neck and it makes us both laugh, but we don't break apart. It's him and me, and I have no idea what this means now, but I know I feel safe. Like anything is possible. Like if it's going to be him and me, nothing can go wrong.

I lose myself in the kiss until a roar of applause forces us apart. My family. Mum, Dad, Alex, Laurie, and Kate are standing by the bottom of the villa's steps, cheering us on with glee. Even Laurie looks happy.

"Finally!" shouts Dad, and I bury my face in Jamie's T-shirt. I'm not embarrassed to be with him, or ashamed that everyone has seen, but the things I want to do to this man sitting beside me . . . I don't want my family reading all these filthy thoughts I'm having. *That* would be embarrassing.

I see that they've all got beach chairs and blankets, the Bluetooth speaker and a cooler of drinks, so I sit with my head on Jamie's shoulder, looking at the sea as they set up a small way from us, laughing and joking and generally carrying on as if the most perfect thing in the world *hasn't* just happened.

Eventually, though, I have to ask, "So . . . are you really leaving?"

Jamie uses a finger to guide my face in his direction and nods. "I am," he says. "It's time."

My heart sinks. "Okay," I reply. Maybe this means we have to put things on pause for a while, then. I can't expect him to drop everything for me. Although I suppose I thought he might. Maybe acknowledging our feelings will have to be enough.

"I think you should come with me, though," he says, eyes alight with mischief.

"Ha ha," I say. "Sure. I'll simply throw my bikini in my bag . . ." I can tell by the way he's looking at me, though, that he's not kidding. "But," I say, because of course this is ridiculous, "I don't know anything about sailing!"

"I can teach you," Jamie says, as if it's the most obvious thing ever. "I didn't know how to sail until somebody taught me."

"Is it even allowed?" I ask. "Won't the boat's owner mind?"

Jamie shrugs. "She's not there," he says. "That's the point. I just have to get the boat *to* her in one piece. I mean, she won't pay you or anything."

"I have savings," I say, before I can stop myself.

"You'll be fed . . ." Jamie adds. "Fuck it, Flo. What else have you got planned? No pressure, okay? But I love you. And you love me.

And it would be a shame not to spend the rest of the summer having more of that lovely sex." I hit his arm. But he has a point. It *is* lovely sex. "It's up to you."

I shake my head, my heart beating out of my chest to let me know what I should do.

"How long do I have to decide?" I ask.

"Half an hour."

I blink. Okay. I've never been impulsive before or jumped without looking in my life. What was it Mum said? Sometimes a pause is better than a misstep? Well, I don't think that's true. Missteps are what life is made of. The adventure of not knowing and trusting I'll be okay is the point. And it's then that it hits me—I don't feel anxious about this one tiny bit. I trust it will all work out. I'm okay. *I'm okay, I'm okay, I'm okay.*

"Sold," I tell Jamie, standing up. I offer him a hand to pull him up, too. "Let me go get my things."

"Not without another kiss," Jamie says, pulling me toward him and gripping me by the butt. "To seal the deal," he insists, planting his lips on mine.

"Get a room!" Laurie yells from across the way.

Jamie and I break apart with a laugh.

"We'll do one better," I yell back. Laurie frowns, not understanding. "We'll get a boat!" I say.

23

Three months later

"Catch!" Jamie says, throwing the rope of our little fishing boat at me.

I catch it easily, loop it round the dock, and wipe sweat from my brow as I stand up, squinting in the sun. I let the warmth wash over me. I never get tired of it. It turns out that I am 100 percent solar-powered. I love being by the water, and I love being in the sun—but hot sunshine *at* the water? It's my actual heaven. Every cell in my body is alive, and I treat it as my job every single day to stay that way. Now that I know what it is to feel content, I work fastidiously to remain that way. And appreciating the little moments is top of the list of "happy management."

I inhale, breathing out heavily, and I can feel his eyes on me. I've got very good at that—knowing when he's watching. He does it so openly, though, I don't suppose it's hard to tune your intuition to it.

"What?" I say, little-moment-appreciation taken care of and eyes now open.

He's standing with the seawater up to his knees, looking up to me on dry land, his handsome face full of affection.

"You're perfect," Jamie says to me. Simple as that. He tells me I'm perfect, or exquisite, or beautiful, or magnificent, on the hour every hour. Sometimes more often. He says it's for all the time he wasn't able to say it. I'm long past trying to stop him.

"You only fancy me because I'm handy with a fishing net," I joke, giving him a bum wiggle.

"Oh, I fancy you because you're handy all right," Jamie retorts.

And I reward him by pulling the fabric of my bikini top to quickly flash my boob.

Jamie yells, "Tease!" and before I know it, he has launched himself up on the dock to chase me. I'm fast, though. Three months of the physical labor that sailing requires has made me lean and strong. I can almost outrun my boyfriend.

Yes. Boyfriend.

We made it official under the stars one night, not knowing when we'll go back to England but knowing that, when we do, we'll do it together.

This has been the best, most freeing three months of my life. Jamie showed me the ropes as we sailed a couple of big boats from one destination to another, and now we've got a gap between gigs to rent a hut on this magical island, fishing for our own supper and going to bed when it gets dark and waking up when it's early, because the electricity is patchy, and surprisingly, I don't even mind. We find ways to stay entertained . . . And Hope is coming to meet up with us next week, with Otto, one of her German lovers.

I'm not ready for it to end yet—the sailing and the sex. *A pause is better than a misstep.* Turns out, this hasn't been a pause. It's been a leap of faith. And I have absolutely no idea how being here fits into the wider picture of my life, but that's what feels like such a triumph: I've stopped worrying about trying to plan. I'm here, now, finally in the moment. And as Jamie grabs me from behind and tackles me to the sand, pinning me down with his weight, I can't help but think, *What a glorious moment to be in, kissed heavy and hard in between shrieks of laughter.*

I can't believe this man is mine, that I can touch him and be touched whenever I want. That we can kiss and fish and make love and talk and just *be*. Because that's the thing. My mind is at peace. My body is exhausted. And down to my very bones, I know this is my happy place. I'm in love. In love with a man, yes, but because of Jamie's love for me I've taken a chance at being in love with my *life*. These past three months I've been an active participant instead of a passive bystander. I've become my own main character and that's not because Jamie makes me braver, but because I've made myself braver. I am vulnerable and unsure, and I know that's not a weakness. Feeling that way and trusting myself is actually a strength. And, honestly, I think knowing that is the biggest win of all.

Acknowledgments

To everyone involved in the making of *Enemies to Lovers*, thank you so very much—from the bottom of my heart. Especially to:

Editorial: Katie Loughnane, Coco Hagi, Laurie Ip Fung Chun, Kate Dresser, and Tarini Sipahimalani
Copy Editor: Madeline Hopkins
Proofreader: Debbie MacPherson
Cold Reader: Laura Meyerson
Production Editor: Claire Winecoff
Marketing: Brennin Cummings and Molly Pieper
Publicist: Kristen Bianco
Senior Managing Editor: Emily Mileham
Managing Editor: Maija Baldauf
Production Manager: Erin Byrne
Interior Designer: Angie Boutin
Cover Designer: Sanny Chiu

. . . and to you, too, for reading.

ABOUT THE AUTHOR

[AUTHOR CREDIT: NADIA MELI 2023]

Known as the queen of the meet-cute, **Laura Jane Williams (she/ her)** is the author of twelve books. Her romantic comedies for adults include *Lovestruck*, *The Lucky Escape*, and *Our Stop*, and she has written several nonfiction titles. She is also the author of the Taylor Blake series for teens. Laura's work has been translated into languages all over the world. *Enemies to Lovers* is her US debut.

laurajaneauthor.com